MY MISSING DAUGHTER

BOOKS BY ELLERY KANE

The House Sitter

The Good Wife

The Wrong Family

ROCKWELL AND DECKER SERIES

Watch Her Vanish

Her Perfect Bones

One Child Alive

DOCTORS OF DARKNESS SERIES

Daddy Darkest

The Hanging Tree

The First Cut

Shadows Among Us

Lucky Girl (A Dose of Darkness Novella)

LEGACY SERIES

Legacy

Prophecy

Revelation

MY MISSING DAUGHTER

ELLERY KANE

bookouture

Published by Bookouture in 2024

An imprint of Storyfire Ltd.
Carmelite House
50 Victoria Embankment
London EC4Y 0DZ

www.bookouture.com

Rumi quotes used with the permission of Rumi Network
www.Rumi.net

ISBN: 978-1-83525-595-7
eBook ISBN: 978-1-83525-594-0

For Gar
My partner in crime

PROLOGUE

Write what you know. That's what they say. Right now, what I know is too much to hold inside. I'm a powder keg. A sparking wire. A shaken-up soda ready to blow.

I can't write, so I run instead. Past the monkey bars, still warm from the sun, and the empty picnic tables, sticky with ice cream and ketchup. Toward the tree line, where the shadows gather like a mob and the smell of the campfire fades like a flower pressed between the pages of a book.

When I reach the edge of the woods, I listen to the roil of the nearby river and suck in a breath. I'm a storm gathering strength. A Category Five hurricane. I let loose a primal yell. A scream that burns my lungs. I can still see the bus from here, and I imagine her inside it. The door stands open, but we're worlds apart. Me on one side, her on the other. It's the loneliest feeling. I reach for the cheap flip phone in my pocket and tap out the number I know by heart, but it brings no comfort. Not anymore. She's stolen that, too. My eyes blurry with tears, I delete each digit and snap it shut.

An angry sob escapes my raw throat. I don't know what to do—where to go. I'm trapped. I tip my head back and prepare to unleash another furious scream. One that will reach her. One that will move her. But a hand comes from behind me and clamps my mouth shut. My scream dead-ends in a whimper, and my legs give way. The flip phone drops softly into the tall grass, just out of my reach...

ONE

NOW

A clap of thunder startles Tracy awake. Moments later, lightning illuminates her bedroom, brightening the rain-streaked window and offering a glimpse of the dark ribbon of asphalt that winds through Kildeer, the Chicago suburb she calls home. Tracy lies still beneath the sheets, the way she had as a girl, counting the seconds before the next furious rumble. Back then, tucked safely in the twin bed in Grandma Ruth's cluttered farmhouse, she'd relished a Midwest thunderstorm. The thirty-nine-year-old version of herself can only worry. About the gutters, the roof. The patio furniture she'd forgotten to secure like a proper homeowner. All the unknowns spring up like weeds in her garden. Pluck one and two more grow in its place.

Though she anticipates the next fearsome boom, she still flinches at its ferocity. She wishes she had a hand to cling to, a warm body to nestle against. But since she ended things with Ray six months ago, it's only her.

As the rain drums on, her chest grows tighter. She can't keep still. Finally, she sits up and reaches for the framed photograph on the nightstand, taking stock of her daughter and cataloguing every detail. The irreverent hot pink daisy she'd pinned to her high school graduation gown. The adorable smattering of cinnamon freckles across her cheeks. The charming half-smile she'd inherited from her deadbeat dad, the only thing of value he'd ever given her. A mere nine days have passed since Willow and her best friend, Amelia, set off on a road trip in the school bus Tracy refurbished herself, but it may as well be fifty. That's mom math.

Another *boom-clap* rattles the bones of the house, and the only light in the room goes out, leaving her staring at the useless, blank face of her alarm clock and the wall beyond, where she hung the signed portrait of John Wayne she inherited from her grandmother. She clutches Willow's photo to her chest and rides another wave of panic.

It will all be fine. Willow will be fine. Still, she checks her cellphone for the hundredth time, resisting the urge to call her daughter again and demand to know her exact whereabouts. Free-spirit Willow doesn't like her hovering. *I'm an adult now, Mom.* As if nineteen years on earth qualifies her for adulthood. A responsible adult would answer her phone. A responsible adult would not leave her texts unread. A responsible adult would never let her mother worry.

Tracy's fears wind through her like razor wire. Each scenario cuts deeper than the last until she tosses back the covers. She rummages through the nightstand for a flashlight, then pads down the stairs and into the kitchen, where she takes her usual seat at the ink-scarred dining table that's seen more homework and take-out than gourmet meals. Willow learned to read at this table, wrote her first story here, too. During tax seasons past, Tracy parked herself on this chair for days, mainlining black coffee and calculating home office deductions for her neighbors. And the burn mark in the wood beneath her hand owes itself to Amelia, a seventh-grade science diorama, and the unfortunate misfire of a glue gun.

Now, Tracy fixes her sandpaper eyes on the screen of her laptop. Grateful for a fully charged battery, she reads the words that bring her a semblance of comfort. *The Road Trip* by Willow Barrett and Amelia Ford, a thriller about two best friends—and true-crime junkies—on the adventure of a lifetime, podcasting their way across the northeast in search of the elusive Great Lakes Slasher.

Tracy scrolls through the red-lined Word document to the last page she'd edited before bed—only five chapters to go—her worries briefly quelled beneath a wave of sheer joy. Her daughter wrote these lines, filled these once-blank pages. She recognizes Willow's voice in every pithy phrase, every unexpected metaphor. Before she'd sold her soul for her nine to five accountant gig, Tracy dreamed of seeing her own name in print. But those days are long gone, mere specks on the horizon in her rearview, as distant as that old farmhouse where she'd grown up and as long-buried as the grandmother who raised her. Tracy prefers the view from her windshield now: the blinding brightness of her daughter's future.

As she reads the manuscript, her breath steadies. Her frazzled thoughts fall in line like obedient soldiers. The storm, too, fades away, until the pattering rain takes on its own lyrical rhythm.

Jenna slinks through the shadowy campground, past the remnants of the fire, toward the tent she shares with Lacey. The hot lava of her anger has cooled and hardened. It weighs heavy in the pit of her stomach, as undeniable as the blade clutched in her hand. She crouches down and tugs gently at the zipper until the tent flap falls open, revealing the soft body of her sleeping friend. Betrayal flares again. How could Lacey steal her dream?

How could she agree to host a podcast without her? It zips white-hot through her fingertips and demands release. In that devastating moment, she understands the rage that drove the Great Lakes Slasher to kill again and again. She raises the knife and—

A sudden light from the street pulls Tracy out of her trance. She turns her head to squint out the living room window, but the downpour blurs her view. Between the slit in the half-drawn curtains, a pair of headlamps go out, and Glendale Street returns to darkness. But Tracy can't look away from the streaked pane. Dread paperweights her at the kitchen table until the doorbell summons her. Its happy tone sounds out of place in the middle of the night in a driving rainstorm, as topsy-turvy as the sunshine at her grandmother's funeral.

Still, she floats toward the entryway as if in a dream, not caring about her bed-head or her bare feet or the rip in the sleeve of the oversized Chicago PD T-shirt that hangs down to her knees. It's the one remnant of Ray she's held on to. It's too comfortable to toss. But Ray would spin it differently, say that she can't let go. That she still needs him.

Tracy opens the door without thinking, without even checking the peephole.

She can't make sense of him. This scrawny young man in a green Taskrabbit tee, who smells of cigarettes and French fries. Rainwater drips from his hair as he raises his eyes, half-hidden behind the fog of his glasses.

"Are you Tracy Barrett?" Clumsily, he wipes his lenses on the hem of his shirt and sniffles. He's soaked to the bone.

Tracy gapes in disbelief at the school bus looming on the street behind him. It might as well be a dinosaur. A sea-foam green T-rex, lumbering through her middle-class neighborhood, with its bicycle rack and rooftop deck for stargazing. From here, it looks no different than it had nine days ago, when Willow stuck her hand out the driver's side and waved goodbye to her.

When Amelia sprang up in the oversized rear window, sticking out her tongue as they drove away. Watching the skoolie round the corner and disappear, Tracy had held on to the porch railing to steady herself. Her daughter's leaving always brought with it a tangible pain, like a cord of her own muscle stretching, stretching, stretching, until it snapped.

"Well, *are you*?" he prompts, apologetically. "Ms. Barrett, I mean?"

Flustered, she nods her head at him and waits for him to explain. There must be an explanation.

Instead, he reaches into the pocket of his khaki shorts and holds his hand out to her. In his palm, the daisy keychain she purchased a month ago. "Here you go," he says, gesturing with his thumb to the bus. "Keys to your skoolie. It's almost got a full tank of gas. I stopped to fill up in—"

"Where's my daughter?"

"Uh..." With a confused shrug, he shoves the keys toward her again. Tracy takes hold of them so forcefully that he steps back. "I don't know?"

"Is that a question?"

"I got hired to do a job, ma'am. Five hundred bucks to drive your bus from Niagara Falls back here." He plucks his cellphone from his back pocket. After a few taps and swipes, he consults the screen. "Deliver to three-thirty-four Glendale Street. Tracy Barrett. ASAP."

"Well, who hired you, then?" She hears the panic rising in her voice. Stabs at her own phone, speed-dialing Willow. They both stare at it as it rings and rings—another unanswered call—then goes to voicemail. She looks at him expectantly. She wants to throttle him.

"I'm not supposed to give out that information. Company policy and all. But you're welcome to contact our customer support line. Maybe they can help." He produces a soggy business card, where she reads his name: Allen Perlmutter.

"*Company policy?* Are you kidding me?" His eyes are fixed on her left hand, where she chokes the keychain in a death grip. Slowly, smartly, he returns the limp card to his pocket. "This is my daughter we're talking about. She's on a road trip with her friend. They aren't due back for another four days, but I haven't been able to reach her. And now you're here. In their bus. So, you can either tell me who hired you, or I'm calling the police."

A sudden gust of wind whips across the porch, shaking the old elm tree and raising goosebumps on Tracy's bare legs. Allen braces himself against it, but it blows his slight frame like a kite.

"Okay, okay. I'll have to pull up the work order. But may I come inside first? It's Stormageddon out here."

Reluctantly, Tracy allows him in and tosses the bus keys on the table near the entryway. He's not moving fast enough. Certainly not as fast as her frenzied mom brain. It's already galloped ten steps ahead to the edge of the unthinkable. Willow, alone. Afraid. In danger. Or worse.

"A name on a credit card is all I've got."

He angles the screen of his cell toward her so she can read the payment details. Unsatisfied, she snatches it from him. Her own device already in hand, she juggles them both, as she clumsily enlarges the print with her fingers.

"Explain," she demands, prompting an audible swallow from Allen.

"The assignment came through yesterday morning with instructions to pick up the bus at White Water Campground. The keys were inside."

Tracy feels as if she's tumbled down the falls herself. She's underwater, drowning. She struggles to hear him above the driving rain and the white noise of her confusion. *Candice Ford.* That's the name on the receipt.

"So, you didn't see anyone?" Tracy knows how she must look to poor Allen, as she flits to the fireplace mantel and retrieves another graduation day photograph, shoving it in his face. "You didn't see either of these girls?"

Allen politely studies the photo, then lifts his shoulders in a half-hearted shrug. "Not that I can remember, but it's early June. The campground was busy."

"Look again. Please." She thrusts the frame at him. "This doesn't make any sense. They have no other transportation, and they should've left Niagara Falls yesterday. They should be on their way home."

He takes another cautious glance. What choice does he have with Tracy bearing down on him? "I'm sorry. I wish I could be more helpful."

She follows a wary flick of his eyes to his cell in her hand.

"May I have my phone back now? I need to call for a ride to the bus station."

She gives no answer but directs him to the armchair. Once he sits, she runs back up the stairs to change out of her pajamas. She tugs on a pair of jeans and sneakers, not allowing herself time to breathe or think or cry, and returns the way she came. Quick and determined. Her heartbeat snare-drumming in her ears.

Stiff-backed, Allen watches her from the safety of the living room. She holds up his precious cellphone and slips it into her back pocket alongside her own. Then, she rifles through the hall closet and tosses him Willow's raincoat. It lands softly at his feet.

"What's this for?"

"What does it look like?"

Pulling on her own trench, Tracy snags the daisy keychain, flings open the front door, and deploys Willow's umbrella. The bus remains where Allen left it, with rainwater running in rivulets around its oversized tires and down the street gutters. Its sad existence seems proof that something awful has happened. Tracy tells herself not to be dramatic. There must be an explanation. A reasonable one. Though part of her still wants to crumple like a balled-up piece of paper, what good would she be to her daughter like that?

"You're coming with me."

Allen doesn't ask where they're going. He must sense that he has no choice. He follows her blindly as she leads him into the storm.

TWO

It's a short walk to the Ford house. A stone's throw across the street and three doors down. Tracy has always suspected that proximity brought the girls together fourteen years ago. God knows, they have little else in common than a Glendale address and the matching red brick façades of their adjacent slices of suburbia. Their single mothers—one by choice, the other by bad luck. Their love of indie bookstores and pineapple pizza. Fundamentally, they couldn't be more different. Like a rock and a bird. Her daughter, Willow, meant to spread her wings. Amelia, alarmingly earthbound. Even in looks, they're yin and yang, light and dark. Willow, wavy blonde and sun-kissed. A stark contrast to her friend's raven and bone.

Tracy fights with the wind, struggling to keep the umbrella open and upright. With every gust, it threatens to take flight, even as the rain-soaked bottoms of her jeans cling to her legs and weigh her down. She glances back, surprised to see Allen has kept up with her. How many times has she walked this route? Countless. But today, it feels like a trek to a foreign land. Every step a reminder that something has gone wrong; something terrible has befallen her. A stranger is wearing Willow's coat.

When they reach the safety of the porch, Tracy lowers the umbrella and approaches the door. It's her turn to ring the bell. To summon Candice from her bedroom. To deliver the news that will break her, though Tracy suspects she won't show it. Cardiac surgeons like Dr. Ford thrive on the worst-case scenario. The microscopic tear in a valve. The blockage in an artery that drops a weekend warrior to the ground. She's been training her whole life for a moment like this.

"What are you doing here? You're drenched." Candice blots her face with a towel. The edges of her dark bob glisten with sweat. Tracy peers behind her, into the dim living room. Of course, Candice would be awake at this ungodly hour. Not only purposely awake but breathy and red-faced, caught mid-workout. *Forty-five minutes a day, no excuses*, she once told Tracy, which explains why she has the body of a woman half her age. On the coffee table, Candice's laptop glows like an orb. On its screen, her cheery instructor remains frozen in a squat, tan quads straining. "My power went out. Thank goodness my laptop still had some juice. You know what a raging bitch I am if I miss my morning workout."

"Have you heard from the girls?"

Candice blinks, momentarily confused. Like Amelia is a plant she forgot to water. It's hard to believe that she chose this life, eggs frozen at twenty-five, surrogacy at forty; whereas Tracy happened on it the old-fashioned way. By being too young, too drunk, and too stupid. While Candice spent her twenties honing her skills on cadaver hearts, Tracy had been knee-deep in diapers. She and Willow had practically grown up together.

"Not for a few days." Candice holds up a finger and darts back into the house. Returning with her phone in hand, she produces the last text she received from Amelia. A photo of her and Willow in front of the rustic White Water Campground sign.

Arrived at Niagara Falls. First stop: barrel shopping. LOL.

"That's more than I got," Tracy admits. "Willow hasn't called or texted since Saturday. She's ignored all my messages."

"Well, that's Willow. That girl lives by her own rules. Am I right?"

Tracy hates that she is. "And nothing since?"

"Two missed calls yesterday. She didn't leave a message, and I didn't get a chance to call back. I got paged for a Code Blue. The patient needed a—" Candice stops cold when she spots Allen. "Who is *he*?"

Allen shrinks behind Tracy's back. And she gets it. Truth be told, she dragged him here as a buffer. She likes Candice, mostly. They're friends, somewhat. But she's never quite sure how she measures up next to her. The Harvard-educated heart doctor, saving the world one clogged aorta at a time. At least Tracy is still on the good side of forty. Candice crested that hill years ago.

"This is Allen," Tracy says. "He works for Taskrabbit. He showed up at my front door thirty minutes ago with the keys to the bus."

"*What*? The girls aren't due back for days." Candice drops her mask of self-possession. Worry tugs at her forehead as she leans out the door for a look. Tracy pinpoints the exact moment when Candice spots the bus parked on the street; she hears the hitch in her breath. "Is something the matter? Was there an accident?"

"I thought you might know, since you paid Allen five hundred dollars to drive it back. Your AmEx was on the order."

Without warning, Candice hammers at her phone screen, then presses it to her ear. Tracy hears it ringing. "How dare you use my credit card! Pick up the damn phone, Amelia."

Tracy recognizes *this* Candice. Brusque, exacting. Intimidating as hell. She ends the call to her daughter with an angry jab of her finger, then turns her focus back to Tracy.

"Have you been inside it yet?"

"No, I thought we should—"

"Well, why the hell not? What are you waiting for?" Candice retrieves her house keys from the ceramic dish on the hall table and pushes past them both, locking the door behind her. Never mind the rain, which seems to have slowed just for her. Now it's nothing more than a sputtering drizzle.

"Am I done here?" Allen poses the question with the delicate precision of a bomb technician.

"No," Tracy tells him, before she takes off after Candice, running down the porch steps, jumping puddles on the sidewalk. By the time she reaches the bus, her lungs burn. Her feet squish uncomfortably inside her shoes. She realizes, too late, Candice can't do a damn thing without her and the daisy keychain in her pocket.

"I think we should call the cops first," she says.

Candice tugs on the locked door. "Do you mean Ray?"

"No, definitely not Ray. That's not a good idea. I don't want to encourage him."

When Candice flicks her eyes to Tracy's oversized T-shirt, her cheeks warm. "Sweetie, he's still obsessed with you. Your very existence encourages him."

"I meant the *actual* police. Like nine-one-one." Ray doesn't count. She's seen him naked. And technically, he's not a cop anymore, though she keeps that to herself. She's grateful the story of his demise hasn't gone viral. Yet. "Anyway, I think Ray's out of town right now."

"Alright. If you really believe it's necessary. Personally, I'm betting those little shits are messing with us. Remember that time they covered all your furniture in bubble wrap." Candice stands on tiptoe to wipe one of the windows with her shirt-sleeve. When she peers inside, her breath fogs the glass. "They probably left a *gotcha* note."

"You really think this is a prank? We have no idea what's going on. And with the girls not answering... c'mon, you must be a smidge worried. I know I am." Tracy winces at her next thought, at the prospect of saying it out loud. But she has no choice, with Candice pretending to be unbothered. "The bus could be a crime scene."

"It looked pretty normal to me," Allen says, with a shrug. "A little cluttered but..."

"But, what?" Tracy prompts.

"Well, there wasn't any blood, if that's what you're getting at. Just a mess. A lot of girl stuff. Clothes and shoes and makeup. And a bunch of torn-up papers."

"Papers?" Frowning, Tracy unlocks her cellphone and dials. She's waited long enough. "Torn-up papers don't seem normal to me. What if the girls got robbed? The bus, ransacked? Are you sure you didn't see anything suspicious?"

Allen grits his teeth, shakes his head. He seems harmless. Then again, so did Ted Bundy.

The interminable ringing finally comes to a sudden stop. "What is your emergency?"

Tracy pictures one-day-old Willow swaddled in a pink blanket in her arms. It's always been just the two of them; she can't remember herself before motherhood. Her chest tightens, squeezing her heart like a vice until she can barely breathe.

She speaks into the phone, suddenly afraid to make it real. "My daughter is missing. She's gone."

THREE

This is not what Tracy expected when she summoned the police. She needed a grizzled veteran in a trench coat to appear on her doorstep with a pocket notebook and a practiced look of concern that would shore up her panic. Instead, Detective Penny Delgado barely looks old enough to drive her unmarked police cruiser, much less track down two missing nineteen-year-olds. Tracy wonders if she's already made a mistake by summoning this novice. Not to mention, she'd called Ray, even though she knew it was a horrible idea. Typical Ray, he managed to make her feel even worse by spouting off, blaming her, and hanging up abruptly. The whole road trip *had* been her idea. A way for the girls to reconnect this summer after a year spent apart and to see Niagara Falls, the setting of their thriller, for themselves. She even helped plan the fourteen-day itinerary that would wind them through the Great Lakes and back, hitting all the hot spots from Chicago to Mackinac Island to their final destination, the White Water Campground.

It's too late to second-guess herself now. Ray can't help her, and Candice's idea to investigate the bus on their own isn't an option either. Detective Delgado had confiscated the daisy keychain ten minutes ago, shortly after dispatching a uniformed officer to take Allen's statement. She holds it in her hand now, her pink nail polish a perfect complement to the happy flower. Tracy can't look away from it. It reminds her of Willow.

"Take a seat, Ms. Barrett. You as well, Ms. Ford."

"*Doctor*. It's Dr. Ford."

Detective Delgado blinks once, twice. A hint of a smirk tugs at the corner of her mouth, then disappears. "My apologies, Doc."

Tracy cuts her eyes at Candice as she positions herself on the sofa alongside her. They need the detective on their side. But more than that, Candice's condescension sets off her alarm bells. Because Dr. Ford only goes full snob when she's in over her head. When she needs to remind herself and everyone in earshot that she's in charge. She's in control. That tells Tracy she must be more worried than she's let on.

"Can we go inside the bus now? Allen said it was a mess. What if something bad happened?"

"I understand your concern. Before we take a look inside the bus, I need to gather some information. I'd like to ask you both a few questions, if that's alright." Detective Delgado turns first to Tracy. For that, she's grateful. She can't sit still any longer. She feels as useless as the throw pillow behind her back. "When was the last time you talked with your daughter, Ms. Barrett?"

"Thursday night. She and Amelia had spent the day on Mackinac Island. They made fudge."

"How did she sound?"

It seems a lifetime ago. The static in Tracy's brain won't let her conjure Willow's voice, and the bit she remembers most she leaves unsaid. "Like herself, I suppose. It was a quick call. Hi and goodbye."

"And you, Dr. Ford? When did you last speak to Amelia?"

"I got a text when they arrived at the campground and

missed a couple of calls yesterday. But actually *talk* to her?" Candice frowns and drops her eyes to the screen resting in her palm. "I'd have to check my phone. My whole life is on this thing. And thank God for that. I'm running on fumes after yesterday's CABG. The poor sucker flatlined twice on the table."

Tracy fights off an eyeroll, explaining, "She's a cardiac surgeon."

"A surgeon. Impressive." The detective sounds blatantly unimpressed. Maybe she's less flappable than she appears. Most of the women in Kildeer oohed and aahed at Candice's accomplishments, at the way she gracefully walked the tightrope between single mother and skilled professional. Tracy had too until she'd seen behind the curtain. The string of nannies and late nights and the lonely little girl who spent most of her time playing Barbies on Tracy's living room floor.

"Found it," Candice announces. "It was a few days ago. Sunday evening. I remember it now. Amelia told me that they'd been invited to a cookout at the campground. That Willow made a new friend. I told her to be careful. She told me to stop nagging. The usual."

"A friend?" Again, Tracy's chest tightens. "Did she say anything else?"

"I don't think so."

"You didn't ask?"

"Why would I? It didn't seem off brand. Willow was always making *friends*." Then, to the detective, she adds, "Her daughter's a social butterfly. Amelia is a bit more reserved."

It doesn't sound like an insult, but Tracy knows better. Candice has never taken Willow seriously. She gets to her feet and paces to the window, watching the first glistening rays of sunlight set the wet pavement afire. "Willow would never intentionally put them at risk. She's smart, well-traveled. She spent her spring break in Europe. She knows better than to just go off with anyone."

"I'm only saying what Amelia told me. Besides, I warned you the trip was a bad idea. The bus too. *Let them enjoy their freedom*, you said. *They're only young once.* Remember all that *carpe diem* mumbo-jumbo?"

Tracy knows how this must look to the detective. Like two clueless mothers, pointing fingers. "I was just trying to make you feel better. They're nineteen. They can make up their own minds."

Candice only shrugs which somehow makes it worse. Tracy wants her to fight back. She needs a place to channel her nerves. Mercifully, Detective Delgado ends the awkward silence. "So, tell me about this road trip."

After retrieving her laptop, Tracy deposits it on the coffee table and pulls up the Writing on the Road Instagram page the girls created for their fourteen-day adventure touring the Great Lakes. The follower count, a meager 325, has grown since she last visited. "After I finished refurbishing the bus this spring, they agreed it would be fun to take a road trip, and I helped them plan the route. They'd written a book together this year, a thriller, even though they were miles apart. Amelia, attending college at Northwestern. Willow, still at home, taking a gap year. The book is actually called *The Road Trip*, and it's set in the northeast, in and around Niagara Falls. They wanted to celebrate their achievement. To edit, to plan their next move. Marketing, agents, publishers, the whole nine yards."

Detective Delgado crouches for a better look at the screen, clicking on the first photo of the girls, arm in arm in front of the school bus. The manuscript clutched between them, their precious spiral-bound baby. "They wrote a novel called *The Road Trip*? A little on the nose, isn't it?"

Irked by the detective's skepticism, Tracy bulldozes over her. "I'm not sure how any of this is relevant. But if you must know, they'd been working on it since senior year. It started as a class project and took off from there. Mr. Spellman always said Willow was the most talented writer to come through Kildeer Prep, and Amelia—"

"Graduated first in her class," Candice adds.

"I see."

"A National Merit Scholar on a full academic scholarship to Northwestern."

"Oh."

Tracy nearly laughs out loud at Detective Delgado's underwhelmed tone. By now, it's surely gotten under Candice's skin. Amelia is the most impressive trophy in her collection.

"Did the girls get along? Were they..." The detective flicks her eyes between them. "Competitive?"

"They're best friends," Tracy replies. "They've known each other since the second grade. Of course they compete. They argue like sisters, but they never stay mad for long."

As the detective scrolls through the remainder of the photos, from the breathtaking Pictured Rocks of Lake Superior to the charm of Mackinac Island, she tosses out another question. "Did they argue on this trip?"

"Nothing major that I heard about." Tracy treads lightly, not wanting to break her daughter's confidence in front of her best friend's mother. "But she's still a teenager. She's not exactly an open book."

Candice makes a noise of agreement. "Same with Amelia. Hell, she's in college now. I have no illusions that I know my daughter at all, if I ever did."

Detective Delgado stops on the second to last photo, dated Sunday. It's impossible to tell which of the girls took it. Backdropped against a starry night sky, the bright flames of a campfire consume the frame. Tracy recognizes the caption as a Rumi quote: *Set your life on fire. Seek those who fan your flames.* She reaches toward the screen and slides her fingers against it, enlarging the image. If only she could conjure her daughter that easily. "I think Willow posted that one. Rumi was a favorite of hers. They read his poetry in Mr. Spellman's class. He taught both girls for Honors English their junior and senior years."

"Spellman," the detective repeats, as she jots down the name. "Have you checked in with the girls' friends, romantic partners, anybody who might know what they were up to?"

Tracy shakes her head. There's no manual for a situation like this. Still, she feels terribly inadequate. Like she's already failed her daughter. She's done everything wrong. "Not yet. But we can put a list together. And I have Sam Spellman's contact info right here in my phone. He was a writer himself, so he's been a mentor to the girls." She looks to Candice for rescue, seeking a sturdy lifeboat in the storm.

"Was Amelia dating anyone at Northwestern?" Tracy can guess the answer to her own question since studious Amelia has always been like her mother. Too practical to have her head turned by some silly frat boy.

But Candice doesn't reply, and Tracy finds her squinting at the laptop screen, laser focused on the cropped edge of the photo. "What's that?" Candice asks.

Tracy leans in for a closer look. She points to the glinting blade, barely visible next to the campfire. "It looks like a knife."

Detective Delgado peers at the screen skeptically before heading toward the front door. She motions to both of them. "I'll have our IT folks enlarge and examine the photos. Do you know if the girls' fingerprints are on file?"

"Fifth grade Safe Kids program," Tracy answers. "They were both fingerprinted."

"Okay, that's good. In the meantime, why don't we take a look inside the bus and see if anything is missing. Right now, there's not much else we can do. You said it yourself; the girls are adults. If they want to go off the grid, I certainly can't stop them."

The detective leaves them alone. The door to the street stands open, letting in the muggy air. Candice doesn't budge, so Tracy stays put too.

"It's definitely a knife," Candice says. "Why would the girls have something like that?"

Tracy shrugs, mutters, "*As undeniable as the blade clutched in her hand...?*"

"Huh? What the hell are you talking about?"

"Chapter Forty?" For a doctor, Candice can be utterly clueless. Tracy doubts she'd skimmed a single page of *The Road Trip*. Countless times, she'd told her she hadn't read so much as a magazine since medical school. She made it sound like a badge of honor. "Maybe it was research for the book. They'd been working on some changes to the ending."

"*Research?*" It sounds unbelievable coming from Candice's mouth, and Tracy's heart starts to pound again, heavy as a boot against her chest. "That seems unlikely. Weren't they finished with all that?"

"I thought you weren't worried." Tracy can't decide how to feel about the deepening furrow between Candice's brows. At least she's not alone anymore.

An unexpected flash of movement in her periphery makes her flinch. Backdropped by the bruised dawn sky, the detective waves impatiently at them through the picture window.

Tracy springs up with a sudden urgency, realizing she desperately wants to lay eyes inside that bus. She needs to see for herself what's happened there. Candice's hurried footfalls echo behind her own, but she doesn't look back.

FOUR

"The door sticks a little, especially when it rains," Tracy warns. She wrings her hands to keep herself from taking hold of the key. Sure enough, Detective Delgado wrestles with the handle until it flies open and sends her stumbling back. All three women peer up into the bus's shadowy mouth.

Some objects have souls. Grandma Ruth had lived by that motto, rescuing all manner of junk from estate sales within a twenty-mile radius of their farmhouse in Lexington, Illinois. Tracy had known it to be true the day she spotted the old yellow school bus while driving home from the grocery store. Marooned on the side of the street like a dying beast, it spoke to her. The dull yellow paint, the dent in the roof. The sign in the cracked front window that read: *$5,000 or best offer*. To Tracy, it said, *Rescue me*. In her head, she'd heard her grandmother's voice, made gravelly from years of cigarette smoking. *That bus needs you.* So, she'd pulled over right then and called the number. Two days later, the bus and its story belonged to her.

Trailing the detective, Tracy climbs the three tall stairs on legs of lead. It smells like Willow—hairspray and bubblegum and the beechwood candle burned to the quick on the foldout table—which only makes it worse. The vacant quiet asks unanswerable questions.

Tracy rubs the goosebumps from her arms and peers over Detective Delgado's shoulder, as she sweeps the beam of her duty flashlight across the interior. A quick tug of the curtains she'd installed lets in the first rays of sunlight.

"Wow, this is seriously cool." The detective lets out a low whistle, admiring Tracy's handiwork. The bright white walls. The banquette cushions made from the foam of the original seats. The bunkbeds and reclaimed lockers, where she'd stenciled the girls' names. Like the fixer-uppers Grandma Ruth carted home, Tracy had painstakingly brought it back to life.

"Thanks, I renovated it myself. My grandmother sold collectibles. Signed vintage portraits, Hummel figurines, artwork. She taught me everything I know."

As the detective approaches the mid-section of the bus, she pulls up short. Candice bumps into Tracy's back, and she jolts forward, steadying herself with a hand to the kitchen counter.

"What is it?" Candice demands.

Already, Tracy spots the first stray sheet of paper lying on the floor of the aisle. It's been ripped in two—a violent tear down its middle—and stripped from its spiral binding. She recognizes it on sight. The typed words at the top of the page read: *Chapter Twenty-One*.

"I'm not sure." Tracy's answer denies the obvious. Allen was right. Papers litter the back end of the bus like confetti; several dents and scuff marks mar the side panel near the bunks; and Willow's laptop lies open on the floor, the screen smashed. She would never leave it behind. This is worse than Tracy expected. It's chaotic. Unhinged.

The detective turns to them with a worried look and gestures to the mess behind her. "Is *this* their novel?"

Tracy nods. Her stomach flip-flopping, she points to a crumpled ball near the detective's boot. "That looks like the dedication page." The girls had insisted on dedicating the book to each other. *Best friends shine a light in the darkness.* "And that's my daughter's laptop. It's broken."

"Alright, ladies. Wait here. Don't touch anything. I'll take a look in the back."

"No way," Candice barks at her. "This is my daughter we're talking about. I'm going with you."

"Me too." Tracy hates the tinny sound of her voice. It's practically a whimper. She wishes she could be so sure of herself, calm under pressure like Candice. Instead, she senses the widening cracks beneath her surface. She wonders how long she can hold it together, and she finds herself stepping aside, surrendering as Candice pushes past her.

Detective Delgado holds firm. "I'm sorry, but I can't let you do that. This looks like... well, it's not what I expected. The gentleman from Taskrabbit didn't mention signs of a struggle."

"A struggle?" Tracy repeats. The word makes her queasy. "Do you think he had something to do with this?"

"At this point, it's too early to say. We don't really know what we've got here."

The detective tries valiantly to maintain her poker face, but Tracy follows her eyes a short distance down the aisle into the shadowy recesses near the bunkbed alcove. The pink pinstriped comforter hangs off the bottom bunk and twists onto the floor, where the worst of the paper-storm gathers. Willow's crossbody bag peeks from beneath the sheets. *Is her ID in it?*

Tracy steps toward it without thinking, drawn by an invisible force. An unquenchable need to know, to understand. But it doesn't make sense. None of it. Just as quickly, she draws back like she's spotted a snake.

Candice gasps—she sees it too. Tracy's knees buckle beneath her, barely able to hold the weight of her own body. Something bad happened here, something sudden and terrible.

Something that will define her life forever, of that she feels certain.

Detective Delgado blocks their view, mercifully shielding them from reality. But what's done is done. Tracy won't ever be able to unsee the black spiral binding that once held these pages together. It's been discarded. Stretched obscenely. And wound in its coils is a clump of sandy blonde hair that she knows belonged to her daughter.

INSTAGRAM

writingontheroad First skoolie selfie on #dayone of an epic road trip with @melthebookworm! Milwaukee, here we come! If you want to follow our route, explore new sites, and get a behind the scenes peek into our soon-to-be-released thriller, visit us at writing-on-the-road-.net. #theroadtrip #bestfriends #harleymuseum
25 likes 4 comments 1 share

ilovepuppies Way to rep Kildeer Prep, girls! Mrs. Johnson, 10th grade biology, is following.

bikerbabe Be sure to check out the mysterious #serialnumberone, the oldest Harley in the world.

> **olderthandirt** @bikerbabe Rumor is the engine was found in a garbage dump and now it's a classic

> **JT77** @bikerbabe don't believe everything you read it's all a lie

FIVE

BEFORE

Day One on the Road: Milwaukee

Willow winds a strand of her hair around her finger, tugging it before setting it free to curl at her shoulder. Effortlessly, her finger finds another strand. Wrap, tug, release, and repeat. Since the fourth grade, it's how she does her best thinking.

"This isn't your mom's Volvo, Will. Statistically speaking, there are forty-three thousand fatal car crashes per year in the US, so I'd prefer it if you kept both hands on that very big wheel."

Startled, Willow glances back to the sofa, where Amelia sits with her feet curled beneath her, her glasses on and the spiral-bound copy of *The Road Trip* on her lap, opened to Chapter One. She pops a potato chip in her mouth, then jabs her finger in the direction of the windshield. "Eyes on the road, too."

"Sorry. Two eyes, two hands. I promise. I was just remembering this dream I had last night."

Amelia groans predictably. Though Willow doesn't look again, she'd bet her life that groan came with an eyeroll. After fourteen years of friendship, she knows Amelia's mannerisms as well as a character she'd written herself, even if they haven't seen each other since Christmas break. "Were you at the grocery store naked again? Riding a tricycle in the desert? Did all your teeth fall out?"

"Go ahead. Mock me. But the subconscious speaks to us in our dreams. Freud knew that, even if he *was* a misogynist tool." Willow shifts into second gear, waving goofily at the FedEx driver as she passes. The open road unfurls like a ribbon, and she can hardly contain her excitement. Since they began their journey an hour ago, it keeps bubbling up inside her. She's worried she might say too much. She might spill her secrets before their first stop in Milwaukee.

"So..." Amelia manages to sound both curious and smug. "What was your subconscious saying, exactly?"

"Well, I was driving a bus."

"Imagine that."

"Driving a bus symbolizes taking a journey in your life. And here we are, on a literal and figurative journey."

When Amelia scoffs, Willow pictures the matching face. A lifted brow, a quirked mouth. "No disrespect to Freud, but you do realize that dreams are a scientific phenomenon caused by electrical impulses in the amygdala and the hip—"

"Yeah, yeah. I get it. The amygdala and the hippopotamus. It sounds like the name of an indie rock band. Or a children's book."

Amelia bursts into laughter. "It's called the hippocampus."

"*Tomayto, tomahto.* I can't help feeling like we're on the verge of greatness." Willow lets out a cheerful whoop to counter Amelia's skepticism and playfully co-opts the tagline from their book. "Just two gals on the road trip of a lifetime."

"A lifetime? Slow your roll, girl. It's just the Great Lakes. We should've convinced our moms to let us drive Route 66 from Chicago to Santa Monica. Now that's the great American road trip. The Mother Road. That's what Steinbeck called it in *The Grapes of Wrath*."

"Your mom would never agree to that."

"And yours would?"

"She let me go to Paris, didn't she?"

"Only because you were accepted into that fancy writing workshop at the Sorbonne, and you convinced Sam Spellman to chaperone. She would never say no to anything writing related. If it meant you had to travel to the moon, she'd be lining up to buy your spacesuit. Speaking of Paris, I'm still mad at you for leaving me alone. You were supposed to visit me in Chicago the week you got back."

"I know. I'm sorry." Willow's chest aches remembering how disappointed Amelia had been when she texted her, blaming her mom for the sudden change of plans. It feels like a lifetime ago, the distance between them widening exponentially ever since. "I tried to convince my mom, but she insisted I stay home. Apparently, I'm allowed to go to the moon and Europe. But Chicago is just too far."

"See. What did I tell you?"

"Fair enough. But still, she's way more laid-back than your mom." As much as Willow admires Dr. Ford, she can be intense. Intimidating. Exacting. Like the time Amelia was ticketed for texting while driving. She'd forced them both to accompany her to the county coroner's office to view the mangled body of a car accident victim. Most of the time, she ignored Amelia in lieu of work, but when the spotlight shifted, even Willow felt the heat. "Anyway, it's fine. Niagara Falls is going to be amazing. Not to mention all the spots along the way. Pictured Rocks Lakeshore, Mackinac Island, and..."

Amelia tromps up the aisle toward the cab of the bus. Wide-eyed, she scrutinizes Willow, then offers her a chip from the bag in her hand. "Are you sure you didn't meet a guy over spring break? Some starving Parisian artist? You sound way too pie-in-the-sky, even for you."

"Hey, don't distract me. Two eyes on the road, two hands on the wheel. Remember?"

She holds on to her secret, guarding it like a precious treasure. Once she speaks it aloud, it won't be the same. It's already different. She feels the momentousness of it, unspoken, wedged between her and her best friend.

"Anyway, I've got plenty to be pie-in-the-sky about. In six months, we could be on the bestseller list. Mr. Spellman says our book has real potential."

"Do you know how many sales it takes to make a bestseller list?" Though Willow ignores her, Amelia presses on. "Last semester, this girl Trixie in my creative writing class told us that her dad sold ten thousand books in a week and still got snubbed. He even had a quote from Stephen King on his cover."

"So, we'll get a quote from someone bigger."

"Bigger than Stephen King? That's impossible." Amelia twists her mouth. A sure sign that she's making a mental spreadsheet, weighing the facts and figures. Calculating the likelihood of failure. It's the depressing logic Willow despises.

"Mr. Spellman could help us," she counters. "He's got connections, right?"

"Sam? Does he know John Grisham? Patricia Cornwell? I doubt it."

"Are we calling him Sam now?"

"*I* am." Amelia wiggles her eyebrows at Willow. She tosses the bag of chips onto the seat and leans against the cab's partition, her cellphone already in hand. "Let me text him." Her fingers fly across the keypad before she reads out loud. "Dear Sam, please make our book a bestseller. Also, did I mention that you are smokin' hot, and I would pay you to read me poetry in bed?"

"You can't be serious." Willow pulls a face. "He's practically my mom's age. I heard Ray call him Harry Potter once."

"I know. But he's not a boy. He's a man. A grown-up Harry. And Ray's way too intense. I can't believe your mom put up with him for as long as she did."

"Me either. I don't know what she saw in him." It's not entirely true. When Ray first sauntered up to the driver's side of the Volvo in his police uniform, her mother's cheeks had flushed. She flirted for the first time in ages, offered to do his taxes. *Wink, wink.* Sure enough, he'd had the nerve to jot his cell number on the speeding ticket. At first, Willow was overjoyed. Her mother deserved to be happy, and she hoped Ray would help ease the sting of the empty nest when she headed off to college next year. But then he'd turned into an overbearing control freak—he'd even tried to recruit Willow for his impossible mission: convincing her mother to keep him around.

"Hey, Earth to Willow." Amelia jabs her with a sharp elbow. "You're about to miss our exit."

Willow curses under her breath, jerking the wheel too fast. Amelia stumbles forward and braces herself against the oversized dash her mother had decorated with tiny potted succulents. "What is with you?"

"Sorry. I wasn't paying attention." Holding the wheel in a death grip, she guides the bus toward the off-ramp.

"I knew it. There *is* a Parisian. His name is Gabriel, and he's a painter. No, *a chef*. Or better yet, a filmmaker. When our book gets optioned, he can direct the movie. You had your first kiss in the Tuileries Garden and picnicked in front of the Eiffel Tower." Clearly enjoying herself, Amelia continues. "Too bad you had a chaperone. Otherwise, Gabriel would've dropped to one knee, and you'd have carted his fine ass back to the US on a K-1 visa."

Willow sighs. "You didn't really send that text to Mr. Spellman, did you?"

"Of course not. I'm not ridiculous." She giggles. "I only sent him your photo with a big heart on it."

"Don't blow it for us, Melly. We need him to take us seriously."

"I'm an English major at Northwestern. If he doesn't take that seriously, screw him. And don't call me Melly. You know I hate that nickname." With a huff, she retreats to the back of the bus to pout. Typical. But Willow *does* know. Amelia had hated that nickname since the first day of fifth grade when Brett Bowman, a popular eighth grader, had christened her Smelly Melly. Willow insisted she couldn't let a boring old football player co-opt her nickname. She uses it still, out of spite for that jerk.

After Willow parks in the lot outside the Harley-Davidson Museum, she finds Amelia with her head down in their manuscript, still pretending to read Chapter One. Willow clears her throat and prepares her peace offering.

"So, you were right. I do have some news."

Amelia presses her lips together, preventing the escape of anything resembling conciliation. It doesn't surprise Willow. She's always the last to give in. "I said, you were *right*. You win. I'm speaking your love language."

Amelia lifts her eyes begrudgingly. "Does it involve a Parisian?"

"*Better*. I got accepted to Northwestern. I'll be joining you there in the fall." She waits for Amelia to emit her usual whoop of excitement. Instead, she's met with a long pause she feels compelled to fill. "I guess that SAT tutor really paid off. I did so much better than I expected."

"Oh, wow. That's amazing, Will." Amelia tosses their manuscript on the seat and grabs her purse, securing the strap over her shoulder. Her gaze drifts past Willow and out the nearest window. "Really, it's fantastic. I can't wait."

"Did you already know? My mom told you, didn't she?"

"Of course not. It just doesn't surprise me, that's all. I knew you'd get in." But Amelia won't look at her. She points to the museum, the first stop on their itinerary. It had been Willow's idea to take a tour of the vintage Harleys since their main character, eighteen-year-old wild-child Jenna, rode a 1959 Hummer she'd inherited from her dad. "Now, are we going inside or not?"

Willow nods. But with every step forward, the knot in her stomach tightens. Her mother warned her this would happen. That she and Amelia would grow apart this year; they'd barely spoken since March. That some friendships aren't meant to last forever. Still, the awkward silence between them hurts worse than she imagined, and the excitement she felt deflates like a days-old balloon. She never realized how lonely keeping secrets would be.

"Four thousand miles. Can you imagine?" Willow snaps a photo of her favorite exhibit: the Tsunami Motorcycle, a 2004 Harley Night Train that was washed away in a storage container in the 2011 Japan tsunami and landed on the shores of a beach in British Columbia one year later. "It's kind of a miracle."

Amelia quirks her mouth again. It's the face of a girl who once called calculus fun. "Actually, it makes sense when you consider the Kuroshio and Oyashio Currents and, of course, the West Wind Drift. The movement of the water would've pushed it east. They found a rowboat too, in Crescent City, California."

Willow sighs. "You're totally missing the point. The wonder of it. If that bike could talk, it would tell a story. The places it's been, the things it's seen..."

Sensing she's lost Amelia already, Willow follows her friend's gaze to the other side of the exhibit's glass case, where she spots dark hair and a chiseled jaw. A black motorcycle jacket. Sensible Amelia has always had an unofficial thing for bad boys, though she prefers to look from afar rather than risk actual face-to-face contact. Once, after Amelia had confided in Willow's mom about a crush she had on a total stoner who'd repeated the ninth grade, her mom insisted they binge-watch the nineties cult classic *My So-Called Life*, calling it her Jordan Catalano intervention. It makes sense to Willow though, her attraction to unavailable men. Amelia can be painfully insecure. Hence, her friend has never been kissed.

"You should talk to him." Willow nudges her. "He looks like the sort of guy who would appreciate the West Wind Drift."

"Very funny. He's wearing two gold skull rings. *Two.* As if one figurative expression of death isn't enough. Why don't you talk to him?"

When Willow waves at him through the glass, Amelia ducks her head and pretends to be fascinated by the floor tile. Her embarrassment splotches across her pale cheeks.

"Don't be shy," Willow says. "He's your type."

"My *type*?"

"You know, trouble with a cherry on top. The sort of guy Dr. Ford would be appalled by."

Hands in his pockets, he gives a slight raise of his head. Like he agrees with Willow's assessment. Then, his face breaks into a lazy smile.

Willow leans in and whispers, "C'mon, college girl. I dare you."

"Seriously? You *dare* me? Are we back in third grade?"

"I *double dog* dare you. What do you have to lose? Worst case, we walk out of here, get back on the skoolie, and never see him again."

The ring of Amelia's cellphone interrupts the moment. Heads turn to look at her, and her flush deepens. She glances at the screen briefly, a fleeting cloud darkening her expression.

"Is everything okay?" Willow asks.

"Fine. It's fine." Amelia waves her away with a flick of her hand and returns her cell to her back pocket. But she stares off for a beat, frowning.

"Your future husband is getting away," Willow teases. "It's a classic meet cute. If only you weren't too chicken to talk to him."

Amelia narrows her eyes, but Willow spots a sudden flash of determination in her annoyance. Once Amelia sets her mind to a goal, she won't be denied, whether it's earning a badge as the top-ranked Girl Scout cookie seller or being draped with the Kildeer Prep valedictorian sash. Willow feels a twinge of guilt for winding her up.

"Watch me."

Past the museum parking lot, the Milwaukee River snakes through the city. Its surface shimmers beneath the streetlights like a dark mirror. Willow tugs at Amelia's arm, forcing her to slow down. "Are you sure about this? We know nothing about this guy. He might not even own a motorcycle."

Amelia wrenches herself free. "Don't be a baby now. You're the one who dared me to talk to him."

"I was trying to break you out of your shell. To say hi to him, exchange a few pleasantries. Maybe hang out later. Not *this*."

"What about getting inside Jenna's mind? You said you needed some details to make her character more believable." Willow huffs at her own words parroted back to her. She had said it. As much as she relates to her main character, she's never been on the back of a motorcycle. "Now, you've got the chance to become a legit biker chick."

"I wanted to see a few Harleys and take some pictures. I never said anything about riding one. I still can't believe you went up to a total stranger and asked if he would give us a ride on his bike."

"I know," Amelia agrees. "It sounds like something *you* would do."

Willow barely recognizes her friend, charging boldly ahead toward the shadowy figure at the end of the sidewalk. As they approach, her stomach drops. She'd convinced herself he wouldn't show. But there's no denying that it's him. He's wearing the same leather jacket. With the same unnerving design on the back. A snake weaving through the eyehole of a skull, its forked tongue extending along one of the sleeves and through the blood-red letters of his name, Jackson. Parked on the street next to him is a sleek black Harley.

Amelia stops short, still out of his earshot. "I'd do it myself, but he was into you. I could tell."

"Right."

"C'mon, do it for the book. For the realism."

When Jackson turns to face them, there's no time to argue. Willow certainly can't confess the truth. That she can't believe Amelia got them into this. That she's terrified of him and his self-assured swagger. That there won't be another book, not for the two of them anyway.

"Hey, you still want to go for a ride?" After pushing a wayward lock of hair from his face, he holds out a helmet to her like he already knows the answer. "There's a cool bar about a half-mile from here that doesn't check IDs. I'm game if you are. I can even come back for your friend."

Amelia pushes Willow forward with a laugh. For a cruel moment, she wonders if Amelia knows what she's been hiding. If she's getting even. But there's no way. She's been too careful for that.

"Just around the block," Willow insists. She tells herself to stop worrying. It'll be fun. "We're meeting some friends for dinner. I don't want to be late."

She fits the helmet onto her head, forcing herself to look at him while he buckles it beneath her chin. From here, she can tell he's got every piece of the bad boy kit assembled to perfection—the scruffy stubble, the gold cross chain, the crooked smirk. The muscles of his chest strain the T-shirt beneath his jacket. He swings one leg over the bike and waits for her to climb on behind him.

Stalling for time, she gestures to the small purse hanging at her side. "What should I do with this?"

"Put it in the saddle bag."

"I'll do it." Amelia slips it from her shoulder as Willow stares at the seat, calculating the slim space that's left for her to squeeze onto. With her purse secured, there are no more excuses.

"What are you waiting for?" Amelia asks. Then, to Jackson, she adds, "She talks a big game, but..."

Willow doesn't know what to say. Only that there's a difference between an adventure and a death wish. As she joins Jackson on the back of his rumbling Harley, she knows she's straddling that line. But she has a plan now—she's going to make the best of this detour—and unfortunately, the first step involves mounting the back of a complete stranger's motorcycle. She hides her fear behind a brave smile that she aims right at Amelia.

"You were saying?"

Suddenly nonchalant, Amelia shrugs at her like she never cared about winning the argument. Then, she directs a glare at Jackson. "Remember, I know what you look like. Better bring her back safe and sound or else."

"Don't worry," Jackson assures her, palming Willow's thigh like it belongs to him. "Your friend will be alright with me. She can hold on as tight as she wants."

The motorcycle zips along the waterfront, blowing Willow's hair behind her. When they arrive at the end of the block, she lets out an indignant whoop that she hopes reaches Amelia. She'll be damned if she lets her friend make her look like a coward. Frankly, she'd rather die.

SIX

NOW

Hours have passed since Allen Perlmutter appeared on Tracy's doorstep. Still, she can't tear herself away from the unblinking screen of her cellphone. She waits for it to speak. To reveal her daughter to her. *Hi, Mom. It's me. I'm here. I'm safe.* The unbearable longing for those words throbs like a toothache. She can't focus on anything else. Not Detective Delgado or the yellow tape or the crime scene investigators who disappeared inside the bus. Not Candice either, who hasn't stopped pacing in front of the fireplace, making call after call to God knows who. Tracy catches a few pointed questions that only twist the knife in deeper.

Have you heard from Amelia?

Do you have a patient by the name of Willow Barrett?

Is this the Niagara County Coroner's Office?

When her phone finally rings, the shrill sound of it shocks her. It falls to the hardwood, vibrating like a living thing. She scrabbles after it, desperate. There is just one name in her brain, and it comes out in a wail.

"Willow?"

The room quiets. Candice looks away from her, pityingly.

But Detective Delgado homes in. "Put it on speaker," she mouths.

"Hello?" Tracy doesn't immediately recognize the man's voice. But it devastates her anyway. It's not her daughter. "It's Sam Spellman. I just got your message."

She can't remember calling. The entire day blurs like a ruined photograph, only the worst parts remain in focus. Strewn papers. Broken laptop. Her daughter's driver's license, still tucked inside the handbag on her bed. The sad clump of her hair. Both girls, vanished without a trace.

She should say something, but she's stuck. No words come.

"You said that Willow and Amelia are missing. You asked if I'd heard from either of them."

"Well, *have you*?" Candice demands from the other side of the room. "This is Amelia's mother. *I'm* the one who called."

Tracy winces at Candice's sharp tone. Poor Sam. Willow adores him. Amelia too. All the kids did. He'd been voted Kildeer Prep's Favorite Teacher three years running. Tracy occasionally let herself wonder what could've been—*a fool's errand*, Grandma Ruth would say—if she'd had a teacher who believed in her literary talent. But in the middle of Podunk, Illinois, nobody used the word literary.

"Really? I'm so sorry, Dr. Ford. I must've gotten confused. I'll admit, when I listened to the message, I blanked out a little. I got in my car right away. You both must be worried sick."

"Where are you?" Tracy blurts, though she already sees him hurrying up the sidewalk toward the house. He looks professorial, clad in a button-down and sweater vest. With his floppy dark hair, wire-rim glasses, and emerald-green eyes, Ray had sometimes called him Harry Potter under his breath. But Tracy found him charming, which only made Ray more insufferable. She's grateful he's not here to question her or Sam.

"I'm outside. I thought I could help."

Detective Delgado gives a nod of encouragement, just as she

had when a few of Willow's co-workers from Chapter and Verse had shown up to offer their support. Even the bookstore manager had been eager to help. But Tracy had sent them all home. What good could they do anyway, with Niagara Falls five hundred miles away? She doesn't want them to see her like this. It's bad enough with Candice taking charge and the detective drilling her with the same pointless questions. All she can think about is Willow. All she can do is blame herself.

Tracy forces herself to walk to the front door, to open it. To arrange her face from *go away* to *grateful you're here*. Truthfully, seeing Sam brings more comfort than she'd expected.

"I hope it's okay that I came." He peers around her, looking sheepish.

"Of course." She steps aside, allowing him to cross the threshold. Usually, Tracy would balk at his mud-spattered Oxfords making tracks on the floor, a leftover quirk from her youth, when she could hardly see the floor, let alone clean it. Grandma Ruth piled her collectibles to the ceiling, buying more than she ever sold, and she sold a lot. Enough to keep the farmhouse and food on the table. But the dirt doesn't matter to Tracy right now. "Detective Delgado, this is Sam Spellman, the Honors English teacher I told you about."

"Please, call me Sam." He follows the detective into the living room and sits on the sofa. Tracy tries not to think about the last time she saw him there, waiting to ferry her daughter across the Atlantic to the Sorbonne. It only reminds her of Willow and what's gone horribly wrong. She drops onto the cushion next to him, suddenly lightheaded. "The girls were special to me. Star students, both of them. They phoned me a few days ago, right after they arrived at the White Water Campground."

"They did?" Candice glares at him. Her eyes, sharp as the blade of a scalpel. "*Why?*"

"He was mentoring them through the publishing process," Tracy says. "You know that."

Seemingly unbothered, Sam shrugs. "Tracy's right. We were in regular contact throughout the year. I was helping them with their novel. That day, Amelia had called me to talk about writing a query letter. We were hopeful that we could secure an agent for their thriller."

"*The Road Trip*, you mean?" Detective Delgado asks.

"That's the one. I suppose it is a bit ironic now, isn't it?"

The detective nods. She doesn't mention the bus. The crime scene, as she'd called it. Tracy wants to lay it all bare. She wants Sam to explain it to the detective. To explain it to her. Surely, someone could explain it. *How could this happen?*

"What do you remember about the conversation? Was anything out of the ordinary?"

"Well, I could tell Amelia was upset. I asked her about it, but she wouldn't really say why. I assumed it was..." Tracy senses the discomfort in his pause. She can guess what he's thinking, and she hopes he won't spill the beans entirely. Candice won't like it. "I thought she and Willow had a fight. Sometimes, Amelia got jealous or vice versa. It wasn't my place to pry. Frankly, it wasn't unusual. Working with teenagers, you get used to the ups and downs. The moodiness."

"You spoke with Willow as well, then?"

"Only Amelia, as far as I can remember. The entire call lasted ten minutes or so." After tapping at his phone screen, Sam holds it out to them. "See."

Tracy stares at the number on his call log. She wonders how furious Candice will be when she finds out about the second book. The one Willow had begun drafting without Amelia. In Tracy's opinion, it shouldn't matter. It wouldn't be any different than *The Road Trip*, for which calling Amelia a co-author seemed overly generous.

"Was that the last time you heard from the girls?"

"Come to think of it, that was it. Nothing since." Looking sick with worry, he glances at Tracy beside him. "Has there been any news?"

Before Tracy can answer, Detective Delgado interjects. "You seem to know the girls fairly well, Sam. What do you think happened?"

He knots his hands together on his lap and delivers his answer without looking up. "I wish I knew."

Candice huffs. "It's a prank, right? It must be. Like the time they filled your desk drawer with ping pong balls."

"It's true that they were jokesters. But this isn't like them. Since you called, I texted both girls repeatedly. I told them the police were involved. I don't want to think the worst, but..."

Tracy can't bear to hear him finish. She stands up and plants her hands on her hips, doing her best to channel authoritative Candice. But she feels like a girl playing dress-up in her mother's heels. She needs ten more years and a few gray hairs. "We should go there. We need to look for them. I can't just sit here and do nothing."

Detective Delgado dismisses her with a shake of her head. She can't even convince a wet-behind-the ears cop. "Local authorities are doing everything they can to track down the girls. If it's necessary, we'll request both their phone records but that can take a few days."

"If it's *necessary*?" Candice parrots. "Of course it's necessary."

"The best thing you can do for now is to stay here and remain calm."

"For how long?" Candice asks.

"I'll check in with you in the morning. In the meantime, keep reaching out to their friends, and call me if you hear anything."

Tracy gapes at the detective. "That's it? You're leaving?"

"I have everything I need from you two, and I can make

more progress at the station. I want to take another crack at Allen, the kid from Taskrabbit. See if there's anything more he can tell us about how the bus ended up back here."

Tracy regrets not grilling him harder. "Is he a suspect now?"

"Like I told you before, we can't rule anything out, including a voluntary disappearance."

Candice scowls at the detective. "You really believe Amelia ran away? She's smarter than that."

"What are you saying?" Tracy asks. "That Willow isn't?"

"I'm sure you'd be the first to admit that Willow doesn't always make the best decisions." Smugly, she offers the detective an explanation that boils Tracy's blood. "She bombed her calculus final last year because she showed up an hour late."

"You know how she gets with standardized tests. She had a full-blown panic attack in the quad. Sam, tell her. You were there."

Sam holds out his hands, trying to keep the peace. "Hey, the last thing the girls would want is to see their mothers going at it. If you ask me, I can't imagine why either one of them would want to run away. They had the world at their fingertips. I'm telling you, their book is something special. It has real potential."

Tracy nods at Sam like he's read her mind. Their book *is* something special. She tries to hold on to that thought, to the fleeting spark of joy it brings. But it lasts only as long as it takes Detective Delgado to cross the living room. She lingers at the front door, suddenly quiet. If only Tracy could swap places with her for the afternoon. Turn into someone who could drive away from here. Who could listen to the radio and eat a tuna salad sandwich at Potbelly's for lunch. Someone whose entire life didn't hang in the balance.

"Mr. Spellman and I agree about one thing. Both of you need to get your shit together. Your daughters are missing. They're counting on you, and you're too busy bickering. At this point, it wouldn't surprise me if they did run away. *From the two of you.*"

The hush that follows hits Tracy like a brick to the face. The quiet click of the door shutting. The detective's measured walk to her unmarked car. The way Sam whispers, "That's not what I meant." It all finally breaks her. She lowers her head into her hands and begins to sob.

Tracy's tears send Candice packing. She hustles for the door, avoiding eye contact as she mutters a goodbye to Sam. *In order to be a good surgeon, you've got to have ice in your veins*, she'd admitted to Tracy once, in a rare display of vulnerability. The girls had been all knees and elbows back then, cartwheeling across Tracy's front lawn in the middle of their gymnastics phase. When Amelia had held up her small bloody palm, punctured by a thorn, Candice had quickly dismissed her tears and pronounced it a superficial injury. *Sometimes, I worry that I can't turn it off. What if I can't thaw out when Amelia needs me?*

Still sniffling, Tracy darts off to find a tissue. She dabs at her eyes and tells herself to pull it together. At least until Sam leaves. Then, she'll allow herself a proper breakdown.

"I'm sorry to drag you into this," she tells him, from the safety of the kitchen. From here, he can't hear her shallow breathing. Can't see the way her hands shake.

"Are you kidding? I'm glad you called." Sam doesn't stay put for long. But he approaches her with the caution of a zookeeper. She's a maimed animal cowering in a cage. "I'm worried too. I couldn't just do nothing."

She risks meeting his eyes, fearing that she might lose it again. With his students, he's been so perceptive. He's always understood when to push the girls, when to pull back. He'll make a great father one day. "What if the detective is right?" she asks. "What if the girls ran away? Maybe we've been riding them too hard with this book. They're still just teenagers. And now, Willow took on the burden of writing a second... and keeping it from her friend. I feel awful."

"I've never seen you push Willow too hard. You've only encouraged her to pursue her passion. She's the one who was eager to start another book, and it was her idea to wait to tell Amelia." Sam squeezes her shoulder with the kind of tenderness that makes her feel less alone, which is its own kind of magic. "And who can blame her? Dr. Ford is so competitive. I imagine she'll be more disappointed than Amelia herself. I honestly think Amelia only did all this in the first place to impress her mom. We all know she's been riding Willow's coattails."

Tracy could easily pile on, but she wants Sam to see her differently than the detective. Not as a crazy lady hellbent on winning a *mompetition*. "Well, in Candice's defense, she is busy saving lives. That's a lot of pressure, and Amelia doesn't require much. She always seems so composed, so practical, so self-sufficient. It's like she's nineteen going on thirty."

Sam removes his glasses and cleans them with the hem of his vest. It reminds her of Willow, the endearing way she twists her hair around her finger when she's nervous or lost in a daydream. "Maybe that's the problem," he says. "Everybody expects her to be perfect, to be grown up. She can never just let her hair down. Lately, it seems like she's starting to crack under the weight of it."

"What do you mean?"

He lets out a heavy breath. "I wasn't sure whether I should mention it to the detective. I don't want to embarrass Amelia in front of her mother."

"I won't say anything, I swear." It's out of her mouth before she realizes what she's promised. She can hear Ray's voice branding her a fool. Candice, too. She used to be better in a crisis. In Grandma Ruth's own quirky way, she'd called her sensible. *Not a man with a plan, but a dame with an aim*, she'd say, flashing Tracy her crooked smile. But who could plan for something like this?

"Tracy?" His cellphone in his outstretched hand, Sam blinks at her with expectation. "I said, I trust you to take a look."

She mutters a broken apology, already scrolling through a series of texts from Amelia. As far as Tracy can tell, Sam had never replied.

Nobody gets me like you do.

As a guy—not my former teacher—do you think I'm pretty?

I wish you were here.

Sam had received the last of the texts a week ago, accompanied by a selfie of Amelia lying atop a rumpled bunkbed in nothing but a lacy black bra and panties.

"Jesus, Sam. How long was this going on?"

"A couple of weeks. Just before she came home for the summer."

"And you didn't tell anyone?"

"I figured it was just a harmless crush. That if I didn't respond, she'd lose interest. But she kept upping the ante."

"Obviously." Tracy places the cellphone on the counter facedown. She can't bear to look at Amelia like that. So vulnerable. It bothers her more than she cares to admit that she doesn't know everything about her daughter's best friend. What she does know unnerves her, and this only makes it worse. "You should've talked to her. You should've deleted the photos."

"Yeah, I should've done a lot of things. But you know how reserved she is. I thought she'd feel humiliated if I confronted her. Honestly, I worried that she'd sabotage the book somehow, mess things up for Willow. Working at the high school, it's not the first time I've received unwanted photos. Girls that age can be unpredictable. I guess, in a weird way, I kept them as evidence."

Tracy can't argue with that. She'd seen the girls and their friends fawning over Sam. "You should tell the detective before the phone records come in. It's going to look bad if you don't."

"It'll look bad either way."

"Candice will lose her mind."

"I know." After a brief pause, the corner of his mouth lifts. "I'm a little afraid of her."

"You're not the only one." Laughing feels wrong but necessary. Like secretly tossing the moth-eaten sweater Grandma Ruth plucked from a Salvation Army bin. Sam has a great laugh. It's warm and boyish, light years away from Ray's rowdy guffaw.

But the silence that follows leaves her empty. She glances at the door. "I keep thinking they're going to walk through it."

He nods. "So, what do we do now?"

Tracy retrieves the contact list from the dining room table. She and Candice had made it together at the detective's request. Three quarters of the names are crossed out, including Sam Spellman. "We keep calling, keep hoping. And we wait."

* * *

Tracy jolts awake. For a precious moment, she forgets her reality. It comes back to her in a rush, and she sits up too fast, leaving her dizzy. The stranger at the door. The bus. And the girls, vanished. Sam Spellman on her sofa with his cellphone pressed to his ear. It's raining again. Raining and dark.

"I fell asleep," she says, mostly to herself, disbelieving.

"Candice called," Sam tells her. "She couldn't reach you. She's coming over."

Tracy's entire world revolves like a game spinner. Finally, she lands on the horror of his words. Candice couldn't reach her. Candice. Couldn't. Reach. Her.

Desperate, she snatches her phone from the coffee table. The screen is horribly black like the inside of a coffin. She jabs at it, already knowing it's dead. Already feeling the thick bile of panic rising in her throat. What if Willow calls? What if she already has? How could Tracy let this happen?

When the doorbell rings, she's halfway there. She throws open the door to the ghost of Candice, pale-faced and shivering. She says nothing, only holds out her cellphone.

Tracy has no choice but to take it. The weight of it feels fateful. Like a stone in a pocket meant to sink her to the bottom of the ocean. She reads the text from Amelia to her mother, sent not five minutes before.

Willow and I got into a fight, and I'm coming home.

INSTAGRAM

writingontheroad #Sals Hawaiian Special in Green Bay is the best pineapple pizza on earth. Call me a liar. I dare you. @melthebookworm nailed it! #daytwo #theroadtrip #bestfriends #pizzaislife
30 likes 7 comments 3 shares

ilovepuppies Looks yummy!

karentjones Hate that place. Bad décor. Bad service. Bad pizza. One star.

> **bobalicious3** @karentjones Your name is Karen. Lololol. Probably never even been there.

> **karentjones** @bobalicious3 And you probably work there. Loser.

roccosristorante You haven't tried Rocco's yet.

packersordie Did you visit Lambeau Field? #lambeauislife

49ersrule @packersordie Lambeau sucks. #goniners

SEVEN
BEFORE

Day Two on the Road: Green Bay

Willow takes another bite of the thin crust pizza from Sal's, an Italian dive a half-mile from Lambeau Field. It's no wonder their Hawaiian special is at the top of Amelia's list of must-eats in Green Bay, Wisconsin. She surveys the lunch crowd, her attention drawn to a group of little girls at the large corner table. They couldn't be more than five years old, with their dirty soccer uniforms and disheveled ponytails.

"Remember when we tried out for youth soccer?" she asks Amelia. "And Brittany Thompson kicked the ball off my head and into the goal." It's a peace offering after their argument last night. But Amelia doesn't look up from the manuscript binder, even after the girls emit a loud, synchronized squeal when their two large pizzas arrive. One of them snags a piece of pepperoni and holds it above her mouth, prompting a round of simultaneous laughter. She and Amelia were like that once. On the same page. That was before Amelia left for Northwestern. Before Willow opted out of their spring break plans and started writing another book on her own. Before they stopped texting and calling and video chatting.

"I'm still not sure about the ending." Willow concedes defeat, ignoring the girls' contagious giggling. "I don't think Jenna would kill Lacey. It's just not believable."

Amelia rolls her eyes but says nothing.

"This pizza is amazing, by the way. Good call." Willow can't try any harder. She's already apologized at least five times for making Amelia worry. Still, she's willing to give it one more go, so long as it snaps Amelia out of her funk. "I'm really sorry about—"

"We can't change the ending now. It's already written. Besides, it's a phenomenal twist. No one will see it coming. And it's James Patterson believable."

"What does that even mean?"

Amelia answers with a dramatic groan that makes Willow feel small. Small and silly. She glances back to the soccer team's table, where the girls are happily munching.

"I keep forgetting how green you are," Amelia says. "We learned all about it in Creative Writing second semester. A plot twist can be outlandish, crazy, completely off the wall. As long as it's not too wild for a Patterson novel, you're in the clear. Anyway, I hate to burst your bubble but plenty of friends kill each other. It's not that far out there. There's a whole docuseries called *I Killed My BFF*."

Willow freezes mid-bite, remembering the wee hours of the morning and the fury Amelia unleashed when Willow knocked on the door of the bus seven hours after Jackson had driven away with her on the back of his bike. Her anger had only escalated when Willow refused to reveal where she'd been. Though Willow should have just spit out another lie, she couldn't bring herself to do it. "Should I be worried?" she asks.

"Only if you insist on changing the ending. You're the one

who wrote it, and I'm telling you, it's brilliant, Will. It's so twisted. I'm still mad at you, but I can't lie. It's really good."

Though Amelia's compliment warms her like the sun, it doesn't ring true. She authored that chapter months ago. She's light years beyond it now. When she reads her old work, it sounds so juvenile. "Alright, but Mr. Spellman thinks it's a bit contrived. He says that—"

"How many novels has he published? Has he even managed to finish writing one?"

"Seriously? After all he's done for us?" Willow tosses the crust of her pizza onto the plate. Suddenly, she's lost her appetite. "He's had five short stories in *The Atlantic*. That's impressive."

"A short story is a far cry from a full-length novel. You know what they say. Those who can't do, teach."

Willow recognizes her friend's haughty tone. She sounds just like her surgeon mom. But she's rarely heard it aimed in her direction. "You're just upset about last night."

"I have every right to be. I didn't know what the hell happened to you. I was about to call your mother. Where did you go, anyway? Were you with Jackson?"

"It was all in the name of research," Willow teases, trying to sound light-hearted.

"Whatever." The way Amelia glances at her phone makes Willow nervous. She's been eyeing it like a ticking timebomb since that call at the museum yesterday. "Maybe I'll just post the photo I took of the two of you riding off into the sunset. Your mom would love that."

"You took a picture?" It's not her mom who Willow's worried about. "You're the one who begged him for a ride. I didn't want to get on that bike, but you gave me no choice. He could've been a legit serial killer. If you ask me, it only seems fair that I made you worry." Now, she really does sound childish, but it's too late to backpedal. "So, don't take it out on me—or

Mr. Spellman for that matter. Yesterday, you wanted to jump his unpublished bones."

Amelia manages a half-smile. "All I'm saying is he's a thirty-something high school teacher. Is he eye candy? *Yes*. But what does he really know about writing to market? Building a fanbase? Producing a bestseller?"

"Probably more than we do."

Amelia looks away from her, at the pizza. She plucks the best slice from the pan—the pineapple perfectly browned on the edges—and takes a delicate bite. "Speak for yourself."

At the soccer table, the girls have finished eating. They gather around a small gold trophy that reads Second Place, and their coach snaps several photos with his cellphone. When he calls out, "Now silly faces!" Willow's stomach sinks. She feels homesick. Not for Kildeer or her mom or Chapter and Verse, but for the girl sitting across from her, close enough to touch.

"Alright," she says. "We can keep the ending. Jenna shoots Lacey with the gun she steals from the cabin near the campground."

Amelia shakes her head and takes another bite, dabbing sauce from the corner of her mouth. "A gun is so cold and passionless. The murder should be more personal than that."

Too exhausted to argue another point, Willow asks, "What do you suggest?"

Playfully wielding her dinner knife, her friend breaks into a smile. Just like that, she's herself again. "Stabbing."

Fifteen minutes later, the soccer team makes an unruly exit, laughing and dancing and goofing off. When the door shuts behind the last straggler, Amelia raises her eyebrows at the table they left behind. "Is that a hundred-dollar bill? That's a huge tip."

"Probably. They came through here like a hurricane. Did

you see the one who threw a balled-up napkin at the coach?" Willow doesn't bother to look at the cash. Instead, she gathers her own money to leave for the server.

"I dare you to steal it."

"*What?*" She laughs nervously. "Why?"

"Why not? You dared me to talk to Jackson, and I did. Now, I dare you to steal the money. It's only fair."

"Who are you?" Willow stares at her friend, pondering her own question. It's the same Melly on the outside, bright green eyes and jet black hair. "Has your body been invaded by an alien?"

"C'mon. I've never known you to turn down a dare."

"Skinny-dipping in Kelsey Scott's pool is one thing, but stealing? That's a hard no." Frustrated, Willow scoots out of her chair, taking the manuscript binder with her. "I'm going to the bathroom. Then, we should hit the road. It's a few hours' drive to Miners Beach."

By the time she returns, Amelia waits for her outside, making a face at her through the restaurant window. At first, she finds it reassuring. But then, Willow passes by their table on her way out. It's not bussed yet, and there's no sign of the ten bucks she slipped under the edge of her plate.

Willow pretends to rummage in her purse, searching for a stick of gum. She side-eyes the corner spot, where the server and the bus boy collect the dirty dishes on two large trays. She scans the mess the girls left behind—the shredded napkins, the wayward straws, the discarded pizza crusts—until she finds the black book with the receipt in the center of the table. She gapes at it in disbelief, then heads for the exit.

Behind her, the server mutters, "This job sucks. They only left me fifty cents."

Still flummoxed, Willow pushes through the front door and into the warm summer air. She turns to Amelia. "Did you take the tips off the tables?"

"Of course not. I'm not a delinquent." As Amelia skips ahead of her, across the parking lot and toward their school bus, Willow's stomach nosedives. She's been so busy building a fortress around her hidden life, she never imagined Amelia might have done the same.

EIGHT

NOW

Tracy closes her eyes, but she doesn't sleep, hasn't. Not since she awoke in a panic yesterday evening to find her cellphone dead. Still, it's a relief to lean her head back against the passenger seat of Candice's SUV. She can pretend she's dreamed it all. She can ignore the looming airport arrivals sign and the clock on the dash. The metronomic clicking of the blinker that signals their approach. She can stay right here in limbo between one day and the next. Between the hope and the reality of her situation.

Twelve hours ago, Amelia texted her mother. One sentence.

Ten hours ago, Amelia bought a plane ticket home. One plane ticket.

Two hours ago, her flight departed from Buffalo Niagara International Airport, non-stop to Chicago Midway. One passenger en route.

Now, the two mothers sit side by side, illegally parked outside baggage claim, as the rest of the world goes on, oblivious to their nightmare. Tracy forces herself to look. She won't be able to pretend much longer.

Candice tried to convince her to wait at home. *It's better I go alone*, she said. *I'm sure Amelia will be frantic. Her friend is missing, and who knows what she's been through?*

What about Willow?

For that, Candice had no reply. Because Amelia had gone radio silent, not answering any of their frantic calls or texts. Tracy didn't give voice to any of the sharp fears whirling through her brain. Every so often, they poked at her, like nails spitting from a tornado. Maybe she should've listened to Candice. She could be lying in her bed right now, albeit not sleeping.

Next to her, Candice takes an audible breath. She stares straight ahead, just as much a zombie as Tracy. "What if Amelia isn't on that plane? What if the text was a hoax?"

"A hoax?" The word catches in Tracy's throat. Yesterday's anger, a fingernail scratch from the surface.

"What if the kidnapper sent it? To buy himself time. To make it seem like she's okay. Like they're both okay. Like they just had a silly little tiff."

"First, you say that this whole thing is a prank that the girls are pulling on us. Then, you insinuate that Willow ran off. And now, it's a kidnapping? I told you that we should've called the detective the moment you got that text."

Candice gives her a look that makes her feel simultaneously stupid and homicidal. "I don't want my daughter interrogated like a common criminal. God knows what's happened to her."

"Don't you think we should at least park the car and go inside?"

The slight tremor of Candice's hands on the wheel gives her away. She's human after all. "I don't want to freak her out, okay? I have no idea what's going on here. This isn't like her. I'm..."

"Scared?"

Candice whimpers. But it's not an answer. She points up ahead, to the sliding doors of the terminal. "Is that...?"

Tracy squints against the rays of sunlight piercing through

the mostly cloudy sky. She knows Amelia as well as her own daughter. The self-possessed way she'd always carried herself, as if she already had everything she could possibly need. This girl, though, looks broken. A bird with a clipped wing. Her sleek black hair cascades like crow's feathers over the sleeves of her Northwestern hoodie. Usually, it accentuates her porcelain complexion, her green eyes. But today, it only highlights the dark circles beneath them.

"Yes," Tracy answers. "It's her."

Already, Candice has flung off her seat belt and thrown open the door. Leaving the SUV to idle, she runs toward Amelia and wraps her in a stranglehold of a hug.

Tracy holds her breath as she scans the busy sidewalk. Strangers rush past mother and daughter—wheeling suitcases, fishing cellphones out of pockets—oblivious to their circumstances. With every passing traveler, Tracy's panic swells, until it threatens to burst like a blister inside her.

She cracks the door, but there's nowhere to go. She can only look numbly at the scene in front of her. That's what it feels like. A scene in a movie. The kind of movie she and Willow would've watched together, sharing a bowl of popcorn and a bag of M&Ms.

Amelia's chin rests on her mother's shoulder. She stares blankly. Her eyes remain fixed on Tracy.

Tracy tries to smile at her, but she can't quite manage it. Instead, she lifts her hand in a wave. Instantly, Amelia buries her face, the way a child might.

She's not Willow. Tracy can't help but hate her.

"She doesn't want to talk about it yet," Candice announces.

"What do you mean?"

"She's upset. Give her some space."

Two steps behind her mother, Amelia doesn't look up. She waits on the sidewalk outside the SUV until Tracy surrenders the passenger seat. She climbs in the back behind Amelia, who cradles her backpack in her lap like a lifeline.

"Amelia." Tracy whispers her name, hoping to coax the girl out of her shell. "Where's Willow?"

Candice gently eases back into traffic, then growls at her, "Jesus, Tracy. She doesn't know. I told you she's upset."

"She doesn't seem that upset." But that isn't true. Tracy would call it shell-shocked—the word Grandma Ruth had used to describe her only son, the uncle Tracy had never known. Two months after returning from Vietnam, he'd drunk a bottle of homemade wine and wandered into the path of an oncoming train. Tracy often wondered if Ruth's antique hoard filled the void he left behind. "And she'll have to talk to the detective anyway."

Amelia sucks in a shallow breath. "Detective? Am I in trouble?"

"No, honey." Candice pats her hand. "Of course not. But when the bus came back, we didn't know what to think. The police are involved."

"I didn't know what else to do. I can't drive a stick shift. Willow did all the driving." With that, she curls her knees into her chest and drops her head between them. Her shoulders tremble, then go still.

Tracy sits back, momentarily conceding defeat. She wants to shake Amelia, to demand answers. But she's not a monster. She closes her eyes and listens to the drone of the freeway beneath the tires. That too reminds her of Willow, five months old and sleeping in the car seat while Tracy circled the block again and again. Anything for a sacred hour of silence. Now, what she wouldn't give to hear baby Willow wailing. Teenage Willow, mouthing off. Nineteen-year- old Willow, singing in the shower after a long day at the bookstore.

"Are you hungry?" Candice asks Amelia. "You must be starving. We can stop for pancakes. Your favorite."

When Amelia doesn't reply, her mother tries again. "It doesn't have to be pancakes. How do bagels sound? Or smoothies? We could go to that new place you like. What is it called?"

"Mom. Stop. Just take me home. I'm not hungry. I'm exhausted. All I want to do is crash."

"*Exhausted?*" Tracy can't help herself. She can't soften the anger in her voice. Can't hide the suspicion. "I haven't slept in over twenty-four hours. You're not going to bed until you talk to somebody about what happened. If you won't talk to me or your mother, that's fine. But you *will* talk to the cops."

Candice shoots darts at her in the rearview. "Do you hear yourself? You're acting like Amelia did something wrong. Her best friend is missing. She's traumatized. She has no idea what happened to Willow."

"How could you possibly know that? You haven't asked her, have you?" Tracy hears her blood whooshing in her ears. She shouts above it, "Well, have you?"

"I don't need to ask. I already—"

"Can the two of you please just..." Amelia's voice wobbles. The rest of her plea dissolves in a sob, leaving Tracy helpless. She can't unsee the strands of Willow's hair, and her imagination wanders to a nightmarish place. A place where Willow is gone forever.

Tracy rubs her temples to push away the thought. Against her better judgment, she taps out a text to Ray. She hates that he's right. That she does need him again. Especially since she'd spent the last six months convincing herself she didn't need anyone. But she has no choice.

Amelia's back. Call me ASAP.

Tracy peers out the living room picture window and down the street to the Ford house. It's been twenty-eight minutes since Candice dropped her off at her own driveway. She didn't even bother to put the SUV in park when she glanced in the rearview and said, "We'll call you later. After Amelia gets some rest." As Tracy slunk toward the house, embarrassed by how easily she'd given up, she risked a look over her shoulder at her daughter's best friend and shivered at the pale face staring back at her.

The dark thoughts had taken hold of Tracy then—*I don't trust her. I never have. She's always been jealous of Willow*—and she'd promptly summoned Detective Delgado and taken up watch.

Each car that passes sends her heart skipping. She distracts herself by speed dialing Willow on speaker. As futile as it may be, it makes her feel better to listen to the interminable ringing. Willow had never bothered with voicemail. Eventually, a robotic voice cuts in to inform her that the subscriber she wishes to reach is unavailable. Unavailable doesn't sound so bad. It's certainly better than missing.

Tracy jumps at the sight of the unmarked police cruiser turning onto her street. Foolishly, she shouts at it through the window. "Detective!"

The car glides to a stop outside of the Ford house. Tracy trips over her own feet, stumbling out the door, and hurries down the sidewalk toward Detective Delgado.

"Detective!" she calls again. "Wait! I need to talk to you."

Though the detective stiffens, she greets Tracy with a sympathetic smile that leaves her wondering exactly how many unhinged mothers have run her down.

"Ms. Barrett, I thought we discussed this on the phone. You agreed to wait at home." She slams the car door behind her and keeps moving, no doubt intent on leaving Tracy behind.

Like a stray dog begging for scraps, Tracy follows at her heels. "I know. You're right. But I can't. I can't sit there while somebody else asks all the questions. Amelia can be so convincing. She knows how to present well. So does her mother."

Detective Delgado heaves a sigh, stopping at the Fords' front steps. "I realize that I look young, but I wasn't born yesterday. For three years, I've been a detective with Missing Persons. Before that, I worked SVU. You need to trust me."

"It's not you I don't trust." Tracy recalls the scantily clad selfie of Amelia that she can't unsee. There are other things too. Things she can't unknow. "She hardly said two words to me on the way home. She told her mother she was too upset to talk about it. I think she's hiding something."

"Why didn't you mention this yesterday?"

"Yesterday I thought they were both missing. Now, suddenly, Amelia turns up. You expect me to believe that she doesn't have a clue what happened to Willow?"

"I expect you to let me do my job." The detective takes the steps faster than Tracy anticipated. She hurries to keep up. "You called me here for a reason, right?"

"Can I at least come inside?" She won't survive it. The not knowing.

"I wouldn't recommend it. But it's not up to me."

Tracy snakes out a hand and stabs at the bell before Detective Delgado can stop her.

Candice and Amelia sit side by side on the sofa. Despite Candice's age, they look more like sisters than mother and daughter. Tracy has always marveled at their resemblance. Once, years ago, she'd joked about it at a PTA meeting, wondering out loud whether Candice had managed to clone herself. Right now, they share the same steely gaze and it's trained on Tracy. Still, what did they expect her to do? Wait around while Amelia caught up on her beauty sleep?

"I was just about to call you, Detective. But it seems Tracy beat me to the punch."

"I'm glad she did. Time is of the essence here. If your daughter has information—"

"I don't." Amelia directs her statement to Tracy. "I want to find Willow as much as anybody. She's my best friend."

"Good. I'm glad to hear it." Detective Delgado motions vaguely toward the stairs. "Is there someplace we can go? I'd like to speak to you privately."

Gripping her mother's hand in her own, Amelia says, "I don't have anything to hide."

"I'm not saying that you do. It's just that Ms. Barrett seems to think you're a bit reluctant to talk about what happened, which is completely understandable. You've been through a lot in the last few days, I'm sure."

Amelia's eyes flick to her mother and back again. Tracy wants to shake the truth out of her.

"My main job here is to get Willow home safely."

"I know. I want to help. I just needed to reset. Take a shower. Put on some clean clothes. Is that bad?" At least that seems truthful. She *does* look refreshed, with her cheeks still flushed from the hot water and spots from the ends of her damp hair dotting the shoulders of her T-shirt. "I didn't want to say the wrong thing."

While Tracy's alarm bells obliterate all rational thought, Detective Delgado nods with understanding. "We just need the truth, Amelia. You won't be in trouble."

Tracy dated Ray long enough to know that cops lie, him better than most, apparently. But Amelia seems reassured. She takes a breath and straightens her spine. Presses her lips together, determined. That's the girl Tracy recognizes.

"On Sunday night, we had an argument. She stormed off the bus into the woods and never came back. I thought she was just messing with me at first. Punishing me for the fight. I mean, she didn't even have shoes on. But she didn't come back that night or the next day. I texted her a hundred times before I realized she'd left her phone on the bus."

"Her phone?" Tracy grips the arm of the sofa, anchoring herself there. She fears she may fly at Amelia at any moment. "Where is it now?"

"In the bus, I guess. I assumed you found it. Didn't you?"

The detective gives a small shake of her head, confirming Tracy's worst fears. Then, to add insult, she scolds Tracy. "Why don't we save our questions and let Amelia tell her story?"

"I'm sorry," Amelia says. "I feel terrible. I should've brought it with me. I was so panicked I wasn't thinking clearly."

"It's okay. I'm sure you did the best you could," Detective Delgado assures her. "So, you had an argument on Sunday evening. What did the two of you fight about?"

Amelia lifts one shoulder in a half-hearted shrug. "Honestly, we just weren't getting along. Every day we were bickering about something. I suppose we started to realize how different we were, always have been. The trip really brought that into focus. Still, it was just a squabble. Nothing major."

Tracy forces herself to bite her tongue. To deny what she saw on that bus. Ray would tell her to be patient. Once the detective locks Amelia into a story, she can pick it apart later. But it's getting harder to hold herself back.

"Okay. So, the skoolie arrived back here yesterday. Wednesday. What happened in between? What did you do the following day when Willow didn't return?"

"I looked for her at the campground. I asked around, but no one had seen her. I thought maybe she'd gotten lost in the woods nearby. But there was no sign of her there. I called the hospitals. The cops, too. They told me to give it a day or two to see if she turned up. That she'd probably just gotten mad and run off with a boy or something."

"What boy?" Tracy blurts again. "Was there a boy with you?"

Amelia grits her teeth. Uncertainly, she turns toward her mother, then to the detective. Tracy knows this Amelia, too. This act she's perfected. As a kid, she'd always been an expert at winning over the adults in any room. For a while, Tracy fell for it, too. Truthfully, she felt sorry for her, desperate for her mother's approval.

"Go on," the detective prompts. "If there was someone with you, we need to know."

After heaving a dramatic sigh, she lowers her head, delivering her answer to the freshly polished hardwood. "I don't want to slander my friend, especially in front of her mom. Maybe we *should* talk in private."

"Amelia, please. There's no time for games. Whatever you have to say, I can handle it. There are no secrets here." Of course, Tracy knows that's a lie. There are always secrets.

"Fine. No secrets then. I won't hold back." The way she cocks her head makes Tracy wish she had earned the right to slap her face. "Willow doesn't have the best judgment when it comes to guys."

"Did she meet someone on the trip?" Detective Delgado asks.

"Someone? More like some*ones*. Plural. Like, in Milwaukee, she took off for seven hours on a motorcycle with this rando we met at the museum." Amelia holds her phone out to the detective, and Tracy cranes to get a glimpse of the helmeted stranger in a black leather jacket. Her daughter's arms, wrapped around his waist. Her chest, pressed flush against his back.

"Who is this guy? Did you get a shot of the license plate?"

Head down, Amelia scrolls through a few more photos. "It looks like that's the only one I took. I don't remember his name. I'm not sure Willow ever mentioned it. She was so into him, she wasn't thinking clearly."

The detective's judgmental frown worries Tracy. Already, Amelia has worked her over. Because this stereotypical bad boy seems more like her type. "Why did she go off with him in the first place?"

"Beats me. I mean, she said it was for research—one of our main characters rides a motorcycle—but I didn't buy it. I wanted this trip to be about us. About our future as co-authors. There was so much to discuss. But Willow made everything about her. That was what started the argument. She didn't want to hear the truth about herself. At first, we couldn't even agree on the ending. She wanted to do a total rewrite and I—"

Tracy can't stomach Amelia's lies. "Willow cared about the book more than you did. She would do anything to make it a success. We both know that it was mostly her who wrote it."

"Is that what she told you?"

"I think I can recognize my own daughter's work. Yours lacks a certain maturity, Melly."

Though Tracy remembers how much she detests that childhood nickname—that's why she used it—Amelia offers no protest, no words at all. Instead, her mother points at the door. "You should leave now. I won't have you criticize Amelia for no reason, and I certainly won't have you blame her for all this."

"Our girls left on a road trip ten days ago. Only one of them came back. There's a knife in that photograph and a clump of my daughter's hair in a police evidence room. So, tell me, Candice, who else should I blame?"

Amelia gasps. But it's the subtle lift of Candice's eyebrows that spikes Tracy's blood. Blind rage propels her from the sofa out the door. She's halfway down the street before she hears the detective calling to her.

She wants to keep running and never stop. Instead, she turns to face her.

"Well, that wasn't helpful. You should've let me handle it."

"You see what I'm talking about, right? She's acting

strangely. She knows more than she's saying. Willow wrote ninety-five percent of *The Road Trip*. You can ask Mr. Spellman."

Detective Delgado groans. "That book is the least of my worries, and it should be the least of yours too."

"I only mention it as proof of her jealousy. I don't want you to buy into her slander. She can be—"

"*So convincing*, I know. You mentioned that." The detective slips a clear plastic bag from her pocket. She holds it out to Tracy. "I want to show you something. Do you recognize this? We found it on the floor of the bus under some of the ripped papers."

Tracy studies the bag. Inside it, there's a thin leather cord—broken at the knot—with an antique brass key still attached. "It looks like an old-fashioned house key."

"Not Willow's though?"

"Not for our house. Could it belong to Amelia?"

"She says that it's not hers. That she's never seen it before." Detective Delgado pauses. A cloud of skepticism passes across her face.

"You don't believe her?"

She shakes her head. "The crime lab doesn't lie. And both girls' fingerprints are on it."

INSTAGRAM

writingontheroad Is this really Michigan? The sandstone cliffs at Pictured Rocks National Lakeshore do not disappoint. Neither does the crystal blue water. Pinch me, I feel like I'm somewhere exotic. #daythree #theroadtrip #bestfriends #ineedatan
50 likes 8 comments 8 shares

ilovepuppies Wear your sunscreen, girls!

bookloverbernstein reminds me of one of my favorite poems the white cliffs of dover by #aliceduermiller

travvvvy35 smokin' hot bikinis

> **ilovepuppies** @travvvvy35 Your comment is inappropriate.
>
> **travvvvy35** @ilovepuppies you jealous, granny?
>
> **ilovepuppies** @travvvvy35 Blocked and reported!

kelseyscott05 looks so fun love the cute suits

rocktrivia Did you know Kid Rock filmed a video there? #bornfree

harleyboy2000 im watching you

NINE

BEFORE

Day Three on the Road: Pictured Rocks National Lakeshore

Willow lies back on her beach towel and closes her eyes. With the sun kissing her skin, her mind wanders to the usual place, the secret place, far from the shores of Miners Beach at the Pictured Rocks National Lakeshore. She slips her hand inside the pocket of her denim shorts to reassure herself it's still there. She runs her fingers down the leather cord and along the smooth edges of the antique key she takes with her everywhere. She can't afford for Amelia to find it and start asking questions. But she didn't dare leave it behind. It's too precious to her.

"Hey, sleeping beauty. Check out Bridalveil Fall." Amelia nudges her with her elbow and passes her a pair of binoculars. She points to the stark cliff face at the west end of the beach, where a thin ribbon of white water cascades down into Lake Superior. "The guidebook says it's Michigan's tallest waterfall. One hundred and forty feet. It usually slows to a trickle in the summer."

Willow peers through the binoculars, marveling at the beauty of their third stop. They'd arrived late last night, parking the bus at the Hurricane River Campground. "It's incredible. We should take a few photos for our page."

"Already done and posted." She flashes a devious grin that makes Willow worry. What if she posts the photo she took of Willow on the back of Jackson's motorcycle with her arms wrapped around him?

"You didn't?"

"Didn't what?" she asks, sweetly.

Willow grabs for Amelia's baseball cap, knowing she'd tucked her phone inside it minutes ago, after ignoring another call. But Amelia retrieves it first. She taunts her friend with it before dissolving into laughter. "Relax. I didn't post it. I told you I wouldn't."

"Fine." She kicks sand at Amelia's legs, and Amelia kicks it back at her until both their towels are covered. Simultaneously, they lie back and sigh, then laugh. It reminds Willow of the way they used to be.

"Why are you so worried about it anyway? It's just a photo. It's not like you banged the guy on the back of his Harley." When Willow doesn't immediately agree, Amelia's eyes widen. "Wait. Did you—"

"No."

"Then, what is the problem? You never take this kind of stuff seriously. You're acting weird." Amelia sits up on her elbow and raises her sunglasses, setting them atop her head. She narrows her eyes at Willow. Willow tries not to look away. Amelia always suspects when she's lying.

"I don't want to encourage him." It's not exactly untrue. Jackson hadn't been too keen on her plan, probably because it didn't involve them swapping spit in a dark corner at that seedy dive bar. But he liked it better when she gave him two hundred dollars. "He follows our page now. If he sees that photo, it'll give him the wrong idea."

"Is this about Milo Bernstein?"

"*Who?*"

"Uh, your boss. The manager at Chapter and Verse. Didn't you say he had a thing for you? That he always scheduled you to work with him on the weekends. Wasn't that why you couldn't come up to Northwestern for Open Mic Night? He posted a comment about poetry on your Instagram post today."

"Oh, yeah. Milo." Willow nods, cursing herself for forgetting yet another half-truth she'd spun. She's no good at this, but she's in too deep to stop. "He actually got transferred to the downtown location last month."

"You never told me that."

"I didn't want to bother you. It was during finals week, so you were super busy." Willow turns her head to the sheer cliffs above the water, imagining herself standing at the edge ready to jump. That's what it feels like to lie to your best friend. To always be one misstep away from plunging headfirst into the cold, dark water.

"What is *that*?" Amelia grabs the binoculars and peers down the beach. Willow follows her gaze to the black lump in the sand.

"It looks like a bag, doesn't it?" Whatever it is, she's grateful for it. She doesn't have to lie again. Not now.

"Or a body." Amelia snickers and tosses the binoculars onto the sand. Already, she's up and moving, waving at her friend to hurry. "C'mon, let's check it out."

As they approach, Willow confirms her suspicion. It's a waterlogged rucksack, half-buried in the sand. A chill zips up her spine while her writer's brain catalogs the details for her next story. She starts to imagine how it got here, where it came from. What's inside.

Amelia starts toward it. She grabs it by one frayed strap and gives it a tug. Predictably, the strap tears away at the seam, and Amelia stumbles backward. She chuckles at herself, then reaches for it again.

"Wait." Willow feels stupidly possessive of the backpack. Amelia can be so oblivious. "We should be careful. It might belong to someone."

"Uh, who, Blackbeard?" She sweeps her hand across the vacant horizon. It's only them on the rockier half of the beach. "Does it look like anyone's claiming it?"

"I guess not. Still." Willow snaps a few photos of the bag with her phone before she drops to her knees and frees it from the sand. "It's soaked. I think it washed up here."

"Whatever's inside we split fifty-fifty." Amelia holds out her hand, ready to make a deal.

Willow looks skeptically at the dingy backpack. "It's not a treasure chest."

"Argh, matey. You never know what loot these lasses might uncover."

With a groan, Willow shakes her friend's hand, only to shut her up, then begins to work the zipper open. She manages to pull it halfway before it gets stuck. She holds the backpack up and peers into the opening.

She gasps, and the bag hits the sand with a weighty thwack. "There's a stack of money in there."

"Stop messing around, Will."

"I'm dead serious."

Skeptical, Amelia retrieves the pack and looks inside. When she shifts the contents with her hand, her eyes widen. "Holy shit."

"Told you."

"We should take it back to the bus." As her friend glances furtively around the beach, Willow rolls her eyes. It's only a white-haired man with a golden retriever and a metal detector. He waves and keeps walking, but Amelia slings the bag over her shoulder. "Now."

Willow shakes her head. "We can't just take it. It doesn't belong to us."

"Well, what do you propose? It's not like there's anybody's name on it. Finders keepers."

"I think we should call the police."

"And say what, exactly?" Amelia doesn't wait for a reply. "Besides, who's going to claim a wad of cash and a big ass knife? Might as well just say, 'Cuff me now, Officer. I'm a criminal.'"

"Knife?" Willow croaks. "What knife?"

She grabs for the bag, certain Amelia's lying. But Amelia holds on tight, and for a moment, they struggle over it. Until Amelia stops cold and lets her end drop. Her mouth follows. "Oh my God. I just realized. It's a *sign*. You love signs."

Willow forces the zipper the rest of the way to get a good look. The fine hairs on her neck prickle at the sight of the long, straight blade—it's at least seven inches—and the worn leather handle. "Yeah. A sign we should leave it where we found it. This is creepy, Mel. It reminds me of *The Road Trip*, when Jenna and Lacey find that knife in the thrift shop. The one that the weird store owner claims belonged to the Great Lakes Slasher."

"Exactly. That's why we need it. It's perfect. It's real life mirroring fiction. This is our version of the knife Jenna plunges into Lacey's chest. We could post the story of how we found it. Now, that would generate some buzz."

"Are you serious?"

"Dead serious. We do need a marketing plan."

"Well, I'm not putting these photos online. In fact..." Willow quickly deletes the pics she snapped. "All gone. If they do belong to a criminal, I don't want him coming after us to retrieve his... *paraphernalia*."

"At least let me take the cash. We can put it toward our next cover. Or add it to our advertising budget. Trixie says online ads are ridiculously expensive."

"No way. It's probably blood money."

Amelia lets out a frustrated huff.

"What is it with you?" Willow asks. She can't help but think of the vanished tip money at Sal's. It's a stark contrast to the Amelia she knows. The Amelia who never so much as abused a hall pass in high school. That ticket she'd gotten texting had sent her into a spiral. "You're supposed to be the cautious one."

"And you're supposed to be my friend. You've been acting all high and mighty since you got into Northwestern."

"*I've been acting high and mighty?* That's rich coming from Miss I Keep Forgetting How Green You Are. Newsflash, you also got into Northwestern, and long before I did." Satisfied that she's won the point, Willow slings the backpack into a pile of driftwood. "We're leaving it here, and forgetting we ever saw it."

"Fine. It's forgotten."

Amelia stalks off toward the lake, where she breaks its glassy surface with her splashing feet. Willow walks along the wet shoreline instead until she reaches their beach towels. By that time, her footsteps have all but disappeared. It's as if she was never there.

Willow wakes to a noise outside the bus. She pulls the comforter up beneath her chin, cursing herself for choosing the most remote spot in the campground. "Mel?"

There's no answer from the bunk above her. Amelia sleeps like a log. When the sound comes again, she recognizes it as the throaty growl of a motorcycle. It grows louder and louder until the headlight streams in through the windows. Then, the light goes out, plunging her back into darkness. Willow can't decide which is worse.

"Wake up!" she whisper-shouts. "There's someone outside."

"Okay, okay. I'm awake." Amelia leans down from the top bunk, peering at her with half-shut eyes.

"What should we do?" Willow asks.

"Ignore them. Whoever it is will go away."

The bike's engine revs. Amelia gasps, and Willow buries herself beneath the covers. Then comes the horrifying crunch of boots on gravel. The chilling drum of a fist against their door. Willow hopes she's still sleeping. That she's dreamed herself into one of her own stories. But when the knocking rattles the bus, she fears this is all too real. It sounds too close.

"Did you leave a window open?" she asks, fearing the answer. When she'd finally returned from the beach, Amelia's fair skin had already turned the color of a strawberry.

"Sorry. I was burning up. The aloe didn't help at all."

"I told you to wear sunscreen."

"I did!"

"Well, you should have reapplied." She wishes she could laugh at the ridiculousness of their argument. But there's yet another knock. Three, to be exact. *Let me in.* He doesn't say it out loud, but his fist makes it clear what he wants.

Amelia hops down and scurries to the couch.

"Don't go out there," Willow hisses.

Ignoring her warning, Amelia lifts the cushion and reaches into the storage below, retrieving her oversized beach tote. Her silhouette creeps toward the front of the bus, low and fast.

Willow looks on, horrified, as Amelia flings open the door and lets out a wild shriek. A panicked scream follows from outside, then the sound of the bike's engine. It only takes a few heartbeats for the roar of the motorcycle to fade into the distance.

"He'll think twice about doing that again." Amelia cackles. "Turns out Jackson is a fraidy cat."

"Jackson? The guy from the museum? With the motorcycle?" Though he's gone, Willow fights off another wave of panic. Her stomach, knotted. Her mouth, bone dry. She tosses back the covers and swings her feet onto the floor. "Why would he—?"

She freezes in place at the sight. Amelia stands in the

middle of the bus aisle holding the tactical knife in her hand. The same leather handle, the same long dark blade. She grins, and her teeth shine white in the moonlight.

"Bet you're glad I didn't listen to you about leaving this behind."

TEN

NOW

Tracy can't sit still. She paces in front of the picture window and studies her cellphone. Hoping to jog her memory, she enlarges the photo she snapped of the mysterious key. Before returning to the Ford house, the detective had confirmed that it didn't fit the front lock or Willow's bedroom door. She studies its ornate head for clues but comes up empty.

Stupidly, Tracy tries Ray again. It's a mistake to keep reaching out to him—he'd hung up on her and left her text unanswered—but she can't stop herself. She needs to hear his voice. In a warped way, he's the only one who can reassure her. It's the cop in him, even if he isn't one anymore. The phone rings only once, then sends her straight to voicemail.

Disgusted with herself and her bad decisions, she tosses it on the sofa and returns to the window, where she watches for signs of Detective Delgado's departure, fully intending to march back across the street and give patronizing Candice a piece of her mind. At least, that's the fantasy. But now that the fire inside her has cooled, she doubts she'll have the courage to tell Candice where to stick it. It's always been this way between them. Once the girls started high school, Candice's competitiveness ratcheted up a notch or ten. From debate team to spirit club and everything in between, Candice always anointed Amelia better, faster, and smarter, which meant she, too, was better, faster, and smarter, by extension. As if being a literal heart surgeon wasn't enough to prove herself.

Tracy hurries to the sofa, where she searches out her wayward cell lodged between the cushions. It's time to call in the reinforcements. She needs backup. But who? She stares at the phone for a moment, accepting the sad realization. Since she left Hirsch and Peterson Accounting years ago to hang up her own shingle, it's been her and Willow against the world. Her only adult friend has been Candice, and *friend* seems too strong a word. Friends confide in each other, take comfort in each other. Friends lend a hand. Candice had done none of the above, had only tolerated her when it fit her purpose. If not for their daughters and their shared street address, they would've remained two distant planets. Different orbits, different galaxies.

Disheartened, Tracy scrolls through her contacts until it hits her. She knows exactly who to call.

Sam picks up on the first ring. "Hey, any news? Is Amelia okay?"

"She's acting weird, Sam."

"Weird, how?"

"Suspicious-weird. She told the detective that Willow ran off with some boy. Which makes no sense."

"A boy? Willow never mentioned a boy. She doesn't have time for that."

Already, Tracy feels a little better. Like she's not crazy. Like she's not a terrible mom who doesn't know her own daughter. "According to Amelia, she had a different guy at every stop and left for seven hours one night on a motorcycle."

"What did Candice say about it?"

Tracy lets out a mirthless laugh, remembering the condescending scowl on her face when she'd pointed Tracy to the door. "Not much. She certainly isn't encouraging Amelia to tell the truth, if that's what you're asking. I just wish..."

"Wish what?"

"I don't want to impose."

Sam tsks at her. "Please, I want to help. Just say the word."

"Would you talk to Amelia? She'll listen to you." She doesn't say the rest of it. That surely Amelia will spill it all to him, her secret crush. The grown man she had the nerve to text, *Nobody gets me like you do*. "If you're alright with it, of course. I wouldn't want you to do anything that makes you uncomfortable."

Sam offers no reply, and Tracy wonders if she's pushed him too far. After seeing the photos Amelia sent, she wouldn't blame him for running in the other direction. He probably should.

"At least come and keep me company while I go out of my mind with worry. The detective asked if I'd searched Willow's room. I don't think I can do it alone."

He doesn't hesitate. "I'm on my way."

Tracy's never been the snooping kind. She didn't need to pry, to paw through her daughter's bedroom like a hungry raccoon. Willow didn't have secrets, not from her. That's what she's always told herself. Standing in the threshold of her daughter's room with Sam by her side, she wonders if she's gotten it all wrong. That key, for instance. What did Willow need to keep locked away from her?

"You take the closet," Sam suggests. "I'll check the usual contraband hiding places. Under the bed, beneath the mattress, in the medicine cabinet."

"Contraband?" Tracy practically laughs at the absurdity. When Willow wanted to try pot for her eighteenth birthday, Tracy smoked it with her. When Willow started dating, Tracy booked the appointment at Planned Parenthood. And when she caught Willow with her copy of a smutty romance novel, she suggested a buddy read. She tried to be the cool mom. A mom like Grandma Ruth, who made her feel more like a partner in crime than a dumb kid.

"What are we looking for?" she asks, wondering what they could possibly find to explain the last forty-eight hours.

"No clue. But I suppose we'll know it when we find it."

Tracy leaves Sam crouched beside the bed, peering into the dark space beneath it, and enters the walk-in closet that holds Willow's quirky wardrobe. The oversized sweaters and ripped jeans. A pair of men's Oxfords strung with bright pink laces. She combs through it all, dipping her fingers into pockets, peering into the open mouths of shoes. She even hauls down Willow's senior memory box. The dried petals of her favorite flower papier-mâchéd across the lid. Daisies everywhere. But it's the letterman jacket that does her in. Willow had rescued it from a thrift shop, à la Grandma Ruth. Tracy touches the soft leather sleeves and presses her face against the dark blue fleece that still smells like her daughter. It's that jacket that finally brings her to her knees.

"Got anything?" Sam calls.

"Not yet." She balls her fists tight to stop from crying. She's glad she closed the door behind her. She wouldn't want Sam to see her like this. "You?"

"Just a few dust bunnies." She hears the shuffle of his boots against the carpet. When she pokes her head out, he's already seated on the edge of the bed, holding out a stack of Post-its and paper scraps. "And some handwritten notes for the book. Early character sketches, plot points. That sort of thing. It's amazing what they accomplished in a year."

She joins him there, appreciative of his company and his timely change of subject. "Did you know that the girls were arguing about the ending?"

"Willow mentioned it a couple of times. It's probably my fault. I told her the best-friend-murder seemed a bit juvenile. I think she took it to heart." He hangs his head, his dark hair flopping across his forehead and onto his glasses. Tracy resists the urge to push it from his face. "Amelia thought the twist had commercial appeal. That it would sell well in the twenty-something female bracket. She's always been more interested in the money and the accolades than the craft."

Tracy knows too well that he's right. "Well, I hoped they could have both. The critical acclaim and the sales. I still do."

"It's a rarity these days, especially in their genre. Ever since *Gone Girl*, it's all about out-twisting the next guy. But if anyone has the talent to do it, it's Willow. She told me she gets it from you. That you used to be a writer."

"Eons ago. Seriously. We're talking prehistoric times."

"Well, I'd love to read your stuff. If you saved anything."

"Gosh, that would be a major excavation. Like an archaeological dig. I wouldn't even know where to look." In the attic, second box from the right, under the one marked *Willow's Baby Toys*. The full manuscript of the novel she'd completed in 2004, typing THE END the day after her eighteenth birthday.

"Are we talking floppy disks or ancient scrolls?"

Tracy grins. She gets it. Why the kids like him so much. "Hieroglyphs, sadly."

"Hieroglyphs. Of course." They share a much-needed laugh. "I'll have to brush up on my ancient Egyptian."

"Don't bother. It's not very good."

"Somehow, I doubt that."

"Willow is a thousand times more talented than I ever could've been. I get to live my dream through her. It's better, sweeter. I forget, do you have kids?" That too, is a lie. When Willow was assigned to Honors English, she'd Googled him, stalked his social media. She wanted to be sure he was a worthy steward of Willow's talent. For a moment, she forgets why he's sitting on Willow's bed, holding a bunch of dusty Post-it notes.

"Not yet. It just hasn't been in the cards. Five years ago, I almost married the science teacher at Dearborn High. Hence, why I'm at Kildeer now. After we broke up, she ran me out of the district."

"I knew there was a reason I hated science."

"Right?" He matches her playful tone. "Who needs penicillin? Electricity? Space exploration?"

A sudden image disrupts Tracy's mirth. Third grade Willow dressed as an astronaut, collecting her Halloween candy in the space helmet Tracy fashioned from a cardboard box. She swallows her embarrassment. How could she be joking around at a time like this?

"Hey, did you ever see the girls with an old key?" She fumbles through her phone to find the pic she snapped.

Sam frowns at it, shakes his head. "Was it on the bus?"

"Apparently, and both girls touched it."

"Maybe it was something they picked up along the way. Like a souvenir or—"

The ringing of Tracy's cellphone interrupts, and her stomach flip-flops at the sight of a familiar number. She answers fast. "Ray?"

"Yeah."

"Oh. Uh... one sec." Tracy holds up a finger to Sam and slips out the door and down the stairs, returning to the picture window. The view of the busy tree-lined street gives her some semblance of control. It grounds her. And she needs it. Because now that she has Ray on the line, she's not sure what to say to him. Truthfully, he owes her a massive apology, but she knows better than to expect one.

"I'm outside."

"You're *what*? Why?"

Just then, Tracy spots him, phone to his ear, cutting a

straight line from his black pickup truck to her front porch. It's been at least a month since she's seen him, but his broad shoulders and scruffy jawline hit her like a gut punch. He marches up the steps with the determined cadence of a soldier sent to rescue her. "I got your text and your call. It seemed like you needed me," he says, before he disconnects without giving her a chance to tell him otherwise.

When the doorbell rings, Tracy's heart quickens. She presses her back to the door to calm herself. "Hang on."

She dashes back up the stairs to find Sam waiting outside Willow's bedroom. "Is everything okay?" he asks.

"Ray's here. My ex. You remember him, right?" The few times they'd met—Willow's graduation and senior prom, which Tracy and Ray had chaperoned—Ray hadn't exactly been welcoming. Between his Harry Potter quips and snide remarks, Tracy had been downright ashamed of him. But Sam had seemed oblivious, which only riled Ray up. He didn't like being ignored.

"The cop?"

Tracy nods.

"Oh. Okay. Should I...?" He gestures vaguely in the direction of Willow's bedroom.

"No, no. It's fine. Come down with me." She starts back the way she came. "I filled him in on everything. But I didn't expect him to show up here."

"I'm sure he's worried about Willow," Sam says. "He probably just wants to help."

The doorbell rings again. Ray hadn't been gifted with patience. At the third singsong of the bell, Tracy flings the door open to find Ray, fuming. But he's not alone. Next to him, Detective Delgado matches his silent fury.

Her eyes ping pong between them. Behind her, Sam clears his throat.

"When were you going to tell me that you dated Ray O'Grady?" the detective asks. "The dirty cop."

With Tracy frozen, Ray takes up her cause. "Why would she tell you a goddamned thing about her personal life? It's none of your business. Her daughter is missing. Now *that's* your business. Me, I'm irrelevant."

"Dr. Ford filled me in on your year-long relationship. The one Ms. Barrett didn't think to mention. I came here to ask her about it, and lo and behold, you show up."

"I guess it's your lucky day," Ray counters. "You're obviously in need of a real detective. I'm happy to offer my investigative services pro bono."

The detective narrows her eyes at him. "I thought you only worked for bribes."

"Ray is right," Tracy says, hoping to defuse the tension. "We broke up months ago. He isn't a part of my life anymore." She can't believe Candice mentioned her ex. But Tracy feels more relieved than angry. For a moment, she'd gone to a dark place. A crazy place. Where she suspected the detective of bugging her phone. Where she wondered what else Penny Delgado could find out about her past.

"Given that his sorry ass is standing on your doorstep right next to me, I would beg to differ."

"So, I don't have a right to be concerned about Willow? I care about that girl. I taught her how to change a flat tire, how to take down a handsy asshole with a thumb to the eyeball. How to unclog the drain in her bathroom. She saw me as a father figure." Now, he's laying it on too thick. Though maybe he's right. For the year that they'd dated, Willow had seemed to like him—or at least tolerate him—until he'd messed it all up. When he'd shown up a few months ago at the bookstore with a dozen roses for Willow to cart home to Tracy on his behalf, her daughter had officially pronounced her dislike for him.

"A father figure?" Detective Delgado scoffs.

"That's right. And you can't stop me from looking for her. With all the time you're wasting on chit-chat, I can guarantee I've got a better chance of finding Willow than you do. You wanna know where I'd start?" With his thumb, he points over his shoulder to the Ford house across the street.

"I should probably go." When Tracy sees Sam behind her, ready to flee with his car keys, she wants to crawl in a hole. Still, she needs him here. Now more than ever, since she's found herself in the middle of a fight between two snapping crocodiles.

She reaches for his arm but stops short of taking hold of it. She won't make a total fool of herself. "Don't leave."

"What the hell is he doing here?" Ray glares at Sam, leveling Tracy with a sudden realization. Had Ray been jealous of him all along?

"I'm just here to help." Sam raises his hands to show he means no harm. "Same as you."

Detective Delgado ignores them both, her eyes landing squarely on Tracy. "I'm sure you're aware that your ex here has plenty of enemies. One of them might be trying to get to him through you. You need to consider that Willow's disappearance could be about something more than a silly fight with her best friend. It could be about you."

"Are you blaming her?" Sam asks. "Her daughter is missing."

"No blame. Just considering all the options. I'm not sure what she's told you about Mr. O'Grady, but he was fired from Chicago PD for—"

"The girls were eight hours from home." Sam waves off the detective's revelation, and Tracy's never been more grateful. She doesn't want to hear it spoken aloud. She doesn't want Willow tainted by Ray's mistakes. Or hers, for that matter. "Are you suggesting someone followed them to Niagara Falls just to get even with this guy? You must realize how far-fetched that sounds."

"Well, damn," Ray mutters. "Harry P. doesn't mess around."

"With all due respect, Mr. Spellman, you're a schoolteacher. For me, far-fetched is just another day at the office. No one knows what happened here. Only that Willow hasn't returned home. All options are still on the table." She glances at Ray like he's something she stepped in. "If you knew anything about Ray O'Grady, you wouldn't be so quick to defend him. And you certainly wouldn't be surprised if someone went to the trouble of driving a few hundred miles for revenge."

The detective lingers on the threshold, but Tracy refuses to invite her in. She can't let Ray in either now. It shouldn't be this way. Not when *her* daughter is the one missing.

Tracy looks over the detective's shoulder toward the Ford house. That's where her attention should be focused. "Did Amelia tell you anything more about what happened? Could she explain the hair at least? What about the knife?"

"After you left, she broke down, totally lost it. She's really upset. I decided to let her get a good night's sleep and revisit my questions in the morning."

Ray utters a scornful noise that makes clear his position on her police work. Frankly, Tracy agrees.

Detective Delgado's jaw hardens. "Do not go over there. Understood? You either, O'Grady."

There's only one acceptable answer, even if it pains her to say it. "Yes."

As the detective crosses the street, Ray curses under his breath. "Damn Penny Delgado. What're the odds?"

"Do you know her?" Tracy watches her return to her car. She stays parked across the street.

"Only by reputation. She's a firecracker." After a brief pause, he asks, "What are they saying?"

"They think she ran off with some boy. That's what Amelia told them."

"Ridiculous," he says.

Sam appears beside her, nodding. "That's what I said."

Ray pretends to ignore him. He lets his gaze drift past Sam into the living room. "Are you gonna invite me in? We should talk about next steps. I know you're shook up. Let me help you."

But Tracy can't unsee the waiting Detective Delgado. It feels like a test. Inviting Ray in will only hurt her case. "I don't think that's a good idea. I'll call you if anything changes."

"I can have a go at Candice. See if she'll let me talk to Amelia. She's bound to know more than she's saying."

Tracy shakes her head.

Ray doesn't protest like she expects. It's worse than that. He reaches a tender hand to touch her face. "I'm sorry," he says, tossing a forlorn look over his shoulder. "I'll go. I don't want to mess this up for you."

Tracy looks on from the picture window while first Ray, and then Detective Delgado, drives away. She senses Sam behind her, his eyes on her back. When she loses sight of the unmarked sedan, she turns to find him sitting on the arm of the sofa.

"I'm sorry about all that," she says.

"It's alright. Like I said, I'm here to help." He waits for her to say something, but how can she explain? Where would she start? "I don't mean to pry, but what's the deal with him? Detective Delgado called him a dirty cop."

Tracy flops into the armchair, the exhaustion of the last forty-eight hours finally laying claim to her. "He's not all bad." She hears the hint of defensiveness in her voice. "Ray and I met about a year and a half ago, when he gave me a speeding ticket. Then, I did his taxes, got him a sweet home-office deduction. He asked me out to dinner to say thank you. About nine months after we started dating, he told me that he planned to retire. Until Internal Affairs showed up to question me, I didn't realize he'd been put on administrative leave."

"So, what did he do? She made it seem pretty bad."

"They never proved anything..." Tracy hesitates. She doesn't want Sam to think less of her. "But they claimed he planted evidence in the Elissa George murder case. He swore the husband, Justin, was guilty of killing her. Then, it came out that the victim's family might've paid Ray to leave traces of Justin's DNA on the murder weapon. After that, all hell broke loose, with egg on the face of the department. You can imagine it didn't make him many friends. They wanted him out so badly that they fired him for making a typo in a police report."

"Whoa. That's wild. I can't believe I never heard about it."

"Well, Chicago PD knows how to bury a story, which, honestly, I'm thankful for. If he'd been dragged through the mud, so would I, and that would be disastrous. My accounting business depends on people trusting me."

Sam nods like he understands. He's a good listener. "Is that why you broke up?" he asks.

"That was the beginning of the end, I suppose. Ray didn't take it well when they fired him. It's hard to have a relationship with someone who's angry all the time. After it happened, he morphed into one of those stereotypical ex-cops. Bitter and full of rage. Then, he became possessive of me. Like he couldn't stand the thought of losing anything—*or anyone*—else."

"It sounds like you made a smart decision. Do you think Detective Delgado could be right? That this could be about him and his connection to you?"

"I'd be shocked if it was. She probably just wants to stick it to him any way she can. Even more reason to keep him out of it altogether. He'll only be a distraction to the investigation." Eager to change the subject, Tracy pushes up off the sofa and heads into the kitchen to retrieve her laptop. She knows exactly what to do.

"You gave me an idea," she tells Sam, as she positions the computer in front of them on the coffee table and opens the Writing on the Road account. "When you found those notes for the book, I started wondering. What if life *could* imitate art? Remember how Lacey's mom starts that campaign to find her killer in Chapter Forty-Seven, and it goes viral?"

Sam cocks his head. She can tell he's on the same page. "Yeah, of course. That was Willow's idea. She thought it would be cool if a stranger broke the case."

Scrolling through the last few posts, Tracy lands on the campfire photo, the knife's blade drawing her attention like a siren. "I don't know Willow's password, but what do you think about typing a comment here from my account? Letting their followers know what's happened. I could post a recent photo of Willow as well."

He nods eagerly. "It makes sense. You should post it on your Facebook page too. Didn't you say that a few of your former work colleagues were armchair detectives?"

Tracy sputters out a half-laugh, remembering how her supervisor, Joyce, had taken an online forensic accounting course five times just in case one of her clients ended up dead. "I hope I'm not relying on Joyce Dudley to find Willow."

She transfers the computer to her lap and types out a message. "How does this sound?" she asks, scooting closer to Sam.

> This is one of the last posts from my daughter, Willow. As you may know, she and her best friend, Amelia, left on a road trip ten days ago in a bus I refurbished for them. Yesterday, a stranger drove the bus back to Chicago, and this morning, Amelia came home with no feasible explanation about what happened. My daughter is still missing, and the police told

me there are signs of foul play. The most unnerving part of all of this is that it's eerily similar to the plot of the girls' novel, The Road Trip, in which two friends embark on the adventure of a lifetime... and one of them ends up dead. Don't get me wrong. I'm not casting stones. I have no idea what happened. I'm terrified, and I desperately need your help to find my daughter. Please share! #whereiswillow

"It's great. Compelling." There's uncertainty in his voice. A nagging question.

"You think I'm being too hard on Amelia?"

"Not necessarily, but Candice won't see it that way." He reads it again, tapping the screen. "The hashtag is a nice touch. It's catchy."

"I certainly hope so. We need as many eyes on this as possible." Hesitant, her finger toggles over the mouse. Once she presses POST, it will all be real. There's no taking it back. With a quick breath, it's done. Just like that, the world knows her pain.

While Sam looks on, she follows his advice and copies and pastes the same text onto her own Facebook page, alongside Willow's graduation photo and a thumbnail of the book cover Sam had commissioned from an artist friend of his. Until now, she's only used her page to keep tabs on her former work colleagues and her Lexington High classmates, most of them still trapped in their small-minded cages in the middle of nowhere USA. She doesn't even have a recent profile picture—just an old snapshot of her and ten-year-old Willow at the Concrete Beach in downtown Chicago.

"Are you hungry?" Sam asks, when it's done. When it's out in the world, traveling the Internet at nearly the speed of light. That makes her nervous. Nervous and hopeful. "I can order a pizza."

Tracy can't remember when she last ate. But she's not

hungry. Still, she doesn't want Sam to leave her alone to constantly refresh her Facebook page. "Sure, I could eat. There's a menu from Lou's in the drawer by the fridge."

Sam leaps to his feet, as if she's just issued his marching orders, and heads off in the direction of the kitchen. The last time she'd ordered from Lou's, Willow had pouted. *What kind of pizza joint doesn't have a pineapple topping?* Tracy half-smiles at the memory. That same night, Willow had received her SAT results, scoring 250 points higher than her first try. An unprecedented improvement, certainly cause for celebration.

"Is the four cheese thin crust alright with you?" Cradling his cellphone to his ear, Sam looks at her expectantly, and Tracy realizes she's been a million miles away for God knows how long.

"Fine. Yes. Four cheese. That sounds great."

When the computer dings at her, Tracy gasps. A new comment has appeared beneath her Facebook post from Alexis Newhart, former head cheerleader and current president of the Lexington PTA. The last time she spoke to Tracy... well, Tracy can't remember Alexis ever speaking to her. She wasn't like the other kids, with her dead parents and her eccentric grandmother, who paid the mortgage on their hoarded farmhouse by selling autographed vintage portraits of celebrities. Grandma Ruth said fitting in was overrated. But what the hell did she know? She died pre-Facebook. She never got to hear the ding.

> OMG, Tracy! I'm so sorry to hear about Willow. If you ask me, the police should be talking to her friend. I'm sharing this on my page. Please keep me informed. Praying for you!

After navigating back to Instagram, Tracy calls Sam over, disbelieving. Tears fill her eyes. "Look," she says. "There are already a couple of replies to my comment. They're using the hashtag. This could actually work."

Sam points to the latest reply from tattedbabe13. *Where can I get my hands on this novel???* "Some people have no tact," he says.

"Ironic, isn't it? That's all the girls ever wanted, people clamoring to read their book."

Side by side, they sit on the sofa in silence, watching the screen. Until finally Sam turns to her. "What if you self-published it?"

"*What?*"

"*The Road Trip*. It would draw more attention to Willow's disappearance. I'm sure Amelia would agree to it."

"I couldn't." Tracy frowns at him. "Willow would kill me. It hasn't been professionally edited. She's coming back, Sam. I won't do anything without her."

"Fair enough." Sam doesn't argue. He's not the confrontational type. Not like Ray, who could pick a fight with a Buddhist monk. His eyes soften. "I didn't mean to upset you. I just feel so helpless."

"Me too." Tracy pats his arm. She lets her hand rest there for a beat before moving it away. As they toggle between the sites and watch the comments roll in, Tracy's chest swells with optimism. By the time the doorbell rings thirty minutes later, she finds that she's hungry for that pizza after all.

INSTAGRAM

writingontheroad I died and went to fudge heaven. #mackinacisland #dayfour #theroadtrip #bestfriends #deathbychocolate #rybathe-fudgemaker #worldslongestfrontporch
150 likes 95 comments 17 shares

ilovepuppies I swear I gained ten pounds just looking at this fudge. Hoping for a souvenir! #fingerscrossed

rybathefudgemaker Thanks for coming by the shop! It was a pleasure to make fudge with you.

kelseyscott05 OMG i just read your mom's post so worried call me #whereiswillow

truecrimelover44 Anybody else find this post spooky? She "just died." It's like she knew what was about to happen to her. #whereiswillow

> **jennyb99** @truecrimelover44 How can you say that? Her mom is probably reading this. Have some compassion.

baronjones @truecrimelover44 that's exactly what I thought #bffdidit

ELEVEN

BEFORE

Day Four on the Road: Mackinaw City

Willow wipes the steam from the small bathroom mirror and blinks at her tired reflection. Bloodshot eyes return her gaze, dark circles beneath. That's what happens when you spend half the night arguing with your best friend again and the other half worrying. About the Ka-Bar knife on the kitchen counter. About the man who banged on the door like he belonged inside. About the next ten days stuck in a box on wheels with Amelia, who, after the last few days, might as well be a stranger she picked up on the side of the road. Frustrated, she tugs on her shorts and slips her precious key back inside her pocket, wishing it could transport her. Soon, she'll be back there, but not soon enough.

When Amelia pounds on the flimsy bathroom door, Willow can only think of last night, of the knife. A shot of rage spikes her blood. Amelia lied to her about taking it.

"Hey, did you fall in?" Amelia asks. "I've got to shower too, ya know. I thought you wanted to get to Mackinac Island by lunchtime."

"I do. There's a ferry at one o'clock." Though Willow knows she could simply toss out the schedule her mother created for the trip, she clings to it like a security blanket. A port in the storm of Hurricane Amelia. "Be sure to let Jackson know our plans so he can meet us there on his motorcycle."

As she tosses that barb at Amelia, Willow catches another glimpse of her own face. Anger isn't her look. She should be dancing barefoot or curled on a bench with a romance novel. Amelia's the one meant for brooding.

"I swear to you. I didn't tell him where we were going. We had a five-minute conversation. You're the one who spent half the night with him."

"Well, he figured it out somehow." Which unnerves Willow for a million reasons that have nothing to do with his fist pounding against the door of the skoolie. If Jackson tells Amelia that she ditched him that night, she'll have a lot of explaining to do. She needs to have a story ready just in case. "And he posted a creepy message about watching us. Didn't you see it?"

Willow opens the bathroom door just in time to catch Amelia mid-eye roll. "He probably just Googled us. It's not like we're in witness protection."

"I still don't buy it. You flat-out lied to my face yesterday. You brought that knife in here. I can't trust you."

"You have to admit, it was kind of a lifesaver." Willow cocks an eyebrow at her. "At least I left the backpack."

"*Did you?*"

"You don't believe me?"

The answer hurts too much to say out loud. Because Willow's been lying too. She despises herself for being such a pretender. Worse, she's got to keep at it. That's the thing about lies, they always snowball. "Let's get out of Miners Beach as soon as we can. We don't even know why he showed up here."

Amelia's face falls.

"*Do we?*" Willow clenches her fists at her sides. She wants to shake her. "Do we know?"

"Maybe." She covers her face, peeking out at Willow from between her fingers. "Don't be mad, but I might've taken something from him."

"What? Why would you do that? And when? How?"

"It was just some cash from his saddlebag. I thought he was too distracted by you to realize." She shrugs.

"You have officially lost your mind." Willow glares at her friend, trying to reconcile it. The girl who'd never earned less than an A minus on her report card. The girl who'd planned the senior trip and co-captained the debate team and turned in a semester's worth of algebra assignments six weeks early. "How much did you take?"

"It's probably best you don't know. Plausible deniability, right?"

"Amelia, I'm not kidding around. How much?" It must be a lot. Too much. Jackson had stalked them online, then driven almost five hours to find them.

"While we were touring the museum, I overheard him on the phone. He was talking about selling some vintage motorcycle parts. When he asked me to put your purse in the saddlebag, it was just sitting there. A wad of cash staring me in the face. I only slipped off a couple hundreds. He should've been more careful."

Willow's stomach churns. "I don't get it. Your mom is a heart surgeon. She drives a Range Rover. She'd give you anything you asked for."

"Like yours wouldn't?" Amelia blinks back tears, lashing out again before Willow can ask what's wrong. "Spare me the hypocrisy."

"My mom wants me to make my own way. To learn to depend on myself. The same way she did after her parents died in that boating accident. After Grandma Ruth died. After my dad left. She's a fighter, and she wants me to be just as tough."

Amelia's twisted little laugh slithers up Willow's spine and makes her skin crawl. She can't believe they're fighting like this. "God, you are so..."

"So... *what*? Go ahead and say it."

"Delusional." She spreads her arms wide, spinning like a deranged ballerina on the vinyl flooring. "Your mom bought you an entire bus. She spent months refurbishing it. This whole trip was her idea. That money in your pocket, I'll bet it's mostly hers. Don't kid yourself. You're just as spoiled as I am."

Willow can't exactly argue, not with her feet planted squarely in the middle of the evidence. But Amelia doesn't understand how her mom grew up. Just like Grandma Ruth, her mom's love language is old junk.

"Newsflash, Will, just because my mom's a surgeon doesn't mean her life is perfect. She has problems too."

"Is something wrong? With your mom, I mean." Willow studies the cracks in her friend's armor, hoping they'll reveal a clue to this new version of Amelia.

Amelia stares ahead, clues stealthily hidden. "Just the usual. She's too busy to notice me unless I'm curing cancer or winning a gold medal or writing a *New York Times* bestseller."

What can she say to that? That sometimes she wishes her mom noticed her less. That her mom had friends her own age, a job that required her to leave the house. Hobbies that didn't involve her daughter. Any of that would make her sound like an ungrateful twit. "Just don't steal anything else, okay? I'd prefer to survive this road trip."

"Me too." Amelia eyes the sleek blade of the knife. "And you're welcome."

. . .

It's only a two-hour drive to their next stop in Mackinaw City. They make the ride in utter silence with Amelia pouting on the sofa and casting furtive glances at her cellphone. Finally, Amelia stalks down the aisle to her bunk and doesn't emerge. Once Willow lands the bus at the campground near the historic lighthouse, she ventures to the back ready to make amends. They can't go on like this, and Amelia has always been too stubborn to apologize first.

"Hey." Willow raises to her tiptoes to peer into the top bunk. She finds Amelia reading the spiral-bound copy of their manuscript. Lately, it feels like the only thing holding them together. "Can we talk?"

She turns her body toward the wall.

"Fine. I'll talk. I'm glad you took the knife. It was a stupid idea, but at least it scared Jackson away. I want us to get back on the same page. Like we used to be. I thought you'd be excited about Northwestern. That we'd be there together. That's what we always dreamed about. But you don't even seem to care."

Amelia snuffles. Is she crying? "I am excited."

"But?"

"The English program is really competitive. Are you sure you can handle it?"

"You're doing alright, aren't you?" Willow risks a touch of her friend's shoulder. Amelia rolls toward her, her cheeks wet. Her nose, pink at the tip. Willow can't remember the last time Amelia shed tears. Fifth grade, maybe. When she bombed a surprise quiz in social studies.

"It's harder than I thought. I had to drop that Short Fiction class. Everybody writes so beautifully. Like Delia Owens and Edgar Allan Poe had a baby."

Willow barks out a laugh and gives her a playful nudge. "Are you worried I'm going to outshine you?"

"No." Her answer comes quick. "Maybe. I don't know."

Willow swallows hard. Once Amelia finds out that she's

started writing another book without her, that she's... well, she can't let herself imagine the rest of it. That's why Amelia can never know. At least not until she figures out a way to tell her without crushing her soul. Her mom has assured her that Amelia won't care, that Amelia isn't as passionate about writing as she is. But Amelia *is* passionate about being the best, and she'll view Willow's snub as worse than a participation trophy. Her stomach churning at the thought of it, she tosses out a trite reassurance. "Writing is an art, and art isn't a competition. There's room for both of us. Together."

Amelia wipes her face with her T-shirt and sighs. "I guess."

Desperate to appease her, Willow whips out her phone and scrolls through their Writing on the Road posts to find the throwback picture she'd posted at the start of their journey. The two of them at seven years old, huddled over a sheet of construction paper, illustrating their first story. "We're a team, remember? Since Ms. Wilmer's second grade fable project."

"You were the better writer back then, too," Amelia laments. "Sometimes I feel like a sham. I even thought about changing majors. Math and science come so easily to me."

"But you don't love them. Don't be like my mom. She sold her author dreams for a CPA license." Taking the manuscript binder, Willow turns to Chapter Eighteen. "*The pale ghost of the moon rides in a cloudless sky*. You wrote that line. Heck, you wrote that whole paragraph. Those descriptions of the campground really set the scene." Never mind that Amelia had stolen the good parts from a poem Willow had penned in the eighth grade. Now wasn't the time to be stingy.

"Mr. Spellman thinks you're the better writer. He probably wants to get naked with you. And marry you. And have babies that you'll name after the Brontës. You know, Charlotte, Anne, and little Emily."

Willow laughs again, hoping it doesn't sound forced. She's not sure what to do with this downtrodden version of Amelia.

She's never seen her like this. "I don't think he's a fan of nineteenth-century lit. He once called it neurotic and depressing."

"That sounds like me." Amelia groans, fake-screaming into her pillow. Then, she turns her face to Willow. A smile tugs at the corner of her mouth. "Thanks for trying to cheer me up. I'm sorry for everything. I've been such a bitch."

"At least you admit it," she teases. "Now, let's get our butts to the ferry. If we hurry, we can still do the fudge-making masterclass at Ryba's."

* * *

With Amelia softly snoring above her, Willow rolls from the bunk and pads toward the cab of the bus, pulling her old Kildeer High sweatshirt over her head. She snags a piece of fudge from the counter and lets herself out into the cool night air. From her seat on the top step, she dials her mom. She needs to hear a familiar voice even if it comes with a heaping side of guilt.

"Hey, honey. It's late. But I'm so glad you called. Your last text had me a little worried."

Her mom sounds tired, stressed. She wonders if Ray's to blame. Though they'd finally called it quits six months ago, he can't leave well enough alone. Her mother, too, seems unable to let go. A month ago, she'd caught them on the phone together. And the following night, her mom agreed to meet him for drinks, telling Willow she felt sorry for him. Truthfully, without the badge and the uniform, he is sort of pathetic.

Willow allows herself a deep breath. She wants to spill it all, to let her mom reassure her. But she holds back. Lately, her mother hasn't been Amelia's biggest fan, and it feels wrong to give her more ammunition against her best friend. "I know. Putting the finishing touches on the book has turned out to be harder than I expected. I think we finally agreed on the ending though."

"You don't sound convinced."

"I want to sell books, don't get me wrong. More than that though, I want to write something real. Not just another knockoff with a shocking twist. But an actual novel that means something to people."

"And you will. You *have*."

"You didn't even read the whole thing yet."

"Well, you're *my* daughter, so I already know it's brilliant."

"Mom. *Seriously*." It feels good to share a laugh, but her heart isn't in it. Even fudge-making hadn't been as fun as she'd hoped. It turns out lying is a real killjoy. "Have you talked to Amelia's mother lately?"

"Not since she yelled at me and called me irresponsible for helping you plan the road trip. Why? Is everything okay?"

"It's fine. Everything's fine." Willow takes a bite to keep her mouth busy. "We made fudge today."

"Do not change the subject. I know that tone, Willow Grace. What is going on?"

"Amelia cried, and I feel like it's all my fault." She selects a small morsel of truth and offers it to her mother. The rest she keeps inside.

"Amelia never cries."

"Yeah, I know. Thanks, Mom." Willow winces at her own barb. She pictures her mother sitting at the kitchen table, her laptop open, or curled on the sofa beneath the afghan. It's always been the two of them, but that's changing, too. She should be nicer. It's the least she can do before she lays a truth bomb on her mother's doorstep and leaves her alone in the fall-out. "She said school is harder than she thought it would be. I feel so bad about keeping the second book from her. I should've told her right away, the moment I started writing it. I should've asked her to help."

"We discussed this at the time. You said that she'd hardly written any of *this* book. That you'd done the lion's share of the work. And the two of you have such different goals, such different skillsets. Leave the popcorn lit for Amelia. You, my girl, are destined for greatness. Why would you let her share the credit?"

Her mom makes it sound so much worse. She sighs.

"Oh, honey. You'll tell her when you get home. She'll be happy for you."

Her mom doesn't really believe that. She knows Amelia too well. "You didn't hear her this morning. Trust me, she'll be devastated. It's the end of our friendship."

"If she can't celebrate your success, then she's not a real friend. Now, get some sleep. You've got an actual novel to finish. You know, one that will *mean something to people*." Willow barely laughs. "And Will? Try to enjoy yourself."

After hanging up the call, Willow leans back and gazes skyward, where a wispy cloud moves across the moon.

"Ten more days," she whispers under her breath. In three days, they'll be in Niagara Falls, and a week after that, they'll be back home in Chicago, where her future will be close enough to touch. Warm skin, brown eyes, soft lips.

She slips her hand into the pocket of her pajamas, savoring the key's familiar edges, its delicious promises. The heady rush of her secret life that won't be secret much longer.

TWELVE

NOW

The ringing of Tracy's cellphone jars her awake. Until she feels the weight of Sam's arm around her shoulders and spots the pizza box on the coffee table next to the four empty beer bottles, she briefly forgets her new reality. She calls his name, embarrassed that her voice sounds like an old faucet, rusted from lack of use, and nudges him in the side with her elbow. She doesn't bother to wait for his eyes to open.

In a rush, Tracy answers the phone, leaving Sam confused and tangled in the afghan on the sofa. He blinks, as it dawns on him too. Where they are. How long they've been sleeping. She wonders if he remembers all of it. The way she'd dozed on his shoulder, told him her favorite Willow stories until his breathing grew deep and even. God, is that a spot of drool on his shirt?

"Tracy, Detective Delgado. We need to talk." Gauzy light seeps through the blinds, reminding Tracy it's morning. Again. Another night passed without word from her daughter.

"Is it Willow? Did you find her?" As she'd started to drift off, someone had tagged Amanda Robles, that famous news reporter from WGN, in her #whereiswillow Facebook post. She taps the screen of her laptop to bring it back to life. "I put the story on social media last night, along with her graduation photo, thinking it might jog someone's memory. Somebody must have seen her. Somebody must know something."

The detective replies with a noncommittal murmur. "I saw your post."

"Oh, wow. That's great. We were hoping it would go viral."

"We?"

"Sam and I. Uh, Mr. Spellman." Tracy finds Sam surveying the damage in the hall mirror. The crease on his forehead from the throw pillow. The mussed nest of his hair. He catches her and shrugs, flashing a boyish smile.

"Dr. Ford sent me the link," Detective Delgado clarifies. "She was less than thrilled with your portrayal of Amelia, and I can't say that I blame her."

Of course Candice would be concerned about *her* daughter. She imagines Amelia tucked in bed, warm and safe, still sleeping. It makes her want to scream. "Well, Amelia hasn't exactly been helpful. What does she expect me—"

"That's not why I'm calling. I'm pulling onto your street right now. I'd like to ask you a few questions about the bus."

Tracy pulls back the corner of the blinds for confirmation. Indeed, she finds the unmarked car with its dark tinted windows parked across the street. "The detective is here," she tells Sam, hoping he'll stay. She needs a buffer from this woman, who seems to hate Ray so badly that she's decided to take it out on her. And she's still holding out hope that she can convince him to talk some sense into Amelia.

"Does she have news about Willow?"

The doorbell rings before Tracy can answer him. Suddenly, they're both face to face with the steely-eyed detective, who wastes no time in rendering her first judgment.

"You're here early," she says to Sam. "Or is it late?"

When Sam's cheeks flush, Tracy comes to the rescue. "We fell asleep monitoring social media."

"Social media. Of course." Detective Delgado manages to make pizza and Facebook sound downright scandalous. She waltzes in like she owns the place, and Tracy tries to tamp down her annoyance. After all, she needs the detective. She's nowhere without her.

"With all due respect, Detective, social media has cracked its fair share of cases. Have you thought about arranging a vigil? Contacting the local networks? Doing a press conference? I believe Amanda Robles from WGN might be interested. Someone tagged her in my post."

"Amanda Robles." She lets out a short, dismissive breath. "Investigative journalism at its finest."

"They call her the Barbara Walters of Chicago, so..." In another life, Tracy met Ms. Robles, but she keeps that to herself. Fingers crossed, the reporter won't remember her or her grandmother or the way she'd once cruelly shoved a mic in both their faces.

"A vigil is a good idea to mobilize the community. We can discuss the media angle later." At least Detective Delgado hasn't completely shut her down. "Let's sit."

Sam lingers by the door, hands in his pockets like a schoolboy waiting to be asked to dance. "Shall I stay?"

"That's up to Ms. Barrett."

Tracy nods at him, grateful when he finds a seat next to her. She should throw away the pizza box. The smell makes her slightly nauseous. But it's too late. Detective Delgado slaps a nondescript folder onto the coffee table, and now, it's all Tracy can think about. Her mind starts spinning the most awful visions. It's a relief when the detective doesn't torture her with it. She flips it open and pushes it toward Tracy.

"Tell me about this secret compartment."

"There's not much to tell." Tracy barely looks at it. "Willow thought it would be fun, so I added a little hidey-hole beneath one of the bench seats. It wasn't a secret. Both girls knew the combination to the lock."

"Before they left on the road trip, was the lock damaged?"

"Damaged? No. It was brand new."

"And was there anything inside the compartment?"

"Not anything that I was aware of, and certainly nothing *I* put there, if that's what you're getting at."

Sam shifts beside her to get a better look. "What did you find?" he asks boldly.

"Well, the outside of the compartment had tool marks. As if someone tried to force it open and failed. Inside, we found cash. Seventy-five thousand dollars."

Tracy hears herself gasp. The room goes slightly off-kilter, and that awful day-old pizza smell floods back into her nostrils. "What? What did Amelia say about it?"

"I haven't talked to her yet. I wanted to start here. With you." The detective pauses then, as if Tracy can add something more than utter shock. Tracy and Sam exchange a bewildered look.

"Who else knew about the compartment?" Detective Delgado asks.

"No one. Unless the girls mentioned it."

"How about Ray? Did he know?"

"Him again?" Tracy doesn't care if she sounds unhinged, a little hysterical. "What does he have to do with it?"

"Well, it's convenient, isn't it? Ray allegedly takes a payoff to plant evidence in a murder case. Months later, a wad of cash shows up in a secret compartment in your skoolie. Are you telling me that's just a coincidence?"

"Ray never set foot inside the bus. He didn't help with the renovations. He didn't know the combination either. You can ask him yourself." She hates that he's not here to answer these questions. That she's between a rock and a hard place, taking the heat for sins she didn't commit. But after yesterday's exchange, it's best that he keeps his distance.

"I intend to do just that, Ms. Barrett. Do you know where he is now?"

Her heart starts to skitter, pattering against the wall of her chest. She picks up her cellphone like it can help her.

"He's her ex-boyfriend, not her child." Sam's indignance surprises her. She didn't know he had it in him. "You should be trying to find Willow instead of wasting your time settling an old vendetta."

"He's right," Tracy says. "Please talk to Amelia. She knows what happened to Willow. I guarantee it."

"I told you I would, but I have to ask. Do you really believe your daughter's best friend hurt her? Because that's what you've insinuated online. Things like that have a way of spinning out of control." She gestures to the laptop on the table, the post still open on the screen at five hundred likes and counting. Tracy resists the urge to snap it shut. It's clear to her now. She can't trust Detective Delgado to be on her side. She's on her own here.

"I don't know what happened to Willow. I want to believe she's safe. That she just ran off with that guy in the motorcycle jacket like Amelia told us. But my mother's intuition is all I've got, and it's been screaming at me since I opened my door at 5 a.m. and saw the school bus parked on the street. Since Amelia flew back alone. Now, this money turns up. What am I supposed to think?"

"I get it. Really, I do. You have your intuition. I have my investigation. I'm not reading tea leaves here. I need to do things by the book, and like it or not, you hitched your wagon to Ray the moment you climbed in bed with him."

Tracy remembers the scratch of Ray's stubble against her cheek the first time they'd kissed. How safe he'd made her feel nestled in the crook of his arm. It hadn't been all bad with him, which was part of the problem. "You'll do what you have to do, and so will I."

"Which is what exactly?"

"Telling as many people as I can about my daughter." With that, she tugs the laptop toward her and scans the Facebook messages, her heart leaping in her chest when she spots one from Amanda Robles herself: *I'm so sorry to hear about your daughter. Would you be interested in appearing on a broadcast...* "Starting with the WGN ten o'clock news."

"I won't stand in your way, but please be cautious with your words. You and your daughter are not the only ones involved here. I assume you care about Amelia as well." She takes a careful pause, waiting for Tracy to respond. Tracy can't tell her the truth. That the way she feels about Amelia is complicated.

"Of course I do. I practically helped raise her. But after she went away to college last fall, we weren't as close. The girls had grown apart too. Predictable, I suppose. Amelia seemed to be struggling with it more than Willow. I didn't want to mention it with Candice around, but Willow told me that Amelia expressed some worry about school. That it was harder than she expected. It makes me uneasy. A girl that tightly wound is bound to go off the deep end eventually."

Detective Delgado studies her intently. Ray did that sometimes, and it made her just as uncomfortable. Like his cop senses could penetrate her soul. "I'll be in touch," she says, finally. "I'll have our community outreach coordinator contact you to schedule a public vigil for next week."

The moment Tracy shuts the door, her knees go wobbly. She starts to second-guess herself. If the past year has taught her anything, it's that you can never really know another person. Not Ray. Not Amelia. Not the handsome teacher standing beside her. Not even her own daughter.

"You alright?" Sam asks, steadying her with a gentle hand at her back. "That detective's not messing around. Honestly, how would the girls get that much money?"

"I don't know. It doesn't seem real. What happened on that trip?" A sense of urgency grips her. It rages through her blood like a fire, won't be denied. "I think I need to go to Niagara Falls to see the campground for myself. To look for Willow. Maybe something there will help me understand."

"You shouldn't go alone."

She gives him a pointed look. "I'm not planning on it."

Sam returns to the house an hour later, holding two extra-large lattes. She purposely takes the first sip too fast, letting it burn her throat. It takes the sting away from the rest of her aching body.

"Well?" she asks, hopeful. Before he'd driven away on his coffee run, she'd watched him walk across the street and ring the Fords' bell.

He shakes his head. "Candice answered the door. She said Amelia wouldn't see me. I think she's protecting her."

"From what?"

Sam considers her question. "Herself."

INSTAGRAM

writingontheroad Road trips are for backroads, and there's no better backroad than Heritage Route 23 with @melthebookworm. Pro tip: Load up on snacks before you go. It's a long way to Saginaw River. #theroadtrip #bestfriends #dayfive #takethelongway
550 likes 100 comments 30 shares

ilovepuppies Drive safely, girls! Don't pick up any hitchhikers.

roadtripper777 You have to visit the Tawas Point Lighthouse. It's our favorite spot.

truecrimelover44 Check out at @melthebookworm's face. She looks guilty. #whereiswillow #bffdidit

> **tedbundyfanxoxo** @truecrimelover44 Right?! Super shady.
>
> **baronjones** @truecrimelover44 Told ya! #bffdidit
>
> **kaykay59** @truecrimelover44 let the cops do their job #inno-centtillprovenguilty

coolgranny1 Praying for your safe return! #whereiswillow

JT77 ive seen this story before #gonegirl #amydunne

aliensrpeopletoo @JT77 exactly... it's a stunt for book sales... duh

truecrimelover44 @JT77 you're going to look like an ass when she turns up dead

JT77 @truecrimelover44 wouldn't be the first time i can live with it

THIRTEEN

BEFORE

Day Five on The Road: Route 23

Willow guides the school bus down Heritage Route 23, the scenic highway that winds along with shoreline of Lake Huron. The afternoon sunlight glistens off the water like a million shimmering stars, but she's miles away. In a cabin hundreds of miles from here. In a bed that smells like the sandalwood cologne she bought him at Macy's with her bookstore money. She sinks into the daydream until a delicious heat spreads through her body, imagining herself there with him. Her first real boyfriend. Not like the boneheads she dated in high school. It's strange and wonderful and achingly romantic, how they'd started as friends, exchanging notes back and forth. How their love had grown deeper with time. Even if she hasn't told anyone just yet. With her mother's break-up still fresh and Amelia perpetually single, it feels safer to keep it to herself. To protect her soft, hazy dream from the spiny bristles of reality.

A flash of black in her side mirror jolts her into the moment, hard and fast. It's so jarring that she jerks the wheel, and the bus rumbles onto the gravelly shoulder. A motorcycle matches her pace in the left lane.

Her heart snaps inside her chest like a rubber band, and she curses under breath, as she steers back onto the road.

"Mel!" she calls out. "He's back. He found us."

"What? *Who?*"

"Jackson." As she checks the rearview, she slows the bus to a crawl. But the rider taps his brakes too, serpentining across the dividing dashes that split the lane in two. He's dangerously close to her. "Look at the jacket."

Amelia appears beside her, her mouth slightly open in shock. "Shit. What're we gonna do?"

"The only thing we can do. Give him his money back."

"Hell, no. Go faster. Keep driving."

"Are you out of your mind?" Neck and neck with the bus, Jackson veers into her lane, and Willow swerves, feeling strangely satisfied when Amelia stumbles forward.

"I need that money," Amelia insists, undeterred by Willow's erratic driving. "I mean, we both need it. Unless we manage to snag a bigtime publisher, we're on our own for advertising, marketing. All of it. We can't even afford a professional editor."

"We don't need one. My mom minored in English."

Willow can't believe they're arguing about this now. It would be funny, if it weren't absolutely terrifying. Eyes glued to the long stretch of highway, she tries to maintain a straight line toward the horizon. It's surprisingly deserted for early summer. But then the guidebook had promised light, easygoing traffic on a two-lane route. What once seemed a blessing, now unnerves her. She prays for a police cruiser, a minivan, a hitchhiker. But there's only Jackson and his beast of a bike encroaching on her lane and miles and miles of tall trees to box them in. Again, the bus tires slip off the road, juddering her bones.

"No offense, Will, but your mom thinks rainbows shine out of your ass. She can't critique your writing."

"Fine, if you won't return the money, I will. Where is it? I'm pulling over." She slows down, surprised when Jackson follows suit. His doggedness terrifies her. "I'll throw it out the window if I have to."

"Like hell you will. We're ten times bigger than him. Don't let him push you around." Amelia gives Jackson her middle finger, as he zips along outside the driver's window. Willow's mouth goes dry at the sight of him, weaving across the divider and into the lane of oncoming traffic. His face, obscured by the dark shield of his helmet. "Can't you go any faster?"

"It's a school bus not a sports car. I have to slow down. He's going to run us off the road."

It happens in a blink. As Willow lifts her foot from the gas, Amelia grabs the wheel, jerks it to the left, and lets out a violent screech. Willow's life cleaves in two, as cleanly and irrevocably as a halved apple.

Jackson loses control, careening wildly through the lane toward a large rock on the opposite shoulder. Upon impact, the motorcycle goes airborne—Jackson clinging to the handlebars like a ragdoll in the rearview—and dead-ends against a massive cedar tree. A fireball explodes into the sky. Willow tears her eyes from the mirror and white-knuckles the wheel.

Though time stops, suspending her like a fly in amber, the bus keeps moving, interminably down the black ribbon of road.

Willow waits for Amelia to speak. To scream. To say something, anything. When she glances at her friend, she finds her staring ahead numbly.

If Amelia won't say it, she will. "We have to call the police. The bike hit a tree. It caught fire. He's probably..." Turns out, she can't bring herself to admit it after all. "Hurt. *Badly*."

"It was an accident. You lost control. If I hadn't grabbed the wheel, we would've gone off the road."

It's an obvious lie. Willow gapes at her, then quickly turns away, squinting into the sun blaring through the windshield.

"Even more reason to call then. We can explain what happened."

"That I took his money?"

"We don't have to tell them that."

"Don't we, though? They'll ask why he was after us. With a bit of investigating, they'll figure it out, and I'll go to jail. Goodbye, Northwestern; hello, Department of Corrections."

"What're you saying, then?" She needs to hear the words from Amelia's mouth before she'll let herself believe that her friend could be so cruel. That the girl she's known since kindergarten could ask her to keep driving.

"They won't let you off the hook either. You're the one who took the ride with him. The one driving the bus too. The cops might think you stole the money."

Willow can hardly breathe. Her chest constricts like a vice. She takes one more look in the rearview at the gray plume to confirm it's real. "But I didn't."

"I know. I'd never let them pin it on you. I'm just saying, is all." After another too-long silence, she adds, "Besides, I'm sure someone stopped to help him."

"The road is deserted."

The *ifs* cloud Willow's brain like the thick smoke she drove away from, making it impossible to think of anything else. It's a wonder she stays on the road. If Jackson *dies*, it's all her fault, and she'll have to live with that. She should turn the bus around right now. Or now. Or now. Or...

If Jackson *lives*, she'll be the one blamed, and rightly so. She left the scene of an accident. She did nothing to save him. For all she knows, the explosion set the entire tree line ablaze. If Jackson *lives*, her life may as well be over.

Please let him be dead. She hates herself for wishing it, but it doesn't change her mind.

Fifteen miles up the road, a police cruiser blazes toward them, siren blaring, then whizzes past, followed by an ambulance moments later. Then a firetruck. Willow veers into a small gas station. Ignoring Amelia's voice behind her, she pushes through the school bus door with urgency. Even the fresh air can't help her now. She doubles over, spewing last night's fudge onto the asphalt. Then she wipes her mouth, returns to the bus, and keeps driving. The road blurs through her tears.

Finally, the roaring in her head quiets. She hears Amelia's voice clear as a bell. "We just have to forget about it. What's done is done."

FOURTEEN

NOW

Later that afternoon, Tracy checks her face in the bathroom mirror. She dabs a spot of concealer beneath her blue eyes and gives her freckled cheeks a pinch. Runs a hand through the hair she hasn't washed in days, straightens her wrinkled T-shirt. *People don't expect you to look your best,* Amanda Robles had assured her, when she'd arrived at the house twenty minutes ago with her cameraman in tow. *In fact, the shittier you look, the better. Give them a mother they can sympathize with.*

Tracy takes one last glance at herself. Mission accomplished, then. Even better that Amanda hadn't seemed to place her. Twenty years has passed since WGN ran the story on Grandma Ruth. Tracy was barely eighteen years old then, and Amanda couldn't have been more than thirty, trying to make a name for herself at the network by dragging Ruth Barrett's through the mud. It's a karmic disaster, her being here now. But Tracy can't be choosy. She opens the door and walks toward the staircase. In her periphery, the duffel bag she'd packed stands at the ready. Sam will be back later to pick her up for the two-hour flight to Buffalo.

"Come, have a seat. We're just getting set." Amanda

beckons to her from down below. She gleams like a bronzed statue, polished to perfection. Her age well-hidden beneath her makeup.

Amanda positions Tracy in the armchair, which production had relocated in front of the fireplace. Pictures of Willow in every stage of life dot the mantel behind her. Though Amanda pronounces it the essential backdrop to tell her story, Tracy finds it an impossible distraction. From the corner of her eye, she spots Willow, age two, with chocolate cake mashed on her face. Age five, running through the sprinkler. Age eight, posing in her astronaut's costume at Halloween. There are seven photos in all, gathered from various rooms in the house, and arranged around the graduation shot of the girls. It's a bit skeevy, the way it's staged, but Amanda insists.

After placing a box of tissues within reach on the coffee table, Amanda passes Tracy a few. "Don't be afraid to cry."

Already, Tracy's eyes begin to well. She looks into the camera and wonders if she's made a terrible mistake.

"Don't worry if you say something stupid. We've got a few hours till airtime. We can edit anything out."

That gives her a modicum of comfort. To know that she has a do-over, a takeback. With these stones in her throat, she's not sure how she'll speak a single word.

"Ready?" Amanda asks.

When she croaks out a noise of agreement, Amanda comes alive and turns to face the lens. The cameraman counts them down until it's too late to run away. She may as well be strapped to her seat and ready for impact. Like one of those crash dummies.

"Good evening, I'm Amanda Robles bringing you a special report for WGN nightly news. Tonight, we're here with Tracy Barrett, whose nineteen-year-old daughter, Willow, disappeared from the White Water Campground in Niagara Falls last Sunday. Willow and her best friend were touring the Great

Lakes in a refurbished school bus when she went missing. There is an ongoing police investigation into Willow's disappearance, which a spokesperson from Chicago PD called suspicious."

Suspicious. Tracy latches on to that word. It's not the right one. It's too soft, too slippery.

"Tracy, this must be an incredibly difficult time for you. What can you tell our viewers about Willow?"

This question, too, feels wrong. How can she explain her daughter in a soundbite? The camera stares at her, unblinking, and demands an answer. "She's smart and kind. A force to be reckoned with. She'd just been accepted into Northwestern for the fall semester, and she insisted on paying part of her tuition with the money she saved this year, working in a local bookstore. She's my only child. My entire world, really."

"Of course." Amanda nods sympathetically. "When did you realize that Willow was missing?"

"On Wednesday morning. When a young man knocked on my door to return the skoolie."

"You must have been horrified. Is he a suspect?" she asks, with feigned shock.

"Honestly, I don't know. The police haven't told me much. I have more questions than answers at this point. But I'm beyond worried. This isn't like Willow. She'd never run away, much less right now. Her future is too bright. Not only did she get accepted to her dream school, but she and her friend have just written a novel together."

"A novel?"

This is the real hook, Amanda had told her. *This book will make your story go viral.* This *is what will find your daughter.* Tracy knows Amanda's right. She has to sell it.

"A thriller called *The Road Trip*. It's about two best friends on the road trip of a lifetime." Tracy laughs a little. It sounds like the clunk of a dead piano key. "Ironic, I know. The girls went on their own road trip to do some last-minute research and editing and discuss the launch. It was Willow's goal to be a published author."

"What an incredible story." Amanda shakes her head in disbelief. "Tracy, I have to ask. We all know about the power of mother's intuition. What do you think happened to Willow?"

It's the question she's been dreading. She looks at Amanda, then back at the camera. But it's Amelia's face she sees. "I don't want to speculate. I only know that Willow's friend returned from the trip without her. I hope that she'll be willing to speak to you as well."

"And if Willow is watching right now? What would you say to her?"

Tracy's chest tightens. She takes in a sharp, painful breath. "I love you, and I'm doing everything in my power to make sure you get home safe, so you can fulfill all your dreams."

Amanda nods sagely, as she collects the centerpiece photograph of Willow and holds it on her lap. Here, the news anchor has already explained, the camera will zoom in on Willow's face. Tracy lets her gaze go there as well, trying to see her daughter the way others might. A fresh-faced beauty with her life ahead of her. Vivacious. Reckless. Daring. Irresponsible. A runaway. A whore. A spoiled little rich girl. She remembers other stories like this one, countless stories. Other missing girls. How people project their own insecurities onto a stranger. Willow will be no different.

"At WGN, we believe our viewers can make a difference. If you've seen Willow or have any information about her whereabouts, please contact Detective Penny Delgado at the Chicago Police Department at the number that appears on the bottom of your screen. We'll be providing regular updates on this story on the network's social media pages using the hashtag whereiswillow. WGN will also be live at the candlelight vigil outside the Barrett home at 7:30 p.m. on Wednesday where the community will gather to show their support and to pray for Willow's safe return. The two blocks surrounding the area will be closed to traffic to accommodate those in attendance."

Tracy wants to wrench the frame from Amanda's hands. She should be holding it. Instead, she sits calmly and reminds herself to breathe until the cameraman gives the signal.

"You did great." Amanda finally relinquishes the photograph and returns it to the mantel. "I'm sure we'll get a strong response from our audience. A couple of years ago, one of our viewers spotted a missing five-year-old girl in a van outside a convenience store. They recognized her right away from the footage we aired during the interview with her mother. That was real tearjerker. Even I shed a few."

Suddenly, it dawns on Tracy how empty she feels. How numb. "I didn't cry," she says, surprised at herself. "I couldn't. If Willow is out there, if she's watching, I don't want her to see me upset."

"Don't beat yourself up. There's no right way to handle a situation like this. The only thing to do is to get through it. It's pure survival. And you're already a survivor, aren't you?"

"A survivor," Tracy repeats, remembering how Grandma Ruth had uttered those words every time she carted home a new treasure. The green glass ashtray. The poodle salt and pepper shakers. The doll with buttons for eyes. Grandma Ruth pronounced all of them survivors, which left Tracy to dream up stories about the rough and tumble lives of the objects they'd rescued. That's when she knew she had a gift for storytelling, a gift that she passed on to her daughter.

"I certainly don't feel like one."

"Trust me, most moms I know would be in throes of a nervous breakdown by now. You're holding it together well enough to advocate for Willow. That's victory." Amanda gathers her notes into an elegant leather briefcase and clasps it shut before passing it to the cameraman. He places it by the door where he waits, as impassive as the briefcase itself. Tracy wishes it could be that easy for her. That this chaos could belong to someone else.

"Do you have time for a few more questions off the record?" Without waiting for an answer, Amanda leads her away from the hall and back into the living room. Tracy needs her, but at the same time, she wants her gone. She's had enough of spilling her guts for one day.

"Only a few. I'm so tired. I just want to—"

"I remember your grandmother." The words nearly bowl Tracy over. She tries not to panic. At least she hasn't said it on camera.

"You do?"

"I could never forget Ruth Barrett. She was my first big story at WGN. The little granny from Lexington who swindled Christie's Auction House with her forged autographed portraits."

"She wanted to make enough to pay the mortgage and my college tuition. Nothing more."

"I heard she died in prison."

"She only lasted one year." Tracy offers nothing more. She thinks of the signed John Wayne hanging upstairs on her bedroom wall. Grandma Ruth had squirreled that one away for herself. She'd always loved the blue-eyed cowboy. Gesturing to the sofa, Tracy says, "Please, sit."

"No need. I'll be brief. When is the last time you spoke with your daughter's friend?"

"Yesterday." Tracy sighs, remembering the way Amelia had looked at her. Her green eyes wide with betrayal. "It didn't go well."

"I figured as much based on your Facebook post. I thought I might try my luck at getting her to talk."

"You'll have to get past her Fort Knox of a mother first, and that's a tall order. Amelia is an extension of Candice. So, naturally, she can do no wrong. Her mother is the only one allowed to criticize her. It's always been that way."

"What about you? Do you see Amelia like that?"

Tracy hesitates. She senses a hunger in Amanda that scares her. Not much has changed in twenty years. "I've never met a perfect nineteen-year-old, if that's what you're asking. Hell, I'm thirty-nine and far from it."

"Word on the street is she's on probation for an honor code violation at Northwestern. Know anything about that?"

Quietly reeling, Tracy pretends to straighten the photographs on the mantel until her heartbeat steadies. "That sounds bad. Willow certainly didn't mention it."

"As a reporter, it piques my interest. One of my mentors at the station always tells me to find the secrets. That's where the story is, don't you think?"

Tracy thinks of the mysterious key and the money hidden in the compartment. The racy pictures on Sam's phone. She senses that there's danger in agreeing with Amanda and even more in not. She chooses to do neither. "I wonder if Sam knew about Amelia's troubles."

"Sam?" Amanda puzzles. "Is he Amelia's boyfriend?"

Suddenly, the room turns warm; a heat rash creeps up her neck for no good reason. "Sam Spellman is the girls' English teacher and mentor. He's helping with the completion of their novel. Lately, well, he's been helping *me*... to cope. He's been a good friend." Tracy wonders what Amanda would think of the two airline tickets in her inbox. Departing Chicago O'Hare at 6:28 p.m., arriving at Buffalo Niagara at 9:07 p.m. Sam had insisted on making the purchase, on coming with her.

"I'm glad to hear it. It's good that you have someone to depend on. Is Willow's father in the picture?"

Relieved to be off the Sam subject, Tracy indulges her. "No, and we're better for it. It's always been me and Willow. Strangely enough, if it wasn't for her dad, I might've been the one writing novels. I minored in English and dabbled with a book of my own. But after I got pregnant, her dad left me high and dry, and I had to take the sensible route. So, I put my dreams on hold and became an accountant, and we never heard from him again."

"Any chance he could be involved somehow?"

Tracy's laugh startles her. Even the stoic cameraman flinches in the corner. "He never wanted kids. I doubt he'd kidnap one."

"You're probably right. My ex is the same way." She offers a sad smile before asking, "What about Amelia's mom? What's her story?"

"Oh, Candice is one of those robots that runs on green juice or something. She once said that women should aspire to a world where they can afford to be as useless as men, if that tells you anything."

"It does indeed. She works out of Mercy General, right? The Cardiology Department."

Tracy nods. "As long as I've known her."

"Alright. I appreciate your time." Amanda presents Tracy with a sleek business card. "I wrote my personal cell on the back. If you hear anything, call me."

Tracy makes promises, gushes with gratitude. Says all the right things. Really, she wants to push her out the door and be done with her endless questions. She wants to beeline it to the airport. Now that she's got the ball rolling, surely, it won't be long. Someone will spot Willow outside a convenience store just like Madeline Gentry, the missing five-year-old Amanda mentioned. That's why she needs to be there. In Niagara Falls. As soon as possible. To do what's best for her daughter, the way she's always done.

Tracy waits by the window, watching intently as Amanda crosses the street. Her cameraman follows at a safe distance, lens atop his shoulder. She charges forward toward the door, bookended by shuttered windows. Tracy's stomach clenches as Amanda raises her hand to ring the bell.

She presses it once, twice, five times. Tracy counts each one. But the door never opens. Finally, Amanda concedes momentary defeat and returns to the news van parked on the street nearby.

Tracy retrieves her cell from the kitchen counter and tries Candice's number. In all the time she's known her, Candice has never turned off her phone. *Job hazard*, she'd joke whenever it rang obnoxiously in the middle of the girls' dance recital or the PTA meeting or the senior awards ceremony. Now, it goes straight to voicemail, reminding her that the world has tilted off its axis. Willow is still missing, and Dr. Ford has taken time off work.

She taps out a text instead.

> *I'm flying to Niagara Falls to look for Willow. This is Amelia's last chance to do the right thing. The story will air on WGN tonight with or without her.*

* * *

Hours later, in her sad motel room in Buffalo, Tracy scrubs the day off in a scalding hot shower and tugs on her usual pajamas—a pair of sweats and Ray's ratty T-shirt. Then, she aims the remote at the television, scrolling through the channels until she finds WGN, and heads straight for the minibar, where she removes a small bottle of vodka. She rarely drinks hard liquor, but she needs something strong to quiet her mind. She's thinking of the broadcast, of course. But tomorrow too. When she'll need a spine of steel to visit the campground. To speak to the local sheriff. The hopeful feeling from the afternoon has dulled to an ache at the center of her chest.

When she hears the knock at her door, she swigs the whole bottle and hides it in the nightstand drawer next to the Bible.

"Do you want some company?" Sam asks, stuffing his hands in his pockets. It's his tell. She knows that now. He's nervous. "I brought reinforcements."

He glances at the plastic laundry bag on the dingy carpet near his sneakers.

"From the minibar," he explains.

"In that case." With a breathy laugh, she steps back from the door. "I started without you."

"So did I." She's relieved when he chuckles. Ray never approved of her drinking alone, but surely even he would give her a pass on a day like this one. Though she feels a twinge of guilt that she hasn't warned him about the news interview or the money in the compartment, it disappears beneath the burn of the vodka in her throat. All's fair, since she'd been blindsided by the police investigation and the way it had changed him.

Sam unloads his haul and pours them each a finger of whisky in a disposable cup he retrieves from the bathroom sink. Clinking his cup against hers, he says, "To Willow. And to you. You're so brave."

She sighs and downs her shot, watching as he follows suit. "It feels like I'm in a bad dream. I keep waiting for someone to wake me up."

"I know what you mean. I blame myself for this. I had no idea about Amelia's problems. But I should've realized there was something off with the two of them, especially after she started sending me those photos. If Willow found out, she might've confronted her and..."

"Yeah, you're right. She would've been furious that Amelia wasn't taking this more seriously. That she was jeopardizing your working relationship. You've been a real godsend to the girls." Tracy flops onto the bed and positions a pillow behind her back. Fisting another small bottle of liquor, Sam joins her. He leaves a respectful distance between them. "I should've never told them to go on a road trip in the first place. Ray said that the whole thing was a bad idea. Candice did too."

"Ray's an idiot." Sam clamps his hand over his mouth and laughs. "I'm sorry. I'm a lightweight, and this stuff is truth serum. But he is. An idiot. I know I only met him a few times, but I always thought you were way too good for him. Besides, you couldn't have stopped Willow. She's a grown woman. She makes her own decisions now."

Tracy wants to tell him that Willow is not grown. She's not a woman. But the truth is that she doesn't want to correct him, not after he's given her a backhanded compliment. Flirted with her even. She likes him. It's shitty timing, but she can't deny it. She tells herself to get it together. Willow would not approve.

But when he offers her the bottle, she takes another sip. "Have the girls' phone records come back yet?" he asks.

"Detective Delgado hasn't mentioned it. She said it could take a few days."

Sam finishes the last of the whisky just as the ten o'clock news starts. Amanda Robles assured Tracy that Willow's disappearance would be the lead story. Still, when her own beleaguered face appears on the screen, she hardly recognizes herself. That ghost of a woman.

They sit in silence, listening to the interview. When the hashtag whereiswillow flashes on the screen in bold white letters, along with the phone number for Chicago PD, Tracy feels relieved. It's over, done with. No surprise mention of Grandma Ruth either, which she wouldn't put past Chicago's Barbara Walters.

But then, "Is that outside the Fords' house?"

Sam gapes at the television screen, where Amanda charges toward a newly emerged Amelia and sticks a microphone in her face. To Tracy's surprise, Amelia remains calm and composed. She's dressed nicely too, in slacks and a black blazer that surely belongs to her mother. This is no ambush.

"Amelia! What happened to Willow? Why aren't you talking to the police?"

As Amelia aims her green eyes at the camera, Tracy thinks of how long she's known this girl, how she's loved her like her own daughter. Hated her too, if she's honest. "Under the advice of my attorney, I would like to give a brief statement. I had nothing to do with Willow's disappearance. During our road trip, Willow behaved erratically. She was... *is*... a troubled person, and I have shared my concerns with police. I have also been questioned about a large sum of money found inside the bus, of which I had no prior knowledge and cannot explain. Given Willow's behavior, I believe that she ran away from the campground of her own volition, and I hope and pray that she is found safely."

"How dare she." Rage courses through Tracy's veins. She thought the alcohol would numb her emotions, but it only sharpens them. She can feel Sam looking at her from the other side of the bed. He's probably afraid of her. "You have to tell the police about Amelia. About those texts she sent you. She's making Willow out to be the bad guy. She's making her sound crazy."

Sam nods. "I will. I promise. As soon as we get back. I should've done it already."

Tracy switches the channel to a mindless gameshow and rubs her temples. Covers her eyes. She can't handle any more surprises.

"Whatever you need, I'm here for you."

She peeks at him through the web of her fingers, and his mouth quirks into a half-smile. It tamps one fire inside her and ignites another. "Whatever I need," she says, shamelessly. "I'll hold you to that."

God, she's drunk.

Slowly, Sam raises a hand to remove his glasses. Then, he sets them on the nightstand and turns toward her.

INSTAGRAM

writingontheroad Just arrived at #saginawriver with @melthebook-worm. Rumor has it that the bass and walleyes are biting! #theroadtrip #dayfive #bestfriends #catchandrelease
708 likes 234 comments 41 shares

ilovepuppies My hubby says I make a mean fried bass fillet. Hope you girls are having fun!

sharkfin77 The bass like the spinnerbait the best. Nothin' better than a day on the river.

truecrimelover44 Did you see @melthebookworm on the news? Wow. Major deflection. And where did she get that awful blazer? #raidedmomscloset #bffdidit #whereiswillow

> **tedbundyfanxoxo** @truecrimelover44 I don't know. It made me wonder what happened on that road trip.

> **winnerwinner4** @tedbundyfanxoxo they both seem guilty to me #spoiledlittlerichgirls

chicagowriter i heard @melthebookworm lost her scholarship to Northwestern... sleeping with a prof... or worse?

> **truecrimelover44** @chicagowriter we need deets and sources stat!

> **chicagowriter** @truecrimelover44 my cousin took creative writing with her second semester and said she's an insufferable know it all #bffdidit

FIFTEEN

BEFORE

Day Five on the Road: Saginaw River

Willow waits until Amelia's breathing sounds even as a metronome. Then, she slides out from her bunk and slips on her sneakers. After unplugging Amelia's cellphone from the charging station and securing it in the pocket of her sleep shorts, she gently pushes the door of the bus open and walks out into the pitch-black Saginaw River Campground. When she's a safe distance from the bus, she sits at a picnic table and unlocks Amelia's phone by typing in her four-digit passcode, her birthday. Then, she pecks out *motorcycle accident route 23* in the search bar.

She ignores the twinge of guilt. Tells herself there's nothing to regret. Not after what Amelia has done. She can't very well search it from her own phone.

Her heart beats faster and faster as she scans the results, until she spots a link at the bottom of the page. It's a sparse post from a local news blotter.

Emergency personnel responded to a one vehicle crash on Route 23 just outside of Indian River. A motorcyclist sustained life-threatening injuries and was airlifted from the scene. Firefighters contained a small blaze that ignited as the result of the crash.

Though it's no different than what she expected, seeing it in print takes her right back there. The dark tint of his face shield. The lightning flash of movement as he swerved. The plume of smoke she left in the rearview. She gazes out into the moonlit spaces between the trees, grateful for the dark that hides her tears. It's strange how she can be numb and raw all at once.

When Amelia's phone vibrates in her hand, she glances down at it without thinking. Then, she drops it onto the ground like a hot coal. Stares at it, as if it's still smoldering.

Her stomach flip-flopping, she forces herself to pick it up. To look at the screen. She can't *not*. To read the thread of messages, which began weeks ago.

The most recent photo, a half-naked Amelia sprawled out on the top bunk of the bus, makes her skin crawl. Worse, that's *her* black bra. The one he bought for her at Fleur du Mal in downtown Chicago. But it's Amelia's text that floors her.

I wish you were here.

Well, not the text itself but the recipient, Sam Spellman.

Amelia, you have to stop this. You're going to get me in trouble.

She reads his response silently at first, and then in a whisper, trying out the sound of it. "You're going to get me in trouble." What did that mean exactly? In trouble, because it's entirely inappropriate for a former student who's half his age to send him sexy pics? Or, in trouble, because he likes it? A subtle but critical distinction.

Glancing back to the bus, she wonders what to do. A part of her wants to hurl the phone into the river. But the other part wins out. The part that needs to know.

Don't you want me? she types, then reconsiders. Deletes. *It's because of Willow, isn't it? She's the one you want. I've seen the way you look at her.* With her blood zipping through her, Willow presses send.

While she waits on pins and needles for his reply, she scrolls up through the rest of the message thread. Her disbelief grows with each text bubble. The messages go back a few weeks, since Amelia had arrived home for summer break. He'd never texted back until now.

Willow's hands shake, as she studies the very first message. There's a bathroom selfie too, of Amelia posing in the bikini she'd worn a few days ago to the beach at Pictured Rocks. Her mouth is painted blood red, a striking contrast to her raven hair, and she's angled her face in the mirror to accentuate her cheekbones. She's stunning. *I'm home and I've missed your lips.*

Words are important. Words are everything. These words shake her to her core, leaving more questions than answers. Questions that tie her stomach in knots and make her throat ache.

Willow hastily deletes the message she sent pretending to be Amelia. Looking at the bus, she steels herself. It's only a few more days till Niagara. But all her excitement is dead now. It's a cold, gray lump inside her. First, the accident. Now, this. It's insane to admit, even to herself, but *this* feels worse.

The phone buzzes again.

You need help, Amelia. You're practically a kid and so is Willow.

She's been so careful. He insisted on it, and she understood. So careful and discreet and patient. Like she could simply lock it all away, all the momentous feelings for him, that had grown too big to deny. But apparently, she's practically a kid, so screw being careful.

She sends one last message, which she also deletes from Amelia's phone, before hurrying back inside.

A kid? Is that how you see me? You told me you loved me.

SIXTEEN

NOW

Tracy wakes in a cold sweat. A vicious beam of sunlight sears her face through the slim opening in the curtains, and she curls like a worm to escape it. Her head throbs at the sound of her own moaning. It's been years since her last hangover. Years since she stayed out all night and spent the morning with her face pressed against the bathroom floor. Back then, she only had herself to worry about.

With great effort, she follows the breadcrumb trail of memory. Sam, standing at her door. Alcohol. The news broadcast. More alcohol. Amelia's cutting green eyes. It all leads to the gentle clink of Sam's glasses against the nightstand, the creak of the bed as he'd come closer. The intoxicating scent of him and his pressed his mouth to hers. Beyond that, the rest gets hazy. A blur of skin and heat and... *Oh God, how did this happen?* She made out with Mr. Spellman. At least they'd had the good sense not to go any further than that.

"Morning." Sam waves to her from the small desk in the corner of the room, and she groans again. Because he looks freshly showered and wide awake. "I brought coffee," he says. "Strong coffee."

Tracy tugs the sheet over her head. She can't look at him.

"About last night," he begins. "I drank way too much. I've been so worried about Willow that I think I wanted to forget everything for a while."

He's giving her an out. A way to save face. "Me too."

"Not that it wasn't enjoyable."

"Right." Beneath her sheet tent, Tracy nods. Thankfully, she's still wearing all her clothing.

"You need to focus on finding Willow. I'm supposed to be helping you do that. I need to be a friend to you right now. Not a guy."

He's right. One hundred percent. Still, Tracy hates herself for feeling disappointed. "Thanks for saying that."

"Of course." She hears him moving. When he speaks again, his voice is so close that she knows he's standing next to the bed, looking over the shape of her. His hand softly grazes her shoulder. "I'll leave your coffee on the nightstand with a couple sugar packets. Just knock when you're ready to head over to the campground."

After the door closes, Tracy throws back the sheets and searches for her cellphone, eager for any updates. This is what she should've been doing, not locking lips like a teenager with her daughter's mentor. Wondering if she's still half-drunk, she stares for a beat in disbelief at the screen. Then, she tosses on her sweatpants, grabs her room key, and makes a beeline for Sam's door.

"Did you see this?" she blurts, the moment he opens it. "ABC News. NBC, too. They're all covering Willow's story. The hashtag is trending."

Sam studies her cellphone, scrolling down the page with his finger. "Did you read this one?"

"I glanced at it." She looks again and swallows hard. Beneath Amelia's photograph, the headline reads: *Best Friend or Worst Enemy?* As she scans the article, certain phrases rise to the surface. *Suspicious behavior. Avoiding the police. Pointing the finger.* "It seems like Amelia's little press conference backfired. Hashtag bffdidit. She's become the villain."

Head buried in his own phone, Sam grimaces. "I'm not so sure about that. People are taking sides, spitting out theories. Read this one."

> Is Willow Barrett the next "Gone Girl?" After vanishing during a road trip with her best friend, sources close to Barrett speculate that her disappearance may be a ploy for attention or worse, a sign of underlying mental health problems.

Tracy turns away, refusing to read any more. She can't stomach it. "That's absolutely ridiculous. Who are these sources? It's probably Candice feeding them lies to take the heat off her daughter."

"Well, for better or worse, you've certainly got everyone's attention. Are you okay with that?" He reaches a hand out to touch her, then stops short and drops it to his side.

"If it helps us find Willow, it's worth it. But thanks for asking. I'm really glad you're here." As she peers over Sam's shoulder at the bed he didn't sleep in, flashes of last night's interlude play out like a bad movie montage. A bad movie she wouldn't mind watching again. Just as her cheeks start to warm, the ringing of her cellphone rescues her from further humiliation.

"Oh, shit. It's Ray. I should probably answer it." She steps away from the door and retreats toward her room. She's learned from experience that Ray's unpredictability is best managed alone.

"Where the hell are you?" he spits at her the moment she answers.

"Hello to you, too." But to be fair, she had left him in the dark. "I'm in Niagara Falls looking for Willow."

"Well, thanks for the heads-up. I really appreciate you keeping me in the loop." What can she do but sigh in the face of his sarcasm? "You tell me you need me, then you send me away. Now, you up and disappear."

"Ray, we talked about this. It doesn't look good. That detective has a vendetta against you. Half the Chicago police force does."

"Yeah, whatever. We talked about a lot of things." He sounds like a scolded puppy. "Are you there alone?"

Tracy glances at her tousled sheets. The balled-up pillow where Sam had laid his head. She wonders if it still smells like him. "Uh, not exactly. I'm with Sam Spellman."

"Jesus, Trace. Again? You know I don't trust that guy. Are you trying to make me jealous?"

"That's what you're worried about? I've got a lot on my plate, Ray. I don't have time to massage your ego."

"Is that so?" He lets the question hang for a moment. Then, "Why didn't you tell me that the cops found a boatload of cash on the bus?"

"I'm trying to be smart, Ray. To put Willow first. How would it have looked if you were my first call after I found out? Detective Delgado already suspects it's yours."

"Yeah, she made that crystal clear when she and her cronies blindsided me outside at six a.m. this morning. She's like a dog with a goddamn bone. What were the girls doing with that much cash anyway?"

"I don't know. You tell me."

"Here we go again." Ray blows out a frustrated breath that makes Tracy want to be rid of him. It reminds her that she ended things for a reason. That she's been stupid to let him back in her life. To give him power over her again. "I told you I thought I was doing the right thing. Just like—"

"I've gotta go." Abruptly, she ends the call, letting herself collapse onto the bed for exactly two minutes. She doesn't have time to feel sorry for herself. Willow needs her. When her phone rings again, she fully expects to see Ray's number. Instead, it's Detective Delgado calling.

"Did you find her?" She sounds as desperate as she feels.

"Are you watching this?"

"Watching what?"

"Turn on WGN. Now."

Scrambling, Tracy races to find the remote, finally laying eyes on it, halfway beneath the bed. A red ticker at the bottom of the screen reads *Breaking news report on missing Chicago girl.* Amanda Robles and her microphone are there too, on a porch in the middle of suburbia.

"We're outside the home of Michigan resident and retired treasure hunter Gene Fairfax, and his dog, Bucky." Sure enough, the camera pans to an elderly man in a rocking chair. Bucky rests at his feet. "Almost two weeks ago, Gene was searching Miners Beach with his metal detector when he came across an unusual scene."

In her head, Tracy starts counting backwards, retracing the girls' route. Miners Beach at Pictured Rocks National Lakeshore was the scheduled stop for day three of the road trip.

Gene turns to Amanda and nods sagely. "I saw that girl. The one who turned up missing."

"Willow Barrett, you mean?"

"That's the one. Looked just like her, and I saw the school bus, too. Someone did a real nice remodel on that old thing."

"What was Willow doing? Was she alone?" Tracy stands in front of the television, as close as she can get. She wants to reach through it and shake him. He's taking too long to spit it out. She holds the phone to her ear still, listening to the detective's shallow breathing.

"Her little dark-haired friend was with her. To tell the truth, Bucky spotted them first. He's got a thing for the ladies. I tried to mind my own business, but they were kicking up a ruckus."

"What do you mean?" It's obvious Amanda already knows the answer to her own question. She's practically salivating.

"Fighting. Like cats and dogs. No offense, Buck." The golden retriever doesn't lift his head, but his tail thumps against the wood planks. "Something about a backpack and a knife. It's a good thing I had my hearing aid in. That thing is my superpower."

"Did it get physical?"

"No, not that I could see, but they ran off pretty quick."

"They ran away?"

Gene nods again. "After Willow threw the bag down, the other gal—Amelia, is it?—stormed off. Willow seemed kind of sad after that. Then, I found a silver dollar. By the time I'd dug it up, she'd vanished. I watched Amelia for a bit. Do you know she walked back down the beach and picked up that backpack? I can't say what was in it, but she snatched it up quicker than a hiccup and put it in one of those beach totes."

"Wow, Gene. That's quite a story, especially now that we know Willow went missing several days later. What do you think happened to her?"

"Well, I'm just an old man. I'm no Sherlock Holmes. But, if I was, I'd want to have words with the girl who took that backpack."

When Detective Delgado huffs in frustration, Tracy startles. She'd forgotten about the phone call. "This is what happens when you take your problems to social media. It makes my job ten times harder. First, I have to deal with the fallout from Amelia's little impromptu speech to the press. Now, this crazy geezer comes out of the woodwork."

"You think he's crazy?"

"He hunts for treasure on a beach with a metal detector. At the very least, he's bored enough to make up stories."

Tracy can barely contain her indignation. It pushes against

her chest, a dam about to break. "Are you going to talk to him? To take his statement?"

"You mean his sales pitch. I think he just gave it." The detective pauses long enough for Tracy to glance back at the television screen, where a grinning Gene holds up his own book, *The Pirate of Lake Michigan: A Guide to Finding Your Own Booty*.

Detective Delgado snickers. "You were saying?"

Tracy stabs her finger at the phone, taking pleasure in the abrupt silence. She turns her attention back to the television just long enough to shut it off. It's gone to commercials, anyway. The detective's voice worms its way into her thoughts. She doubts herself, doubts her instincts, until she logs in to her Facebook account and reads the latest in a steady stream of comments on her post. Complete strangers are on her side, praying for her and her daughter. Complete strangers are looking for Willow. Complete strangers have branded Amelia a cold-blooded murderer.

INSTAGRAM

writingontheroad @melthebookworm and I are up early on #daysix for a sunrise hike at Saginaw River Campground. Send coffee stat! #theroadtrip #bestfriends #notamorningperson
1,002 likes 575 comments 63 shares

ilovepuppies Sunrise hikes are the best… nothing like seeing the world come alive! Enjoy it!

momofeight8 Heartbreaking that you're still missing. I'm praying for your poor mom. #whereiswillow

truthseeker007 Anybody local to Niagara Falls? Thinking of setting up a search. DM me. #whereiswillow

> **thetaylorshow** @truthseeker007 i'm in

truecrimelover44 Gene Fairfax is my hero. Did he just witness the prelude to a murder? BTW I take a deep dive into this case on my next podcast!!! #genethepirate #bffdidit #whereiswillow

tedbundyfanxoxo @truecrimelover44 Or he was the murderer #genedidit???

winnerwinner4 @tedbundyfanxoxo no do not badmouth gene dogs are a good judge of character #buckyknows

tanyagirl63 Anybody else obsessed with this story? I need a big whiteboard and a red marker #murdermap #whereiswillow

ibrakeforturtles @tanyagirl63 How much do you want to bet that @melthebookworm flees the country? Mommy's a doctor. #canadianfugitive

jaredm30 @tanyagirl63 ur not alone the struggle is real can't get any work done #downtherabbithole

darkdoctor79 @tanyagirl63 Have you seen the old WGN footage from 2003? Is Tracy Barrett's grandmother the #swindlinggrandma?

tanyagirl63 @darkdoctor79 What?!?!? On my way to check it out… thanks for the tip!

SEVENTEEN

BEFORE

Day Six on the Road: Saginaw River

Heavy with regret, Willow spends the night at the Saginaw River Campground tossing and turning. She can't shut her brain off. She desperately wants a take-back, but a text message can't be undone. With Amelia snoring above her, she slips her hand beneath her mattress as far as she can reach and powers on the burner phone he bought her. *For our eyes only*, he'd said. Of course he called her a kid. He had to cover his tracks. They can't go public yet. Not until she tells her mother and he quits his job at Kildeer Prep.

When the cheap flip phone comes to life, she's relieved to see ten missed calls, all in the span of the last five hours. He's just as panicked as her, maybe more so. *This is what you do to me*, he'd say. *You make me crazy*.

"You awake?"

"Uh..." Willow scrambles to turn off the phone and stuff it back in its hiding place. "I am now."

"Wanna do a sunrise hike?" Amelia hops down, as if she's been awake for hours. Maybe she has. That makes Willow nervous. "Put yesterday behind us, you know? Take some photos for the page."

It's an unspoken invitation. A silent demand. To never speak of Jackson and the accident that wasn't an accident again. "Alright. The guidebook says that there's a trailhead just north of our campsite. But we should probably hurry. Sunrise is just before six."

"You're the one still lying down." Amelia strips the comforter from the bed, leaving Willow cold and exposed. She tugs it back over her bare legs and glares at her friend. As hard as she tries, she can't unsee those pictures. She can't unread those words. Can't stop thinking about all of it, the whole disastrous trip. From the mysterious backpack on the beach to Jackson's crash landing. And now, Amelia sexting Sam, the literal love of her life. It's too much to handle.

"What?" Amelia asks. "You're staring at me."

"I'm just tired. I didn't sleep well last night."

"Well, suck it up, buttercup. We've got a new day ahead of us and a sunrise to see. You know, early bird, worm, et cetera, et cetera."

Willow nods, managing a half-smile. Amelia's right about one thing. It is a new day, which means it's one day closer to the end of this road trip. One day closer to her getaway at the cabin with Sam. But more than that, it's the start of their life together. The life where he resigns from Kildeer Prep—he's already written the email—and together, they tell her mother. How they fell in love slowly over their shared love of literature. How they're moving in together. How they found the cutest little brownstone in Logan Square. Her heart swells at the promise of it. Yes, a brand new day.

Ten minutes later, Willow follows Amelia down the stairs of the bus and out the door. She takes a deep breath of the dewy air to center herself. Then, she points her cellphone flashlight in the direction of the trailhead. "It's a twenty-minute walk to the lookout point. That'll put us there right on time, but we have to keep a steady pace."

"Perfect." Amelia charges ahead, with Willow playing catch-up. "We should take a few selfies at the top. We didn't post anything after we arrived yesterday."

That's because we killed someone. Willow bites the inside of her mouth hard to stop from blurting it out.

"It might look weird," Amelia adds.

"To who?" she bites back. The unspoken answer—*the police*—burns in her throat.

"You're not still upset, are you?"

"I thought we weren't talking about it."

Amelia stops and tosses a look over her shoulder. At this rate, they'll never make the sunrise. "But you're moping."

"*Moping?*" The word seems painfully inadequate. "Do you even care what happened to him? He's probably—"

"Of course I care. But it was an accident, Will, and one hundred percent his fault. He was chasing us down the road and driving recklessly. He might've been high on something. Who knows?"

Willow wants to tell her exactly how insane she sounds. Wants to ask her what kind of monster she's become and why. But all her replies and retorts and cheap shots vanish, chased away by the beam of a flashlight at the trailhead. A figure waits there, dressed in dark clothing. Big black boots. Thick, unkempt beard. Suddenly, Willow feels small and unsure of herself. Like a newborn fawn hiding in the grass.

"Morning." He's friendly, too friendly. She feels it in the clench of her gut, telling her to run. Instead, she freezes. "Have you gals seen a black rucksack around here?"

"A rucksack?" Amelia repeats. Willow detects a hint of fear in her voice, which only deepens her own unease. Amelia sent racy photos to their teacher unsolicited. Amelia stole money. Amelia killed a man. If she's afraid, there's no hope for Willow.

"Yeah, like a backpack. Military style."

"Did you lose it?"

The stranger takes a step forward and lowers his flashlight, leaving his face in near darkness. "You could say that. But lucky for me, it had one of those AirTags in it. It's been pinging around here since last night. I thought maybe you'd found it, since your skoolie is right up there."

"We didn't," Willow hears herself say. Because it's true. Three days and three hundred miles ago, she'd tossed the bag herself and watched it land amid the rocks and driftwood at Miners Beach. But she can tell the man doesn't believe her.

"Sorry, we have to go." She wills her sneakers to move, but her leaden legs won't budge. "We're trying to get to—"

"What was in it?" Amelia interrupts. "You know, in case we run across it. Was it something valuable? Are you offering a reward?"

His throaty laugh sounds menacing. "What are you girls playing at?"

"I just asked a question. You don't have to be a creeper about it."

Willow cuts her eyes at her friend. The gut punch of the truth leaves her breathless. Amelia took the backpack after she'd promised to leave it behind. That means the stack of cash is on the bus right now. No wonder he's been tracking them since Miners Beach.

"You know good and well what was in it, because it's in your goddamned school bus. You stole my property, and you *will* return it."

"Your property? That stupid backpack washed up on the beach. It certainly didn't have your name on it. Haven't you heard of finders keepers?"

With another broad step, he's way too close to them. He

raises the hem of his shirt to reveal the butt of a gun in his waistband. "We can do this the easy way or the hard way, and I promise you that you're not going to like the hard way."

When he reaches for his weapon and fires off a crisp warning shot into the air, Willow grabs Amelia by the arm and yanks her down the footpath. She moves as fast as she can, thankful that a sliver of orange light has breached the horizon to light the way. She doesn't dare turn around, but she senses him in pursuit at her back. Hears the thud of his boots, the ragged hitch of his breathing. She fully expects him to end her with a bullet.

The school bus beckons like an old friend. If only they can get there.

Another shot cracks the air like a whip, and then, another.

Willow watches, horrified, as he takes aim at the bus's front passenger tire. Lucky he's an awful shot, and the bullet ricochets off one of the stones that borders the firepit and grazes the bus's large metal rim. He grunts in frustration and fires off another errant round, just missing a bird perched on a rotting tree trunk. It only stokes his fire.

"We're in trouble, Mel." Willow curses under her breath, searching the trees for a place to hide.

But Amelia is gone.

"I just want what's mine." The stranger's long strides make quick work of the distance between them, and she's frozen stiff again anyway. She forces herself to look at him, to try to memorize his features. Her fear turns him into a blur of teeth and muscle. "I won't hurt you, but I need that money back. It's a life and death situation."

"I swear I didn't know she took the bag or the money. I told her to leave it behind."

"No biggie. Once it's back in my hands, we can forget about all this. We can be friends."

Willow swallows a lump. "The problem is that I'm not exactly sure where she put it. I only saw the knife."

"Doesn't hurt to look, does it?" He stands guard by the bus door, expectant. The gun hangs at his side. "Go on. I'll be right out here in case your friend tries something."

Still breathing hard, she lets herself inside and climbs the steps into the cabin. She'll check the secret compartment first. Worst case, she'll grab the knife. At least she'll be armed.

"Don't do anything stupid," he calls, practically reading her thoughts. "I'll give you ten seconds, then I'm coming in. Ten, nine..."

He's toying with her, batting her around like a frightened mouse. Her hands shaking, Willow removes the cushion and lifts the seat. Beneath the extra blanket, she finds the sun-bleached backpack with the stack of cash inside.

"Eight, seven, six..."

She roots around the bottom until she finds it. The small, circular AirTag, sealed tight inside a plastic baggie.

"I've got it!" she yells to him, as she slips the knife from the counter into her back pocket. Her heart thumps wildly in her chest. If it came to it, could she stab him? It's one thing to write about murder, but to do it? That's something else entirely. Besides, he would surely shoot her first.

"I'm waiting," he singsongs. "Five, four, three..."

Taking a deep breath, she walks toward the door, stopping just short of the steps. She can't see him, but she knows he's there waiting. He won't leave without the money. What will he do with her now that she's seen his face? "Promise you'll take it and go?"

"Cross my heart—"

A meaty thwack cuts him short. Stifling a scream, Willow inches forward, eyes wide. Amelia stands over the man, a large rock in her hands. He's not moving.

Amelia meets Willow's eyes before she speaks. "And hope to die."

EIGHTEEN

NOW

When the White Water Campground sign comes into view, Tracy inhales a sharp breath. Only days ago, Willow had texted her a photograph in front of that sign. This is the place she needs to be right now, she's certain of that.

Sam parks the rental car in the lot outside the main lodge. In the spot nearest the door, Tracy spots a dusty police cruiser. "That must be the Niagara County Sheriff," she says. "He promised he'd meet us here."

"Let's hope he's more helpful than Detective Delgado," Sam says.

"That wouldn't take much." Tracy blames Ray for that. Making friends was never his forte, even before he got booted from the force. "I just hope she hasn't poisoned Sheriff Gibbs against me."

As they walk toward the lodge, Tracy surveys the busy campground and finds herself drawn to two girls playing on the monkey bars. Their laughter reaches her and transports her back in time. Rewind ten years, and she could be looking at Willow and Amelia. Thick as thieves back then, despite their differences. But now, the fracture between them keeps widening. It would be a lie to say she hadn't seen it coming, encouraged it even. The reminiscing makes her sad, nonetheless.

Sam follows her past a carousel of tourist brochures and into the office, where a woman waves to them from behind the desk. With her bangles jingling around her wrist, she flashes a friendly smile that puts Tracy at ease. Her gold-plated name tag reads, *Bea*. "Welcome to White Water," she says. "Are you visiting the Falls?"

Grandma Ruth had called it the eighth wonder of the world, though it wasn't on any list. Tracy can still remember leaning against the viewing rail, with her grandmother at her side, both tasting the mist on their mouths. It was a magical place, the last place she and Grandma Ruth had visited together before the cops had carted her away and Tracy had to start over. Again.

Sam nudges her forward, back into the moment.

"No, we're not here on vacation," she says. "My daughter, Willow, is missing. She stayed here."

"You're Tracy Barrett? I can't believe I didn't recognize you." Bea looks starstruck. "I saw your interview on WGN. You're even prettier in person. And so brave. I can only imagine how you must be feeling. It's a wonder you're still standing."

Uncertain how to respond, Tracy mumbles a thank you. She's grateful that Sam seems distracted by the taxidermy wild turkey in the corner. He wanders to the window and peers out into the parking lot.

"Listen to me rambling on. Sheriff Gibbs told me you'd be stopping by. He's just down in the mess hall—that's what we call our café—grabbing an early lunch. Would you like me to show you the campsite your daughter rented with her friend?"

Tracy flinches with surprise. "You remember my daughter?"

"I remember them both. Pretty little things and sweet, too. They asked me to take their photo in front of the sign the day they arrived. But I must admit, it's mainly because of the knife that they stuck in my mind."

That's not what Tracy expected to hear, and it rattles her. She calls to Sam—"She remembers Willow!"—then fishes out her cellphone to show Bea the campfire photograph. The menacing blade glinting in the firelight.

"Could be. It's hard to make out." Bea tries her best though, holding the photo beneath a small desk lamp. Finally, she shrugs. "The black-haired one tried to sell it to me the day they arrived."

"Amelia, you mean?" Sam asks.

Bea nods at him gravely. "Your daughter didn't like that one bit."

"Oh." Sam's cheeks turn the color of her lipstick. The color spreads down his neck. "Willow isn't my daughter. She's my..."

"He taught Willow in high school," Tracy blurts out, eager for Bea to continue.

"Willow was very upset. She grabbed the knife and stormed off with it."

"Do you know what happened to it?" Tracy senses Bea's hesitation. "Please tell me. It could be the key to finding out what happened to her."

Bea wrings her hands, her bracelets softly clinking. "I didn't want to get the girls in trouble. I didn't even tell Sheriff Gibbs, and we went to high school together. You don't get to run a top-rated campground for thirty years by spilling the secrets of your guests."

"I understand. But I need to know. My daughter is missing."

Teary-eyed, she beckons Tracy around the desk and into the break room, shutting the door behind her. It's just the two of them now. But even so, Bea speaks in a whisper. "Willow threw it in the Niagara River. It runs behind the campground."

"You saw her?"

"She looked so upset that I sent my son after her. I was

worried that she might try to hurt herself. We get all kinds around here. Last summer, one fella got drunk and impaled a park ranger with a s'mores stick."

"Is your son here? Maybe I could speak with him."

"He's off leading a nature hike." Bea gestures over her shoulder to a wall display of employee photographs. She finds her voice again. "My pride and joy. Second from the right." As Tracy approaches the framed picture, she adds, "I believe you spoke to him already. His name is Allen Perlmutter. He drove your school bus back to Chicago."

"Your son is Allen? The task rabbit?" Sure enough, it's him. The scrawny young man who greeted her on her doorstep. "He lied to me. He told me that he couldn't remember seeing the girls, and he certainly never said that he worked here."

Bea drops her head, avoiding Tracy's eyes. "That's my fault. I didn't want him to get mixed up in anything, so I told him that the less he said, the better. To be frank, I didn't want him to go to Chicago at all. And in that behemoth of a bus, no less. But Amelia agreed to pay double his usual rate. Plus, she threw in a cash tip to cover his bus fare home. Things have been tight the last few years. He's working two jobs. We need the money."

"Does Detective Delgado know what he saw? Did he tell them everything?"

"Oh, hun, I assumed that fancy detective from Chicago would've told you. She had him at the station for three hours, interrogated him like a common criminal. The poor kid hadn't slept at all. It was almost as traumatic as the day his daddy died of a heart attack."

Bea has some nerve calling out Allen's trauma, but she ignores the urge to tell her just that, knowing it will get her nowhere closer to the truth. "Did Amelia tell you that Willow was missing?"

A dark cloud passes across Bea's face. "She said they'd had a fight, and that Willow ran off in the direction of the river again, just past the tree line down there. We looked for her all day, called the hospitals. I hate to say this, but..."

"Say it. Please."

"Well, for a day or two, I wondered if she fell in and drowned or... jumped. But the bodies always wash up eventually."

Tracy winces and shakes her head fast, trying to chase away the image of her daughter fished out of the water like an old boot.

"I'm so sorry. I shouldn't have said that. You must be worried out of your mind. Such a beautiful girl with a bright future." Bea gazes off, as sounds of conversation drift in from the lobby. When the service bell dings, she jumps. Wide-eyed, she reminds Tracy of Allen, the way he'd blinked at her from her doorstep. A deer caught in the headlights. Is it all an act? Is Bea covering for him?

"Duty calls, huh?" Tracy watches Bea with suspicion, as she moves toward the door. "Thanks for your help. Willow would be grateful."

Again, Bea's eyes go watery. "I tell ya, I can't wait to read that novel of hers. It's sure to be a bestseller."

Tracy plants herself in the seat of the playground swing and rocks back and forth, letting her feet drag through the sand. From here, she can smell the remnants of last night's campfire. She can count the steps to the campsite where Willow and Amelia had parked the school bus. She can feel her daughter's energy keeping her upright, spurring her on, even if they're no closer to finding her. Sheriff Gibbs had spent the afternoon with her and Sam, walking the campground and talking to employees. He assured them that his deputies had done a thorough search of the entire site and the surrounding areas. Had talked to every witness they could locate. Had even called in the K-9 unit, who tracked Willow to the edge of the forest.

"Ms. Barrett?" Tracy turns to look over her shoulder at the young woman who summoned her. She's not Willow. Of course she isn't. But she exudes the same energy, with her vibrant smile and bouncy curls. Tracy remembers her from the mess hall, where she offered them warm sugar cookies that reminded her of the ones Willow baked for her Chapter and Verse co-workers at Christmas. Everything reminds her of Willow.

"Britt, is it?"

The girl nods, pointing to the name tag clipped to her uniform. "I'm on break, and I saw the two of you sitting out here and..."

Sam stands and graciously offers her a seat on the swing next to Tracy. She takes it.

"There's something you should know about Bea's son, Allen. I didn't want to say anything in front of the sheriff. I'm sure he's harmless, and he can be really sweet. But he's super awkward around girls, and he gets the wrong idea. Like after I started working in the mess hall, I saved him a slice of apple pie one night. His mom told me it was his favorite. I swear, he followed me around like a puppy for the next two weeks. I had to flat-out lie to him and tell him that I have a boyfriend. Then, one night at the campfire, I caught him taking a sneaky photo of me. I didn't say anything, but it made me uncomfortable. It's happened to a couple of the other girls too."

Tracy and Sam exchange a worried look. "Earlier, you said that you remembered Willow and Amelia. Did you see them interacting with Allen?"

"Like I told Sheriff Gibbs, I saw them talking to him at the campfire. Then, Willow sort of pulled him away. He liked her. I know that much."

"How do you know?"

"With Allen, it's obvious. Then, the day after he came back

from Chicago, he offered to go out searching with the dogs. It seemed like he wanted to be the one to find her. Like the hero, you know?"

"The hero." That word makes her uneasy. Ray has a hero complex too, and look how that had turned out. With him tossed off the police force and branded a criminal. The line between hero and villain can be razor thin.

Ten minutes after Britt leaves them on the playground, Tracy stops her nervous swinging. There's nothing she can do about Allen. Not right now. She says to Sam, "I think I'll walk down to the river. Maybe Willow left something out there. Something the dogs didn't pick up on. Something the cops might have overlooked."

"But the sheriff said—" Sensing her disappointment, he quickly reverses course. "It's worth a shot though, right? Especially since Bea said she saw Willow run down that way before."

"We've covered every other corner of this campground. It makes sense to at least take a *look* at the river."

He gives her arm a comforting squeeze. "I'll come with you. The Niagara River is ferocious, especially in the spring and early summer. It can sweep you off your feet if you're not careful."

She tosses him a quizzical look. "Have you been here before?"

"Oh, yeah. I thought I mentioned that my granddad owned a cabin near Lake Moodie. It's on the Canadian side about thirty minutes from here. As a kid, I came up here every summer. This is where I fell in love with the outdoors. Nothing beats camping as a stress reliever. I still do it as often as I can."

"Wow. That must've been amazing. I divided my summers between thrift stores and swap meets, and the occasional trip to the junk yard or Goodwill. That was the real highlight."

He laughs without a hint of judgment. "Now that sounds like an adventure."

Together, they walk the hundred yards toward the tree line, where the dappled light promises relief from the summer sun. Tracy scans the grass, searching for God knows what. For something to reassure her that she's done the right things. That Willow will come back to her soon and unscathed.

"Do you hear the river?" Sam points into the woods, awestruck. "It's exuberant."

"It looks it, too." As the sounds grow louder, the water comes into view. Fast-moving as a snake and just as unpredictable, shifting and roiling. "No wonder Willow came here. It's so alive."

Sam joins her at the edge. "You don't think she..."

Tracy can hardly believe what he's suggesting. She thought he knew her daughter better than that. "She would never."

"Yeah. Of course. I'm sorry I said it." But he fixes his eyes on the river and keeps talking. "It's just that the girls were out of sorts, and we haven't heard from her. There haven't been any sightings or ransom demands. The police haven't found her body. It's like she just disappeared from the face of the earth."

Her body. Tracy feels sick, overwhelmed by it all. She's afraid to think about what will happen next. Without a word, she takes off in the direction of the campground, stumbling over the uneven ground like a spinning top out of control.

When she reaches the forest's edge, she stops and listens to her own ragged breathing. She gazes back toward the campsite, imagining it's the skoolie parked there instead of a beat-up Winnebago.

"Hey, are you alright?" Sam finally catches up to her, breathing hard himself. He stands there, arms at his sides, and shrugs. "Ignore everything I said. I'm a total jackass."

"You're not wrong." Tracy takes a step toward him and then another. Suddenly, she wants to kiss him. To forget everything else in her life but this moment. This man. She wants to be rescued from herself.

Then, her foot knocks against something hard. She bends down to find a nondescript cellphone buried in the tall grass. The old flip style no one uses anymore. "It's a phone," she says, declaring the obvious.

Sam frowns at it. "It's not Willow's, though. That thing looks ancient. Who knows how long it's been here?"

Tracy attempts to power it on, but it's dead, and she briefly considers leaving it there. It terrifies her, the thought of the unknown. But what would Sam think of her if she walked away from it? "I should turn it over to the sheriff, don't you think? It could be important."

After pondering for a moment, Sam nods. "You're right. Too bad it's broken."

"I'm sure it's only a dead battery. The cops will figure it out. Just like they do in *The Road Trip*." Tracy remembers that particular late-night conversation with Willow, months ago, talking through the plot—Jenna's cellphone, a pivotal clue in solving Lacey's murder—while a late February snow dusted the front yard. The promise of their fireside chats shimmers like a golden mirage, just out of her reach.

Tracy grips the phone tight in her hand, as they make their way back across the field. With the campground in their sights, she pulls up short at the sight of a commotion near the picnic tables. Flanked by three deputies, Sheriff Gibbs stands at the center trying to calm a small, frenetic crowd.

"What's going on?" she asks.

There, in the dirt, in the middle of the melee, lies Allen, wriggling like a worm. A fourth deputy drags him to his feet. His cuffed hands, useless behind his back.

Sheriff Gibbs approaches her. "He had Willow's cell—"

Stuffing the flip phone into her pocket, Tracy takes off at a full sprint, charging toward him. She grabs hold of the collar of his White Water Campground polo and shakes him hard. It scares her a little, how unhinged she must look. But what mother wouldn't be?

"You lied to me! What did you do to my daughter? Why did you have her phone?"

Allen's lips tremble, but nothing comes out, so she ups the ante. Whatever it takes.

"I know you saw her the day she disappeared. Were you watching her? Did you follow her into the woods?"

After Sheriff Gibbs pulls her off him, Allen manages to squeak out, "I didn't hurt her." To Tracy, it doesn't sound convincing at all.

From the safety of the rental car, Tracy and Sam watch Allen get escorted across the parking lot and shoved into an awaiting police cruiser. Now that she's come back to her senses, she removes the flip phone from her pocket and places it on her lap.

"I forgot about that old thing," Sam says. "Why don't we look through it together first? No need to bother the sheriff with it, if it's nothing."

While Tracy turns it in her palm like a stone, the police car coasts past the White Water Campground sign and disappears around the bend. She thinks of the money hidden on the bus, of Amelia's strange silence. Of all the unknowns that might turn up on that phone and how it might impact her daughter. She thought being the cool mom gave her an advantage but really, she's no better off than the next sucker. As Sheriff Gibbs approaches the passenger window, she slips the phone into the console.

"You alright?" he asks her.

Though her pulse still hasn't slowed, she nods. "I lost my cool."

"To be expected."

"Has he said anything?"

"Not any more than what you got out of him. His mother is coming down to the station too. She'll talk some sense into him. I've gotta say, he's a peculiar kid, but—"

"So, he had Willow's cellphone," Sam interrupts. "Has he been charged with a crime?" It's the question that's been burning in Tracy's brain since she spotted Allen wriggling in the dirt.

"Not yet. He's been detained for questioning. We didn't plan to cuff him, but he put up a fight when we searched his fanny pack. He wouldn't let us touch it."

"How did you find the phone in the first place?" Tracy asks.

"Cellphone data. According to Chicago PD, Willow's phone made the trip to Chicago and back. That could only point to one suspect. We found it powered down under Allen's mattress."

Tracy shudders at the thought of him sitting, rain-soaked, on her sofa, with her daughter's cellphone alive in his pocket. "And in his pack?"

Sheriff Gibbs shrugs. "His dad's Eagle Scout medallion. Apparently, it brings him good luck."

INSTAGRAM

writingontheroad @melthebookworm tweaked her ankle in the first half mile of our sunrise hike. She's as good as new, but we had to enjoy the view from our firepit. There's nothing like the peace of the Saginaw River. #stilldaysix #stillnotamorningperson #theroadtrip #bestfriends #changeofplans #niagaraorbust
5,899 likes 887 comments 90 shares

ilovepuppies Ouch! Rest, ice, compression, elevation. That's what I learned in my Girl Scout days.

truthseeker007 It's a good five hours from Saginaw River Campground to Niagara Falls. Wonder why the #changeofplans?? Maybe the beginning of the end? #bffdidit #whereiswillow

truecrimelover44 OMG!!! Freaking out here! Did anybody else see the news out of Niagara? Who is Allen Perlmutter? #bffdidit #whereiswillow

tedbundyfanxoxo @truecrimelover44 His Facebook account

is active. He works for the campground where @writin-gontheroad was last seen. #helookslikeaserialkiller

tanyagirl63 @truecrimelover44 His LinkedIn says he's a task rabbit. Didn't a task rabbit bring the bus back to Chicago? My head is exploding. What if @melthebookworm didn't do it? #whereiswillow

ibrakeforturtles @tanyagirl63 Not ready to give her a pass. Why isn't she talking? Why is she hiding out? Maybe they did it together. #bffdidit #whereiswillow #whereisamelia

stephenkingfan3 Anybody else dying to read this novel? #truthisstrangerthanfiction

truecrimelover44 @stephenkingfan3 YAAAAAAASSSS! #whereiswillow

tedbundyfanxoxo @stephenkingfan3 Instant bestseller. Guaranteed. #whereiswillow

happyfeet @stephenkingfan3 is it wrong to say hell yes but also im a little scared

NINETEEN

BEFORE

Day Six on the Road: Saginaw River

From the rocky shoreline, Willow stares out at the Saginaw River. The glassy, smooth surface gives nothing away. But beneath it lies a rock. The blood that once stained it has already dissolved in thin threads, carried downstream toward the bay. A man lies there, too. Amelia rolled him onto their spare blanket, dragged him the twenty yards to the riverbank, then pushed him in, watching as the current took him. She tossed the gun in too. The river had erased it all, and the rest Amelia incinerated in the firepit, including her blood-spattered hoodie. It never happened. Except, it did.

"C'mon." Amelia prods her, more insistent than the last time. She used to listen to her friend. She used to consider her the voice of reason. "We need to get out of here. Now. Someone could've heard those gunshots."

"I already told you I'm not leaving." Willow glances down at her cellphone, willing herself to do the impossible. To dial the damn numbers. 9-1-1. But her fingers feel as disconnected as the rest of her. They don't listen to her at all. "I'm calling the police. You can do whatever you want."

"What am I supposed to do?" Amelia steps in front of her. There's desperation in her eyes. A current of fear hums through Willow, pricking the hairs on the back of her neck.

"I don't care. Take the skoolie if you want."

"You know I can't drive a stick shift."

"Then call an Uber or a taxi. It doesn't matter to me. But I'm not getting back on that bus with you. We're done."

A laugh clunks out of Amelia's throat, one-note and slightly hysterical. "Wow. I save your life—not once, but twice—and *this* is how you thank me. Not to mention everything else I've done for you."

"Oh, yeah. Like what? Did you off someone else? The kid who used to call me *Willow Tree*? That Starbucks barista who was rude to me?" Willow can't believe her own words. She can't believe the cold expression on Amelia's face. The way she'd rolled the unresponsive stranger into the river with a merciless grunt.

"Trust me, you don't want to know what else. You couldn't handle it." Vaguely reptilian, Amelia's green eyes dart to Willow's cell. She fights the urge to flee from her, to run and never look back. But where would she go, now, after what she's done? She can't claim innocence anymore.

"Whatever it is, I didn't ask for it. I never asked for any of this. I want to go home. I don't know you anymore." Without thinking, she finds herself echoing Sam's text message. "You need help, Melly. I saw the photos you sent to Mr. Spellman."

It's a small comfort that she can still shock her friend into momentary silence. Amelia gapes at her, then glowers. "You went through my phone?"

"I had no choice. I was going out of my mind about Jackson, and I wasn't going to use my phone for a Google search."

"What do you think happened to him?" Amelia wields each

word like a weapon, cutting her off at the knees. Willow had glimpsed this side of her before—calculating and exacting; practical but never cruel. It terrifies her that she's overlooked it somehow. This essential part of her friend. "He died, Willow. He hit a tree trunk, and his bike went up in a plume of smoke. Nobody survives that kind of thing. Why would you search for it at all?"

"Because I'm not a psychopath."

"Are you saying that I am?"

Willow can't look at her. She watches the soothing motion of the river instead. "Two men are dead because of you."

"Because of *me*? Are you saying you did nothing wrong? Who fled the scene of an accident? Who threw the rock in the river?"

Fifteen minutes ago, with the firepit still smoking, Amelia had dropped the rock onto the grass and collapsed next to it, pointing at it with a shaky finger. Willow had tried her hardest not to look, but the blood stain wouldn't be denied. Standing on the shoreline, she'd felt like Lady Macbeth, unable to see anything else but that damned spot. She'd reared back and slung the thing as far as she could manage. Now, she can only wonder if Amelia set her up. "You told me you couldn't lift it again. That it was too heavy. That your arms were shaking too much."

"I didn't want to hurt the guy," Amelia says, skirting the issue. "He was coming after you. He had a gun. I acted in self-defense. No one can deny that."

Willow's strength drains from her. Instead of running, she turns her back to the river and slogs up the bank toward their campsite. Amelia chases after her.

"Look, if you call the cops, it's all over, and you know it. Everything we've dreamed about. Everything *you've* dreamed about. Northwestern. A big-time career as an author. The stupid second book that you think I don't know about. Our entire lives. All of it. Down the drain."

Willow blinks at her. "You know about the second book?"

"You're not the only one who can snoop around. I saw the file on your laptop."

She can see that Amelia's hurt. She flings the door to the bus open. The backpack sits on the bottom step, where she'd dropped it in surprise. She casts it out and watches Amelia scurry to retrieve it. "Just tell me why. Why did you steal Jackson's money? Why did you take the backpack when I told you not to? And the tips from Sal's? You took those too, didn't you?"

Her face reveals the answer. "I don't know why. It was just an impulse."

"Bullshit." Willow dials the first digit. Then, the second. She holds the screen up to Amelia and waits.

"Go ahead," Amelia taunts. "But I won't be the only one who takes the fall." She doesn't have to say it. Willow already knows what's at stake. She drops her hand to her side. Still, she can't imagine climbing those steps into the bus. Driving away from here like nothing happened. Sleeping below a killer.

"I'm calling my mom, then. I'll take an Uber to the airport in Detroit and fly home. She can deal with getting the bus back since you can't drive it."

Before Willow dials, Amelia grabs for the phone. Clawlike, she seizes Willow's wrist instead, pinning her into place. "Wait. What about our Insta page? We can't stop the trip now. Our followers are expecting us to wind up at Niagara Falls, right?"

"I don't care." Willow wrenches her hand free, alarmed at the red marks on her skin. "I don't trust you."

"Think about it, Will. Think about how it's going to look. Innocent people don't run away."

Through the radio static swirling in her head—panic and dread and desperation—Willow can hardly think at all. But Amelia has a point. If the cops catch wind of any of this and start asking questions, she'll be the one who turned tail.

Evidence of a guilty conscience. She doesn't trust Amelia to have her back.

After one more moment of agonizing indecision, she bites out, "Alright, but I'm driving straight through to Niagara Falls. No more stops. We'll finish the revisions there. Then, I'm done with this road trip... and with you. I'm bringing this bus back alone."

"Fine." Amelia unzips the backpack, tossing the tracker Willow discovered onto the dirt. She stomps it like a spider, then carts it to the nearest trashcan and drops it in.

Willow turns the key in the ignition. Once she starts her new life with Sam, none of this will matter, and she can't very well do that from a prison cell. A willing accomplice, the bus revs to a start, ready to take them far, far from here.

TWENTY

NOW

Tracy wipes ketchup from the corner of her mouth and inhales the last bite of her cheeseburger. She deposits the wrapper inside the empty paper bag and balls it up, tossing it into the motel room trashcan.

"Feeling a little better?" Sam asks her. He's hardly touched his own meal.

"Marginally." Refreshing the newsfeed on her cellphone, she groans. "There's another one."

"Mother of Missing Girl Attacks Campground Employee Suspect, Demands Answers." Sam reads the headline aloud, then scrolls down to the cesspool below. The comment section. "At least everyone's on your side."

"Everyone?"

"Well, minus a few nutjobs and crazies."

"I don't know what got into me. I'm an accountant, for God's sake. I should be level-headed."

"Nobody's level-headed when it comes to their kids. A student's mother once threatened to put a hex on me if I didn't raise her grade one full letter."

"Was she serious?"

"Dead serious. She stole one of my ink pens to use for the spell."

Tracy lets herself laugh along with him, enjoying a brief moment of normalcy before the gravity of the day knocks her down again. "I can't believe Allen kept Willow's cellphone. Do you think he could've hurt her?"

"Knowing Willow, she would've knocked him into next week. She's a capable young woman. She can hold her own."

"But what if he heard them arguing and followed her into the forest? He could've ambushed her. Or scared her so badly that she fell into the river."

"If any of that happened, I'm sure the cops will get it out of him. We just have to be patient. They'll find the evidence, just like they found the cellphone."

"Speaking of cellphones..." Her eyes drift to the flip phone on the table, still dead as a rock. After dinner, Sam had promised her they'd find a dollar store that sold the right sort of charger. They'd look at it together and decide what to do. "I'm almost scared to look. What if it belongs to Allen? What if...?"

When Sam doesn't immediately answer, she cringes. "Do you think I overreacted?" Tracy knows she overreacted. She'd left a scratch on Allen's face. A long, bright river of red across his cheek that popped on camera.

"I think it's understandable, even if you did." When he puts his hand on hers, she pulls away, conscious of her greasy fingers. Of her outburst that will live forever on the Internet. Of her growing attraction to her daughter's mentor.

Sam turns his attention back to his phone screen. After scrolling for a bit, he glances up at her nervously.

"What now?" she asks.

"Was your grandmother really a swindler?" He shows her the post she's already seen with the link to the old news footage. She hoped no one would notice, but it's grown to 10,000 likes. "She forged celebrity signatures?"

"It's a long story. I don't really talk about it. Most people don't understand."

Sam raises his eyebrows, then walks to the restocked minibar, where he plucks two small bottles of vodka to share. "I'm a good listener, and if you get me drunk enough, I probably won't even remember."

She laughs and takes a generous swig. "It's not as glamorous as it sounds. She did it for my college fund. I was her responsibility after my parents died, but she never made me feel like a burden. I was her best friend, her scavenging buddy. Anyway, the whole scheme ended her up in prison, where she died. You know, she would've gotten away with it if she hadn't gotten too big for her own britches by trying to pass off that art at Christie's."

"Christie's, huh? That's bold. Your grandma sounds like a force to be reckoned with."

Tracy remembers arriving on the doorstep of the farmhouse at seven years old, deposited there by a taxi driver who complained that the gravel road would scratch up his finish. Grandma Ruth flung open the door and wrapped her in the kind of hug that made her believe her life wasn't over. "For better or worse, she's the reason I am who I am. Willow never met her, but she certainly has her moxie."

Sam settles back in the chair, propping his feet up. "Tell me about her."

An hour and two bottles later, Tracy wraps up her favorite Grandma Ruth story. The afternoon they scavenged an antique pool table from an estate sale and found a kitten in the corner pocket. "That was a good day," she says, smiling. "We named him Cuey."

"Cuey." Sam giggles. "That's cute. Cutey Cuey."

"Say that five times fast."

Of course, he tries, which only leads to more giggling. Until Tracy flicks on the television and sees her daughter's face leading the local six o'clock news. Allen appears in handcuffs, the cut on his face as nasty as she imagined it would be.

Sam sobers, too. "Have you heard from Dr. Ford or Detective Delgado?"

"Radio silence. I still can't believe the things Amelia told that reporter about Willow. I realized the girls had grown apart this year, but I never imagined she'd lie like that. As far as we know, she and Allen could both be in on it. When we get back, you'll talk to the detective about the texts, right?"

"I promised you I would." Sam sighs. His shoulders droop. He pushes a soggy French fry across his fast-food wrapper, his lip curling in disgust at it.

"Do you not want to? I know it's asking a lot—"

"No, it's not that. I just keep thinking of all the promises I made to Willow. About her writing, her career. Northwestern. I promised I'd always be there to support her, and I feel like I let her down. Like I didn't show up when she needed me most. I don't want to let you down, too."

"You won't. Already, you haven't, in every way that counts. You're here in this dumpy hotel with me."

Without thinking, she lays her palm on his stubbled cheek. She leans in, wanting to forget about Amelia Ford. About the dead burner phone on the table. And if she's being honest, even about her daughter, who's vanished without a trace.

A knock at the door sends Tracy scrambling. Guilt smacks her across the face, sobering her up quick, as she drops her hand and steps away from Sam. She's no stranger to guilt. As a single mom, she knows it like an old friend. She never wanted to end up like Grandma Ruth, selling antiques to pay for Christmas presents and buying school clothes at the Goodwill. That's why she'd worked twice as hard to earn every end-of-year bonus for Willow's college fund. Why she'd left Hirsch and Peterson and struck out on her own. Why she'd sworn off dating until Willow had insisted she get a life.

Now, when it counted the most, she'd let herself get drunk and distracted by a silly crush, when she should have been screaming Willow's name from the rooftops.

The knock comes again. "It's Sheriff Gibbs. Anybody home?"

"Coming," she calls.

She unfastens the deadbolt and opens the door. "Is everything okay?" she asks, with a hitch in her voice. Surely, he'll read between the lines and understand what she's not saying. He's a lawman, for Christ's sake.

"No news on Willow, if that's what you're asking. We've still got Allen down at the station, and we're searching his cabin. So far, he's sticking to his story. He only kept Willow's phone to look at her photos. He thought he could find her somehow. When he realized how much attention the case was getting, he panicked and shut it down. I've already been in touch with Detective Delgado. Chicago PD has a press conference planned for the morning." The sheriff lets his words settle. "That's not why I'm here."

"What is it?" Sam appears at her side, sounding worried. She hopes the sheriff can't smell the vodka on them.

"We got a call from Lakeview Hospital, just outside of Indian River, Michigan. Apparently, a gentleman there saw your story on the news today. He's asking to speak to you."

"Michigan?" It's the last place Tracy expected. The girls had passed through there just over a week ago. "Does he know where Willow is? What's he saying?"

"Well, he's not exactly talking." The sheriff removes a folded sheet of paper from his shirt pocket. "I got a fax from Indian River PD about thirty minutes ago. You're welcome to take a look."

Tracy takes it from him and works it open. She can barely

read the scribbled writing. The misshapen letters spell out, THATS HER and GREEN BUS DRIVER.

"Apparently, he wrote that down during the twelve o'clock news segment about Willow and gave it to the nurse. The medical staff reached out to the local cops, and here I am. My buddy's ex-wife is a detective down there."

"He wrote it down?" Tracy hates playing catch-up. "What aren't you telling me?"

Sheriff Gibbs sighs. A part of her wishes she could shut the door in his face and hide out here forever.

"Up until yesterday, he was in a medically induced coma. They think Willow tried to kill him."

INSTAGRAM

writingontheroad We have arrived at White Water Campground. Took the obligatory photo in front of the adorable sign. Now, bring on the falls. #howisitstilldaysix #theroadtrip #bestfriends #niagarafalls #getmeabarrel #finaldestination
10,876 likes 3,501 comments 254 shares

ilovepuppies My hubby and I honeymooned in Niagara back in the day. It's the eighth wonder of the world. You girls are so lucky to get to do this together!

> **truecrimelover44** @ilovepuppies This comment did not age well... lol
>
> **ilovepuppies** @truecrimelover44 You don't know these sweet girls like I do. Keep your opinions to yourself.

truthseeker007 Another cryptic post. #finaldestination... sheesh! #bffdidit #whereiswillow

truecrimelover44 Allen Perlmutter is giving me Gary Ridgway vibes. #whereiswillow #newsuspect

> **tedbundyfanxoxo** @truecrimelover44 Did you see Willow's mom take him down? Is she an accountant or a WWE wrestler? #tracykicksass #dontmesswithmoms

> **niagaracutie** @truecrimelover44 i used to work at #white-water i swear that guy has bodies in his basement

> **joeydon4** @niagaracutie you sound like a woman scorned #donthateonperlmutter

> **sammyjo66** @niagaracutie I think he's kind of sexy #nerdyguysdoitbetter

stephenkingfan3 Still waiting for the release of #theroadtrip! Give the people what they want!

> **truecrimelover44** @stephenkingfan3 AMEN BROTHER

TWENTY-ONE

BEFORE

Day Six on the Road: Niagara Falls, White Water Campground

"Let's get a quick photo for Writing on the Road." Amelia points to the cheesy sign at the entrance to the White Water Campground and tugs Willow by the arm.

As Willow lets herself be pulled down the dirt path, she suppresses her rage. Her horror. Her desire to be anywhere but here. Well, not just anywhere. She needs Sam's arms around her, his body pressed against her own. For a moment, she lets herself go back there. To spring break. To his cabin. To the first time they made love. She shoves a hand in her pocket and touches the key. She still can't believe her mom had bought the whopper of a lie that she'd been in Europe for the break. Amelia, too. *Someday, we will go to Paris,* he'd told her. *There are so many places I want to take you.* And he'd been right. Pretending to be overseas meant that her mother wouldn't demand a phone call or a text every five minutes and they'd be free to do whatever they wanted. Which it turned out wasn't much of anything at all. They'd hardly left the four-poster bed.

A few more days, and she'd be right back there, in what he called their own little slice of heaven.

"Can you at least try to smile?" Amelia shows Willow the dismal selfie she'd just snapped. "It looks like I kidnapped you. Like I'm holding you hostage."

While Willow tries to force her face into a semblance of normalcy, a woman approaches. She wears a bejeweled campground T-shirt, hot pink lipstick, and too many bracelets that jangle when she walks. Instantly, Willow likes her. "Would you gals like me to take your picture?"

"Could you? That would be amazing." Amelia smiles brightly, then gushes, "You are so kind, Bea."

The woman beams, glancing at her nametag.

"I'm totally obsessed with your bracelets and sequins. My mom could never pull off that look."

Willow stares at her, trying to figure out what's real. Who's real. This saccharine sweet version of her friend. Or the heartless bitch who left two bodies in her wake.

"Do you want to be in the picture as well, dear?"

"Oh, sorry. Yeah. I was just daydreaming."

"Easy to do in a place like this. If you'd like, my son can give you a tour of the property. He knows all the hidden spots away from the tourists. He's up at the lodge right now."

Willow joins Amelia by the sign and the girls link arms. "That would be great. We've got this Insta page called Writing on the Road, and we need—"

"Only if it doesn't take too long. We have a deadline for our revisions, remember?" Willow cuts her eyes at Amelia, wishing she could say how she really feels. Let down and hurt and mad as hell. Ten minutes into the five-hour drive, Amelia had fallen asleep, leaving Willow to mull her unanswered questions. If only she can get through these damn edits. Finish the book and drive home, sans Amelia. Then, her new life awaits.

"You'll have to excuse my friend." Amelia sidles up to Bea

like she's known her forever. Not five minutes. "She hasn't been sleeping well. But I'd love to take the tour while she naps. What time should I be there?"

Minutes later, with Bea out of earshot, Willow hisses, "Are you planning to kill him too?"

Slinging her bag over her shoulder, Amelia stomps off in the direction of the lodge and leaves her alone with her own hateful words echoing in her ears.

Screw Amelia. Willow spends the next hour alone, writing the revised ending they'd discussed, where an enraged Jenna sneaks into the tent she shares with Lacey and stabs her as payback for agreeing to host a nationally syndicated podcast behind her back. Willow hasn't written in days. Hasn't had the stomach for it. But now, the words seem to flow from outside herself, and her fingers glide effortlessly across her laptop keyboard. She writes all the ugliness as if she's lived it. The sheer strength it takes to plunge a knife through flesh, through bone. The metallic smell of it. The blade slick with blood. The weight of a lifeless body. The unmitigated betrayal.

When she's done, she collapses onto the pullout sofa, exhausted and relieved that she's cut the final cord binding her to this trip from hell. She doesn't bother texting Amelia. Instead, she sends off the draft to her mother with a note: *All done! We eagerly await your feedback.* Then, she holes up in her bunk with the burner phone.

Her finger hovers over the call button. It's a bit of a risk with Amelia so close by, but she's stopped caring entirely. She's in a total freefall and can't quite work out if it's terrifying or exhilarating. Besides, she can keep an eye out for her through the small porthole window her mother had built in at her request.

The phone rings only once, and he's there, breathing hard

on the other end. Like he's been running all night to find her. "Why didn't you call me?"

"I couldn't get away." It all flashes back at once—the stranger, the rock, the roiling river. The splash of the water before it swallowed him whole. "We've been really busy working on the book."

"Willow, please. I told you I don't like childish games. Are you really going to pretend you didn't send me that drama queen text?"

"Well, you called me a kid, didn't you?"

"Only to get her off my back. And how did you find out? You didn't say anything, did you? I shouldn't have to remind you what's at stake here." He takes that tone she despises. The fatherly scolding. She deliberately ignores his worry. Let him suffer. Let him think the whole damn world knows.

"Your text made it sound like more than that." Knowing that she has this power over him makes her suddenly brave. "Have you ever... done anything with her?"

But not too brave. She can't say what she really means.

"What? Of course not. How could you ask me that?" She doesn't answer. Amelia's blood-red mouth is all she can think of. Her text, *I've missed your lips.* "I told you that you are the only—"

"I know, I know. The only student you've ever done it with."

"*Done it?* How old are you, *twelve*? That is not what I said. You're the only *former* student I've ever *loved.* The only one I've ever slept with. I'm in *love* with you, goofball."

She admires his effort. She lets herself be convinced. It's best to ignore her doubts. What do they get her? "I love you, too. I just wish we could be together. Like really together. In public. For everyone to see. Amelia included."

"We will be. Soon. I told you that I have to deal with a few things first."

"You already have your letter of resignation prepared. What else is there to deal with?"

"Don't you want to get this book published first? Get your big-time career started. We can always wait a little longer. I like having you all to myself."

"There's always something to wait for. Some reason why. It's getting exhausting."

He sighs, and it irks her. Because he sounds like her mother, years ago, when Willow still threw tantrums at the dollar store. She always wanted the one toy her mother couldn't afford. "C'mon, it's only been a few months, and I'm risking a lot for you," he says. "You have to be patient."

Willow grits her teeth. She wants to tell him what she's been through, but how can she? He'll never look at her the same. "I can't wait forever. Imagine how many hot guys I'll meet at Northwestern. Guys my own age. Maybe you're right. Maybe we shouldn't tell anyone. In fact, maybe it's stupid for me to go off to college with strings attached."

"What exactly are you trying to say?"

"I don't know." She wants him to fight for her. To tell her he can't live without her and he wants the world to know it. No more waiting, no more excuses.

"If you don't want this anymore, just say it. Be an adult, Willow. Have an adult conversation. None of this hard-to-get bullshit. You're better than that."

Just then, Willow spots a flash of movement through the porthole. Amelia stands by the campfire circle, extending her arm toward Bea. In her hand, she holds the stranger's knife.

"Are you still there?" Sam asks.

"Guess what, Sam? You don't know me as well as you think, because I'm *not* better than that." She hangs up abruptly and scoots out from the bed, hurrying down the aisle and outside. Her heart pounds against her ribcage, asking the question. The only question that seems to matter anymore. What has Amelia done now?

"Melly, what are you doing?" She wants to rip the knife from Amelia and hurl it into the trees, but then she notices Bea's eyes widen and tries to keep her cool.

"Nothing. I was just telling Bea that we found this knife. Did you know the Marines use this brand. Cool, huh?"

Willow looks at her flatly. Inside, her blood boils.

"Anyway, Bea's son collects knives, and he thinks it could be worth something. Bea was asking how much we want for it."

"It's not for sale. You know that."

Sensing the tension between them, Bea raises her hands and takes a step back. "Oh, I didn't realize. I do understand, though. It'll make a nice camping knife for the two of you, and if you ever need to scare anybody off, that thing will do the trick. A knife like that is nothing to mess with."

"You're right about that," Amelia says. "But we'd really like to get rid of it. Your son can have it for free if he wants it."

Now, she's crossed the line. Her words are like a poke to the eye. Willow wants to clamp a hand over her mouth. Instead, she snatches the knife from Amelia's grasp and tromps into the field toward the tree line, picking up the pace when she hears Amelia behind her.

"Hey, where are you going with that?"

She's done explaining herself, so she runs faster. Deep into the forest, where the light doesn't reach. Small twigs snap beneath her feet, but the roar of the river swallows the sound. Out of breath, she stops at the edge.

She thinks of throwing the knife. It only reminds her of what she's already done. The unthinkable.

She thinks of wading in, wonders how far the water would take her. About the long plunging drop at the end. It doesn't seem so bad.

"Are you okay?" The voice startles her, and she's not sure

how to answer. She imagines how she must look, standing here, breathless, with a knife in her hand.

"I've been better."

The boy nods at her. The rest of him doesn't move. Two skinny legs stay anchored to the earth like saplings. Maybe he thinks she's skittish. That she might bolt into the water and disappear downstream. That she might be a mermaid. "My mom sent me out here after you. She said you were upset."

"I am. I was. I'll be okay."

"You're not gonna hurt me, are you?" His eyes move to the knife, and she can't help but laugh. She throws her head back and lets herself go, laughing, laughing, laughing. Until she starts to cry.

TWENTY-TWO

NOW

Tracy can't believe this is what it's come to. This is her life now. A quick nap and a cold shower to sober up. A long drive in a rental car to a trauma center in the wee hours of the morning in the middle of nowhere Michigan. With Sam at the wheel, she monitors social media, taking notes on the tips that sound halfway sane, ignoring the snark, and responding to as many well-wishers as she can. Though she ducks a call from Ray, who surely only wants to lecture her about her irresponsible campground antics, she reaches out to Candice at least once every hour. She listens to the single ring on repeat and the authoritative greeting that follows. She even leaves a pathetic voicemail.

"You should try calling the hospital," Sam says. "Maybe they have another way to reach her."

Tracy pulls up the number for the Cardiology Department at Mercy General. After a series of prompts, a beleaguered woman answers the phone. "This is the operator. How can I direct your call?"

"Um, I'm trying to reach Dr. Candice Ford. It's an emergency."

The woman huffs. "Don't you reporters ever sleep?"

"I'm not a reporter, I swear. It's Tracy Barrett, Willow's mother."

"The missing girl?"

Sadly, Tracy can only say, "Yes. That's me. Could you just patch me through to her voicemail or page her or something? It's important. She's not answering her cell."

"I wish I could help you. I really do."

"Then, why don't you? I'm not asking for the impossible."

"Actually, you are. I shouldn't tell you this, but Dr. Ford doesn't work at Mercy General anymore."

"Since when?" Tracy scrambles to catch up. Her brain fog doesn't help. But when the clouds begin to part, she knows for certain that Candice told the detective she'd saved a man just days ago, after he'd flatlined twice on the operating table. Had she quit since then? "That doesn't make sense. Are you sure we're talking about Candice Ford?"

"I really can't say any more. It's against hospital policy to disclose information regarding an employee's termination. Have a good day, ma'am, and I hope your daughter is found safely."

"Termination?"

With a click, the call is severed. She's gone.

"What was that about?" Sam asks.

"Candice quit or got fired. I don't know what to think. But she doesn't work at the hospital anymore." Tracy confirms it on the hospital webpage, where she finds that Candice's bio and headshot have been removed. "Did Amelia mention it to you?"

Sam looks just as confused. "Not a word. Do you think there might be some truth to the online rumors?"

"Which ones?" Over the last few days, the online rumors had multiplied like the worst virus. Each one more ridiculous than the last. But then, isn't the truth stranger than fiction?

"That Amelia is on the run. No one's seen her since that interview with Amanda."

As Tracy weighs the possibility, a memory rises to the

surface. Her and Candice, at the senior banquet, listening to the other mothers gossip about the latest Netflix hit. A documentary about a rich kid that fled the country, with his parents' help, to avoid being charged with the murder of his girlfriend. *I would never do something like that*, Kelsey's mom pronounced. *My child will take responsibility for her actions.* Candice had turned to Tracy, low-talking so no one else could hear her. *No way in hell I'd let my daughter spend a day in prison. Amelia would be on a plane to Morocco.* Morocco? Tracy wondered. Candice had explained before she could ask. *Nice beaches and no extradition.*

"She's probably halfway to Morocco," she says to Sam, only partly joking.

The road rolls on like a black river into the night, and Tracy tries not to think about the stop at the end. About the man who summoned her to tell a story she doesn't want to hear. Amelia should be here too to face this, whatever it is. Instead, she's holed up at home, which seems a preferable alternative, even with the throng of reporters circling the door like vultures. A few crazies showed up too, brandishing signs with WHERE'S WILLOW? written in red paint. Tracy had seen them on the WGN morning broadcast. So far, there's been no mention of Bobby Jackson or the accident or the ridiculous accusations he made. But Tracy knows it's only a matter of time before the mainstream media gets wind of it. Sheriff Gibbs had already phoned Detective Delgado and the local authorities, and the story had begun circulating on the Internet, growing bigger and more outlandish with each post and repost.

Tracy looks over at Sam. "Are you sure the girls didn't say anything to you about an accident? A guy named Bobby?"

"Trust me, I would remember something like that." Sam graciously answers her question. Again. "Maybe he's confused.

Sheriff Gibbs said the accident was nearly fatal. That his wounds were catastrophic. A head injury could cause all sorts of memory issues."

"He wrote *green bus* though. How many green buses are out driving on Route 23? And Amelia said that Willow had gone off with a guy on a motorcycle. This could be him."

"I'm just saying, don't jump to any conclusions. He could've passed the girls right before the accident. It might be the last thing he remembers. That doesn't mean they did anything wrong."

"Willow would never leave the scene of an accident."

"I agree." He takes her hand and gives it a reassuring squeeze. "Try not to worry about it. Let's stay focused on finding Willow. That's the most important thing. He might be able to help with that, especially if he had some sort of interaction with the girls."

Tracy nods, but she can't shake her growing dread. It reminds her of Willow's metaphor in Chapter Fifteen, when Jenna and Lacey had wandered into a thrift shop with a creepy owner who offered to sell them the Great Lakes Slasher's knife. *A pit of snakes writhing in her stomach.*

As the nurse leads them through a long corridor toward the Intensive Care Unit, those snakes turn to vipers. Tails lashing, teeth gnawing at her insides. Sam must sense her discomfort because he stays close, nudging her with his elbow and calming her with a half-smile.

"Is he in bad shape?" Tracy wants to prepare herself for what she might see. But mostly, she's stalling.

"It's a miracle he's alive, to be honest. Luckily, a couple of kids were playing in the woods near the scene. They heard the explosion and were able to call for help. But the fire caused third degree burns to his neck, torso, and legs. His windpipe was crushed on impact. And—"

"Crushed?"

"That's what happens when your motorcycle goes airborne and crash lands into a tree trunk." The nurse points to a single room with a closed door and a plastic chair out front. "He may not be awake for long. He comes in and out."

"Is he on a lot of medication?" Sam asks.

The nurse answers with a pointed look.

"I think what he's asking is, can we trust what Bobby is saying... or *writing*? I have some questions about my daughter."

"Well, the cops seemed pretty interested." Tracy reads the undertone of judgment in her voice. This woman is not on Willow's side. Suddenly, the prospect of coming face to face with Bobby Jackson doesn't seem so bad. "If he's telling the truth, maybe your daughter had a good reason to disappear. At least that's what they're saying on TikTok."

Tracy swallows hard. *TikTok?* She's barely mastered Instagram. It scares her to imagine another platform of strangers spinning theories about Willow. With a quick breath, she takes a step forward and places her fingers on the door handle. "Please don't say anything about this."

But the nurse has already left them. When Tracy calls to her, she doesn't turn around.

"It's probably best that I stay out here," Sam tells her, lingering at the doorway.

"Are you kidding?" Tracy can't fathom going in alone. Already, she's overwhelmed by the antiseptic odor of the hospital. The lingering notes of blood and fear. "I can't do this by myself. I need backup."

He nods at her but keeps his distance. Like he might bolt at any moment. Tracy doesn't blame him. She wants to flee this place, to forget it ever existed. But she's a mother. She can't run away.

Slowly, softly, carefully, she crosses the room toward the pitiful figure beneath the sheets. Only his eyes and his swollen mouth are visible beneath his bandages. Tubes and wires connect his broken body to machines that beep and whir in methodical confirmation. Proof of life.

A notepad and marker rest on a tray table. She wonders where Bobby's parents are. Who they are. She doesn't even know his age. For a moment, she curses herself for not asking the nurse. It makes her seem cold and disinterested. Then again, the nurse is probably in the breakroom posting a TikTok video right now. About her. About Willow. About this poor, injured boy who could turn the whole world against them.

Tracy can feel his eyes on her, as she approaches his bedside. They're sky blue like Willow's, and her heart aches just looking at him. She glances back at Sam, still hovering two steps from the door, and he gives her a nod of encouragement.

Unsure how to begin, she raises her hand in a small wave. "My name is Tracy Barrett. I'm Willow's mom. She's the missing girl who's been on TV."

Bobby's eyes flick urgently to the notepad, and an awful wheezing sound comes from his throat.

"How do you know my daughter?" she asks, placing the marker between his bandaged fingers.

It's painful, the waiting. The arduous scrawl. But finally, he stops.

"Tried to kill me?" she reads aloud, awaiting his confirmation. She takes an audible breath. "How?" Her clipped tone cuts through the quiet hospital room. "How exactly did she do that?"

Again, the writing. The waiting. "Ran off road."

"I don't believe it," Sam says, mostly to her. "He just came out of a coma. He's barely alert."

But Tracy can't look away. There's only one question to ask. "Why?"

Bobby pens a simple dollar sign.

"Money?"

He taps the page again, writes, *Mine.*

She thinks of the secret compartment, the seventy-five thousand dollars that materialized there. "How much?"

5000.

"I told you not to allow anyone in the room without prior approval." From outside the door, Tracy hears raised voices. "I leave for ten minutes, and you let the suspect's mother in there? Have you lost your mind?"

Suspect. Tracy hates that word and the accusation behind it.

As the nurse argues her case, Tracy steps away from Bobby's bedside. When a uniformed officer barges through that door, she wants to be as far away as possible. Not standing close enough to smother the poor guy. That's when she sees the jacket draped on the plastic chair in the corner.

It's slightly melted in places. When she picks it up, the smell of smoke bites at her nose. A large tear mars one sleeve.

It's black leather like the one in Amelia's photograph.

Above the painted-on image of a snake slithering through a skull, the lettering reads *Jackson.*

Tracy hurries to get out a last question. Something that will make it all add up, like a column on one of her spreadsheets. But when she turns to look at him, he's staring intently at Sam. Then, he presses the marker to the notepad and writes.

Tracy hears a scuffle in the hallway. A voice asks, "Were you making a video? *For TikTok?*"

"Hey, that's mine. You can't take—"

"I just did."

Sam opens the door to reveal an Indian River police officer on her tiptoes, holding a cellphone in the other, as high as she can manage, just out of the nurse's reach. In the other, she balances a steaming cup of coffee. "What is going on?" Sam asks. "Was she trying to record us for social media?"

"I need you to step out of the room, sir. You too, ma'am. Hospital's orders."

"We had no idea that—" Tracy's excuse gets stuck like a burr in her throat. Already, she can imagine the nurse's secret footage leaked online. How virtual strangers will spin it. She hadn't really thought any of it through. She'd only thought of the people who would want to help. Of the parents who would cry for her and hold their own children a little tighter. Of the girls who would see themselves in her daughter and share the post on their own pages with a heartfelt message. But she'd never imagined the ones who would doubt Willow, would blame her. Or worse, would use her story for their own gain. She feels silly.

"We should probably go." Sam enunciates each word as if he's said it before, and she hasn't heard him, which is entirely possible.

She nods her head and waits for him to clear the doorway. With Sam out of view and the officer busy with the nosy nurse, Tracy hurries back to Bobby's bedside. He looks at her helplessly, as she rips the top page from his notepad and stuffs it in her jeans. The last three words he'd scrawled burn in her brain.

U were there.

Another night in a cheap motel room, and Tracy can't sleep. After leaving the hospital, she begged to drive the six hours back to Chicago. She needed to stare at the ceiling in her own bedroom. To toss and turn in her own sheets. To figure out what the hell she would say at her missing daughter's candlelight vigil. To read and reread Bobby's scrawled message.

But Sam insisted it wasn't safe. They were both too exhausted to drive. So, they'd stopped at the first no-tell motel with a lone vacancy. A single room with two twin beds. To be fair, they *were* dog tired. So tired, neither had bothered to change out of their clothes or crawl beneath the covers. She dropped into a dreamless sleep that lasted all of forty-five minutes until her eyes opened and the dark thoughts came to life. The worry turned to terror. The uncertainty, to the black hole of the unknown.

She turns her head to study Sam in the dark. A lock of hair curls across his forehead. Without his glasses, he looks so young. So much younger than she feels, but then again, single motherhood has aged her in dog years. A seed of doubt breaks open. Its twisted little shoots grow like weeds, strangling out the daisies, until she can hardly breathe.

The racy photos and texts from Amelia.

Sam's empty promises to tell the detective.

The fighting between the girls. The dead flip phone he'd encouraged her to hide from the sheriff. And now, this.

She needs to see it again, to hold it in her hand. She reaches into the pocket of her jeans and rolls onto her side, away from Sam, to reach the page in the light of the alarm clock.

U were there. *You* were there. Had he meant…?

"Sam." She nudges his ribs with her elbow, summoning him from sleep. His eyes shoot open, and he sits straight up.

"What is it?" Frantically, he scans the room, then he turns to her. "Did you hear something?"

"I need you to be one hundred percent honest with me."

"Okay."

"Were you sleeping with Amelia?" She hadn't intended to blurt it out like that, but now that she's gone and done it, she's glad she's caught him off guard.

"*What?*" He sounds shocked. Looks it, too. But so had Ray, when she first confronted him about the allegations of police misconduct. She hadn't known until the Internal Affairs agent came knocking on her door. *Some folks can lie as easy as breathing*, Ray had told her once. *They'll look you right in the eye when they do it.* "Are you seriously accusing me of that? After what happened between us..."

"It was just kissing. We agreed it was a mistake." Still, she flushes at the thought of it, embarrassed by her own recklessness. "I want to see what's on that phone," she says. "We need to get a charger."

"Now?"

Her pointed look answers for her.

"Okay, now. We'll get one right away."

"But you've been putting it off. Putting me off. You promised you'd tell the detective about those messages from Amelia, and you haven't. You didn't even try."

Sam hops up from the bed and flicks on the light. Tracy withers beneath it, wondering if she's gotten it all wrong. If she's about to lose the only person firmly in her corner.

"I haven't seen Detective Delgado since we left for Niagara Falls, and I don't want to call her up out of the blue. I know how these things go. I've watched *Forensic Files*, too. I don't want to end up as the prime suspect."

"But you've got nothing to hide, right?"

Tugging on his sneakers, Sam marches to the door. "Let's go."

"Where?"

"To find a goddamn charger."

Tracy hurries after him, toward the lobby. The red no-vacancy sign casts an eerie pall over the parking lot. The white-haired desk clerk nods at them, seemingly unbothered by the interruption. By the odd hour. By Tracy, still in her socks.

"Do you have a charger that will fit this?" Sam surrenders the phone, placing it on the countertop. She tries not to overthink it, not to act paranoid. But the questions remain. *Why was it in his pocket? And what did he do with it while she was asleep?*

The old man studies the phone through his glasses. Then,

he raises them to his forehead, squints, and looks again. Finally, he shrugs. "What do I look like, a Radio Shack?"

Disappointment weakens her knees. She lets out a small, pathetic groan.

"I'm just joking with you, doll. I'll take a gander in the lost and found. You'd be surprised what people leave behind."

He disappears into the back, leaving them alone. Sam stays at the desk, avoiding her eyes.

"When we get back to the room, I'll call the detective. Hell, I'll call 911 if I have to."

"It's okay. We can wait till—"

"No. It can't wait. I don't want you to doubt me a second longer." He takes a deep breath and faces her. "I did not have sex with Amelia."

"I believe you." Still, she's glad to hear him say it out loud. Her relief only grows when the desk clerk returns, grinning ear to ear. He holds up the charger like a proud fisherman.

"You're in luck. I got one."

"We'll bring it right back," Tracy says, resisting the urge to snatch it from his hands.

"Don't bother. It's yours now. Nobody's coming back for that dinosaur."

Back in the room, she inserts the connector. She watches Sam silently pace the worn carpet, as she presses the power button. The screen lights up in a glowing green.

"Well?" Sam peers over her shoulder. "Check the call log. The messages."

Tracy can't remember what she ate last. A convenience store hotdog outside of Niagara? But as she searches the phone, that last meal pushes its way back up. There are no calls. No messages. No photos. Nothing. "It's been wiped clean."

"Probably never used," Sam suggests. "Maybe it fell out of a hiker's backpack. Something they kept for emergencies only."

It sounds logical, reasonable. Completely believable. She

closes the phone and focuses her attention on breathing. In and out. In and out. Until her nausea passes. "I suppose that's possible. But I should turn it over to the police anyway. Don't you think?"

He nods. "Cover all your bases. That's the smart thing to do."

"Smart, right." Clutching the flip phone in her hand, Tracy sits on the edge of the bed. She doesn't feel smart. She thinks of Bobby Jackson and the words he'd painstakingly written. She feels incredibly stupid. Stupid to think she ever really knew her daughter at all.

"What do you make of this?" She reaches into her pocket and passes Sam the torn sheet from the notepad.

"He wrote this?" Sam squints at the paper, regarding it just the way she had. With disbelief. "Why didn't you tell me?"

"I didn't know what it meant. I still don't."

"You thought it meant *me*. That *I* was there?"

"Kind of." She shrugs, embarrassed. "*Were you?*"

Sam joins her on the bed and locks eyes with her. "Where? At the scene of the accident? That makes no sense."

She knows it's the truth. Still, she can't let it go. "He looked at you when he wrote it."

"I don't want to be cruel, but this is bullshit. The guy suffered a severe head injury. Not to mention the burns, the trauma. All the meds they're pumping into him." Tentatively, he puts an arm around her shoulders. "I don't think we can believe anything he says. Including his accusations about Willow."

Tracy desperately wants to believe him.

"Remember the time she thought she hit a squirrel on the way to school."

Tracy chuckles at the memory. "Yeah, I remember. She spent the next forty-five minutes searching for it in the bushes.

She missed her biology test. Her teacher thought she'd made the whole thing up."

"I can't imagine that girl hurting anyone intentionally. Can you?"

His reassurance feels like a warm blanket she wants to curl up in. "Thank you for being here. I couldn't have gotten through any of this without you. But, will you..."

"Yes." He speaks softly, tentatively. He's probably afraid to set her off again. "I'll call the detective now."

INSTAGRAM

writingontheroad Rumi said it best: Set your life on fire. Seek those who fan your flames. #isdaysixoveryet #theroadtrip #bestfriends #niagarafalls #finaldestination #countingstars #makingwishes
15,765 likes 3,532 comments 651 shares

ilovepuppies That fire needs a marshmallow stat!

kelseyscott05 have a smore for me!

kelseyscott05 can't believe ur still gone... praying for you willow

tracythetaxtamer This is one of the last posts from my daughter, Willow. As you may know, she and her best friend, Amelia, left on a road trip eleven days ago in a bus I refurbished for them. Yesterday, a stranger drove the bus back to Chicago, and this morning, Amelia came home with no feasible explanation about what happened. My daughter is still missing, and the police told me there are signs of foul play. The most unnerving part of all of this is that it's eerily similar to the plot of the girls' novel, *The Road Trip*, in which two friends embark on the adventure of a lifetime... and one of them ends up dead. Don't get me wrong. I'm not casting stones. I have no idea what happened. I'm terrified, and I desperately need your help to find my daughter. Please share! #whereiswillow

> **papabear33** @writingontheroad @tracythetaxtamer Praying for you and your daughter! #whereiswillow

> **trixiepie1** @writingontheroad @tracythetaxtamer I'm so sorry. I'd be a wreck too. #whereiswillow

jenniferbudowski13 @chicagopd this woman's daughter is missing why isn't amelia being questioned harder? #whereiswillow #cast-ingstones

truthseeker007 Peace loving Rumi? Really? Was this before or after you tried to kill that guy on a motorcycle? No wonder you disap-peared. #whereiswillow #willowisontherun #canadaorbust

> **billygoatgruff** @truthseeker007 Gotta wonder what happened on day 6? Is there a knife in this photo? #whereiswillow

> **truecrimelover44** @truthseeker007 Why isn't @melthebook-worm talking? #whereiswillow #bffdidit

> **truthseeker007** @truecrimelover44 Did you see that nurse's video? #whereiswillow #willowisontherun

> **truecrimelover44** @truthseeker007 Yeah, and it's obviously doctored. Check out her bio. She's an aspiring influencer. #eyeroll #thatsaysitall

> **chicagowriter** @truthseeker007 I agree with @true-crimelover44. How do we know which girl was driving the

bus? Word on campus this week @melthebookworm stole money from her roommate.

stephenkingfan3 Anybody going to the vigil in Kildeer? #whereiswillow

billygoatgruff @stephenkingfan3 Kildeer sounds creepy. But hell yes, save me a candle! #dontkilldeer

truecrimelover44 @stephenkingfan3 I'll be there recording for the podcast. #whereiswillow

truthseeker007 @stephenkingfan3 It's gonna get wild. #whereiswillow #bothgirlsrshady

TWENTY-THREE

BEFORE

Day Six on the Road: Niagara Falls, White Water Campground

Willow lies back in the grass and takes in the expanse of night sky with its confetti sprinkle of stars that twinkle at her like they know a secret. The campfire flickers at her feet, warming her legs, and she can still taste the sticky sugar on her lips from the marshmallows she roasted. On the other side of the fire, Amelia sits across from her, singing along to a guitar rendition of "Brown Eyed Girl," without a care in the world. This is how she'd imagined their road trip. The two of them together had always been their own special brand of magic. But now, that's all over, and her excitement at the prospect of being with her best friend at Northwestern next year has turned to a dull ache. A pit of dread she keeps tumbling into.

Her throat constricts. A sure sign that the tears are coming. Swallowing hard, she sits up and joins in the singing. The song only makes her think of Sam though, because every song reminds her of him. That only makes her sadder. Since their argument earlier, he hasn't called or texted like she thought he would. She feels stupid for how she acted. He's right. She should act like a grown-up. Now, she worries that she's ruined everything. That he won't even want to meet her at the cabin. And then what?

A little desperate, she snaps a photo of the crackling campfire and writes a caption meant for him. To remind him that they belong together. That they'd once lain in bed, reading poetry to each other. That he'd whispered Rumi's words against her skin. Then, she posts it to Writing on the Road, a secret grand gesture that she hopes will move him.

She casts her eyes skyward to find the perfect wishing star, flinching with surprise when Allen taps her on the shoulder. She hadn't seen him sitting there. He mumbles an apology and flashes her a goofy smile. She hopes she didn't give him the wrong idea earlier.

"Are you feeling better?" he asks.

"A little. Thanks for talking me off the ledge."

"It was my pleasure." The red deepens on his already-flushed cheeks. "I mean, that's what Eagle Scouts are for, right? I couldn't leave a damsel in distress."

"I didn't know you were an Eagle Scout."

Chest puffed, he fishes a rusted medallion out of his fanny pack. "I'm official. Do you wanna hear the Scout Oath?"

Willow waits patiently while he recites the lines with his hand held over his heart. When he grins broadly, showing all his corn kernel teeth, she knows for certain. She definitely gave him the wrong idea.

Allen points proudly to the edge of the fire. To the Ka-Bar knife. Willow's heart skips like a stone.

"What is that doing here?" she whispers, hoping Amelia won't notice. "I told you knives make me uneasy. You promised to keep it out of sight."

"I will, I will. But I needed it to sharpen my sticks for

tonight. Did you know I start all the White Water Campground campfires myself with two sharp sticks and a little patience?"

"Wow. That's amazing." She pretends to be impressed. Really, she's worried. She should've tossed the knife in the river when she had the chance, not left it in the hands of a wannabe Bear Grylls. But, once he'd spotted her there on the bank, she'd had no choice. She couldn't risk looking any more suspicious.

"I could show you how to do it tomorrow if you'd like. There's sort of a trick to it."

"Matches?" she offers.

He laughs way too loudly, drawing Amelia's attention. She stops singing and walks over to them. "I didn't know you'd met Allen, too. His tour was excellence, bar none. He even knew about the debate surrounding the origin of the name of the Niagara River."

"Spouting little-known facts is the way to Amelia's heart," Willow says, with a smile. "Allen came after me today when I..." She waves toward the woods though she can hardly spot the tree line in the pitch black. A coyote yips in the distance.

"Had a meltdown?" Amelia suggests. "Believe it or not, Allen, she's known as the free spirit of the two of us. But on this trip, she's been nothing but a mopey stick in the mud."

"Oh, really?" Allen seems to relish being caught between them, roped into their drama. His eyes flit to the blade. It shimmers in the glow of the fire. He'd already broken his vow not to show it around, and especially not to Amelia. Willow can't stomach the thought of another argument, more words they can't take back. She needs it hidden out of sight. Now.

She links her arm through Allen's and leads him back toward the fire, intent on distracting him. "I'll bet Eagle Scouts have the best ghost stories."

He beams back at her, Amelia and the knife all but forgotten. "Have you heard the one about the hook-handed killer?"

With an exaggerated shudder, she tucks the knife safely beneath Allen's rucksack. "Ooh. I can't wait to hear it."

TWENTY-FOUR

NOW

Tracy gapes at the reporters on her front lawn, as Sam slow-rolls by the house. A six-hour drive home, and this is how it ends. With a camera lens shoved in her face and an endless stream of questions she doesn't want to answer, but can't avoid. The sight of the WGN van twists her stomach. It means Amanda Robles waits among them. After Tracy's mom-attack on Allen and Detective Delgado's morning press conference, the reporters will be more ravenous than usual.

"Keep driving," she tells him. "Make the block. I need a minute to prepare myself."

"Are you sure you don't want to stay at my place? I have a spare bedroom."

"I don't think that's a good idea right now. Not with all the attention Willow's story is getting."

Another group of reporters gathers on the Fords' sidewalk. Tracy keeps her head down, but casts a sideways glance at the front door, where a stack of uncollected newspapers, a slew of broken eggshells, and a spraypainted sidewalk tell the story. #WHEREISAMELIA? It's a far cry from the makeshift shrine to Willow that's popped up near the Barretts' mailbox. Teddy bears and handmade cards and bouquets of pink daisies, presumably inspired by her graduation photo. Tracy isn't sure whether to feel grateful or paranoid.

Once Sam pilots the car around the corner, she checks her face in the mirror. She blends the concealer that's caked into the wrinkles beneath her eyes and freshens her lip gloss. Better. Sad though it may be, she knows the ugly truth. The more attractive she appears, the more airtime she gets. But it cuts both ways. She can't appear too put-together. She needs to strike the right balance of exhausted and determined. Of crazy and sane. So far, she's been walking the tightrope. The last few days have aged her. She can feel it in her bones.

"Are the cops pulling me over?" Sam taps the brakes and glances worriedly into the rearview.

Tracy turns to peek over her shoulder, suppressing a groan. "It's the detective. You should probably stop."

He slows and pulls alongside the curb. They wait there, passenger window rolled down, while Detective Delgado approaches, wearing her usual unreadable expression. It quickly turns sour when she reaches them.

"Follow me back to the station. We need to talk, and I don't want to send the vultures into a feeding frenzy." She's not asking, but Tracy pushes back. It's the last place she wants to go right now. She'd rather take on a wake of vultures than face the detective's questions. Surely, she's heard about the unauthorized visit to Lakeview Hospital by now. Tracy doesn't want to explain herself.

"Is that really necessary? We've been driving for hours."

"If it wasn't, I wouldn't say so." She leans in and looks right at Sam. "You, too. And bring your cellphone."

As Sam tails the police car through the city streets, they hardly speak. Tracy wishes she knew what he'd told the detective about Amelia. About those half-naked photos and the unhinged texts. She'd stepped out of the room to give him privacy, taking an impromptu walk around the perimeter of the cheap motel. When she finished ten laps, she'd returned to the room to find Sam asleep. His face, peaceful. His breathing, even. He hadn't moved when she nudged him.

Now, he white-knuckles the steering wheel. "Do you think they found Willow?"

"She would've said." But, then again, cops lie. Take Ray, for example, and his insistence he'd done nothing wrong. "Oh, God. What if she didn't want to say? What if it's bad? What if—"

"Just breathe," he tells her, taking a deep inhale of his own. Tracy follows his direction. Whatever it is, they'll know soon enough.

Twenty minutes later, a uniformed officer escorts them inside the station and points them to an interview room, where he collects Sam's cellphone and passcode. Witness or suspect, it's the same dingy quarters. Tracy counts four gray walls. Three plastic chairs. Two anxious faces. And one detective who's making them wait. But, for what? Why?

Finally, Detective Delgado opens the door and breezes inside, greeting them as if no time has passed. As if Tracy's stomach hasn't twisted itself in knots. As if Sam hasn't bitten his thumbnail down to the quick. Ray had once told her that these rooms are time warps. Seconds turn to minutes turn to hours turn to days. He'd once questioned a murder suspect for eight hours straight.

"Glad to see you made it back safely and without totally ruining my investigation by interrogating an injured witness. On his death bed. Against hospital's orders." Her long pause has the intended effect. "Oh, wait. You did. All of that."

"We didn't know," Sam says. "No one told us about the

hospital's orders or that the officer was on break. That nurse set us up for views on TikTok."

Detective Delgado all but rolls her eyes at him, then sets her sights on Tracy. "Well, what do *you* have to say for yourself?"

Tracy is tired. Tired of sitting here. Tired of answering questions. Tired of being treated like she's in the way. "My daughter's life is on the line here. What did you expect me to do? Sit back and say nothing? You're not exactly making progress. It's been five days since the bus came back. Five days!"

The detective stanchions herself in the doorway like a small but mighty statue. The sort of knickknack Grandma Ruth would've called punchy, paid way too much for, and propped in a position of honor on her cluttered nightstand. The sort Tracy would like to smash to bits.

"I expect deference to authority. At a minimum, I expect you to notify me. To wait for me." She lets out a shaky breath that leaves Tracy more anxious than ever. "Bobby didn't make it."

"What do you mean, didn't make it?" The room starts to close in, until those four walls seem to press against her. Tracy reaches for Sam to ground her. The weight of his hand on her shoulder brings her back.

"As you saw, his injuries were extensive. Shortly after you left the hospital, he went into cardiac arrest. The doctors weren't able to revive him."

Bobby's blue eyes. That's all she can see in the two-way mirror. She starts to cry, slowly at first, then harder.

"I know this is difficult, Ms. Barrett, but you need to tell me what he said to you. *Everything* he said to you. It could help us find Willow."

"He didn't say anything," Tracy manages. "He couldn't speak."

"Don't get cute. The nurses said he'd been writing messages

on a notepad about Willow running him off the road. It looked like a page was ripped out. We couldn't find it."

"I don't know anything about it." It comes out before Tracy can think what to say. Above all else, protect Willow. It's all she's known since her baby girl was a speck on an ultrasound. Nothing changes that. Not even the awful accusations Bobby made.

"Mr. Spellman, you were there. Is that true?"

Sam nods. "He seemed pretty out of it to me. I never saw him write a word."

Tracy snuffles and wipes at her eyes. "Is that why we're here? To answer questions about Bobby?"

"Among other things." A world-weary Detective Delgado finally slumps into the third chair. They've worn her down. "Between us, this investigation is turning out to be a real shit show."

"Did you find something?" Sam asks. "Please tell us. We're worried sick."

"Sheriff Gibbs phoned me this morning. While executing the search warrant of Allen Perlmutter's cabin, his deputies located a Ka-Bar knife. We believe it's the same knife as the one in the photograph on Willow's social media. Both girls' prints are on it."

Tracy can still feel Allen's fleshy neck beneath her fingertips. Can still see the trickle of blood. The hangdog look on his face as the deputies carted him away. "Has he been formally charged?"

"Not related to Willow's disappearance. At this point, we don't have enough evidence. But the deputies found other illegal weapons in his cabin, including two hand grenades and a sword. Buffalo PD will hold him on those charges while we complete our investigation."

"A sword?" Tracy and Sam exchange a worried look, but Detective Delgado has moved on. She enlarges a mugshot on her cellphone. The eyes are two soulless marbles. The nose looks like it's been broken more than once. "Do you recognize this man?"

Befuddled, Tracy takes a second glance at the photo. She still comes up empty. "No."

"We found another set of prints on the knife. They belonged to this man. Jeffrey Wilkes. He's a career criminal. He paroled from Metropolitan Correctional Center last year."

"What does that have to do with Willow? Do you think he kidnapped her?"

"We don't know yet, but we have to consider it as a possibility. His family reported him missing a few days ago."

"Missing? From where?"

"The South Side of Chicago. Apparently, he'd fallen back into his old habits, trafficking girls and drugs in Riverdale. He had runners up and down Lake Michigan. Right before he disappeared, he told his brother that one of his guys got ripped off. Then, he left town to look for the bag. It had an AirTag inside it." Instantly, Tracy remembers the cash in the secret compartment. She tries to push the thought of it from her mind. "We tracked the spending on his debit card, and some of the charges match up with the girls' route. The last purchase he made was at the Saginaw River 7-Eleven. There's been nothing since. But the local police took a report of gunshots out at the campground. Officers are following up."

Sam springs up from his chair and lets out a frustrated growl. "Trafficking girls? Obviously, this guy is your suspect. Who knows what he's done to Willow? Where he's taken her."

"We're doing everything we can to find him. And Willow, of course." The detective knows what she's doing. She takes a reassuring tone. Tracy doesn't trust it. "It did cross my mind that the money we found on the bus could belong to him."

"Well, yeah. He probably stashed it there."

Grateful to Sam for speaking up, Tracy murmurs her agreement. Her tired brain is still playing catch-up. This is exactly why she would've preferred to be picked apart by the vultures.

"That's one theory," Detective Delgado says.

"It's the only theory that makes sense."

"Unless you believe the dying declaration of Bobby Jackson. I'm not saying I do, but we did find an interesting Google search on Amelia's cell for *motorcycle accident on route 23.*"

"A single Google search? On Amelia's phone, not my daughter's? A dying declaration?" Tracy finds her voice, and it comes out angrier than she expects. "I doubt any of that would hold up in court."

"Is that what Ray told you?"

Now, Tracy jumps out of her seat. "I haven't spoken to Ray in days. No matter what Bobby wrote on that stupid notepad, Willow is the one who's vanished. Willow is the one whose hair you found on the bus. Willow is the one whose best friend is hiding out, avoiding the police. For all we know, she's fled the country. Have you even laid eyes on her since Friday?"

The detective doesn't answer. She seems shocked by Tracy's outburst.

"That's what I thought. That's three days ago. My daughter is the victim here. Yet, you seem more interested in accusing her of a crime than finding her. So what if she did run Bobby off the road? Where the hell is she? And when are you going to start demanding some answers from the one person who's got them?"

"We're trying our best, but as you know, Amelia doesn't have to talk to us, and we don't have enough evidence to—"

"Let me out. I'm done here." Tracy pulls on the locked door. There's no way she's giving up the burner phone now. She'll handle this herself. "I don't want to hear from you again until you find my daughter."

"But we need to discuss security for the vigil." Detective Delgado speaks to her in a soothing tone, as if she's a caged animal biting at the bars. And that's exactly how she feels. She pounds on the door until her fist hurts. Finally, the detective relents and opens it. Tracy bursts into the hallway and doesn't look back.

Tracy braves the vultures alone, convincing Sam to drop her off in the driveway. With her in their sights, they're more like hawks. Screeching through the sky, talons splayed. Somehow, she manages to slip through the door unscathed. Inside, she watches them through a crack in the blinds. They circle on the sidewalk for a while, then settle. Birds of prey, indeed. It will only get worse after tonight. After what she's about to do.

With twelve hours till dawn, she carts her laptop to the sofa and opens the last file Willow sent her: The Roadtrip_Final Draft. In another window, the ominous book cover Sam had commissioned from an artist friend of his, with the girls' names sharing billing in large font at the bottom. A long, winding highway zigzags across the dark background. She can only pray it's not a one-way road to hell.

INSTAGRAM

writingontheroad Eighth wonder of the world with @melthebook-worm! #dayseven #theroadtrip #bestfriends #niagarafalls #finaldestination #aweinspiring
18,001 likes 6,803 comments 699 shares

ilovepuppies I just showed my hubby. We took a photo in that exact spot! #honeymooners

stephenkingfan3 What an underwhelming press conference. Way to tell us nothing. #detectivedelgadoishotthough

> **girlsrule77** @stephenkingfan3 What an underwhelming post. Way to be a misogynist. #stephenkingwouldnotapprove

> **truecrimelover44** @stephenkingfan3 They know more than they're saying. #bffdidit #whereiswillow

> **chicagowriter** @stephenkingfan3 it's been how many days since we've seen @melthebookworm? #whereiswillow #whereisamelia

truecrimelover44 @chicagowriter 3 by my count #bffdidit #whereisamelia

truthseeker007 Did anyone else see @useranon88's TikTok video? Remember #crookedray? #whereiswillow

truecrimelover44 @truthseeker007 Damn, I hoped that guy was dead. #raysucks

boomboom4 @truthseeker007 unpopular opinion: #crooke-dray got a bad rap. @justingeorge is, was, and will always be GUILTY!!!

chaosismyfriend Doesn't @melthebookworm live in Kildeer too? #whereisamelia #letsfindher

boomboom4 @chaosismyfriend I'M IN! #whereisamelia #letshuntherdown

useranon88 @chaosismyfriend #whereisamelia #letsmake-hertalk

girlsrule77 @chaosismyfriend @boomboom4 @useranon88 Someone should report you! #unhinged

TWENTY-FIVE

BEFORE

Day Seven on the Road: Niagara Falls

Willow awakens with a start, the burner phone buzzing beneath her mattress. Before Amelia hears, she hurries to silence it. She'd left it on vibrate with the hope Sam would reach out. That he would answer her last text: *Will you still be there like we planned?* That he wouldn't let her down. Not after all this waiting. She'd already lied to her mother, inventing a mandatory three-day bookstore staff retreat.

She fishes the phone out and takes an anticipatory breath. Her whole world rests on his answer. She's never been one of those girls. Until now. Without him, without their future together, it all turns to dust. She'll be left with nothing but the horror of this cursed road trip. What she's done. What she's allowed Amelia to do.

I like your photo. You still fan my flames.

Then, one minute later.

I'll be there.

Three words that hit her bloodstream like the strongest drug. There's no going back to sleep. Instead, she calculates the time, starts the countdown. Seven days, twelve hours, five minutes, thirty-five seconds. She holds the key in her hand tightly, as if it's Sam's flesh and blood. When he gave it to her, he told her to think of it as a promise. A promise that they'd be together again soon and then, forever.

Now that it's almost real, she imagines them telling her mother. Maybe she'll ask Sam to start the conversation. He'll know how to handle her and her unavoidable questions. Like when it started between them. Twelfth grade field trip to the Lincoln Park Zoo. On the bus back to Kildeer, he offered her the seat next to him and grazed her thigh with his knuckles while they talked about their favorite authors. She pretended not to notice. She wondered if she'd read it all wrong.

Like when he first kissed her. February of this year. He'd invited her to be a guest speaker to his seventh period seniors' Honors English class. She still remembers the click of the lock of his classroom door after the last student packed up and left. How he leaned up against his desk, waiting for her to make the first move. How she hoped she wouldn't mess it up. Wouldn't give herself away.

Like what she planned to do next, starting with forgetting the road trip ever happened. Move into their Chicago brownstone, with its picture window and the quirky coffee shop down the street. Write books together. Have snowballs fights in the winter and jog the Lakefront Trail together in the summer. She wants it all at once. She can hardly wait.

Willow stands on the observation deck overlooking the Falls. This morning, she thought she would feel relieved to be here.

To have reached the final stop of the trip. But her chest hurts, and she can't silence the nagging voice in her head. She worries about what the next week will bring. That Sam will look at her and know. She isn't the same naïve girl who met him six days ago outside a hotel in downtown Milwaukee—a quick ninety-minute drive from Chicago—convincing Jackson to leave the bar and drop her off there on his bike. *Oh, I get it. I'm being ditched,* he'd said, spotting Sam waiting on the sidewalk. She's different now, so different she hardly recognizes herself.

"It's awe-inspiring, isn't it?" Amelia yells above the roar of the cascading water. "I can't wait for the cruise tomorrow."

Willow nods flatly. She hasn't told Amelia that she finished the revisions. That she has no intention of going on that cruise. By this time tomorrow, she'll be halfway back to Chicago.

"What's wrong with you? We're at Niagara Falls. You said it yourself, it's like an unofficial wonder of the world."

"I'm fine. Just tired." She hopes Amelia will leave it alone. That she won't make her put the final nail in the coffin of their friendship. Even with all that's happened, she keeps waiting for the real Amelia to show up. The girl she thought would be her maid of honor, her baby's godmother, her friend for life.

Amelia shakes her, shouts into the void, "But it's Niagara Falls!"

Willow forces a smile. Inside, she feels empty and numb.

"C'mon," Amelia says, tugging at her arm. "Let's go to the gift shop. I want to get my mom a cheesy souvenir."

"I'm right behind you." Willow waits there a moment longer to enjoy the Falls alone. She imagines the terrifying plunge on the way down. The bone-juddering crash into the water. The peace beneath it, cold and soundless like a tomb. She shakes off a shiver and goes to find her ex-best friend.

. . .

Willow can't sit still. She can't outrun her bad mood either, the impending sense of doom that's been nipping at her heels since they left Niagara Falls. Amelia must feel it too, because she spends the afternoon hiding out at the mess hall while Willow tidies the skoolie from top to bottom. When she finds her friend's stolen blood money still secreted in the bench seat compartment, she changes the combination to the lock. She knows it's cruel and childish—that she'll have to tell Amelia eventually anyway—but it gives her a momentary satisfaction.

Willow showers at the lodge. She lets her hair air dry and ties the key around her neck, no longer caring if Amelia sees it. Practically wanting her to. Tonight, she'll tell Amelia that it's done. They're done. The trip is over. Tomorrow morning, she'll start the long drive back. Alone.

"Don't forget about the cookout." Willow tries to make small talk, so their last hours together won't be unbearable. She shuts the door behind her and listens for Amelia's response. "I ran into Allen on the way back. He said he's looking forward to seeing you there and that he's making his extra-spicy chili dogs."

Amelia finally says, "He was my friend first, you know."

"Who, Allen? We literally just met the guy. I'd hardly call him a friend." Willow peers into the top bunk, screwing her face up at Amelia. "Are you seriously jealous?"

Willow positions herself in front of the full-length mirror near their beds and starts to apply her makeup. Amelia hops down. Hands on hips, she stands behind her. It makes Willow feel cornered. "It's not about that. I just don't understand why you have to want everything that I do. Why you have to take it all from me."

"Like what?"

"Writing, for one thing. I was the one who took that creative writing class at sleepaway camp in the fourth grade. No one seems to remember that. I was the one who wanted to go to Northwestern since we went to that college fair. And I know it's stupid, but in the third grade, I said I wanted a Barbie party and you laughed at me. But then, you stole my idea, and your mom bought all those cute pink sunflower favors."

Willow dabs a bit of makeup on her sunburned nose, then turns to face her friend. "You're mad about a birthday party my mom threw eleven years ago?"

"That's not the point and you know it. It's like you're always trying to one-up me. For once, I want to have something for myself."

"Fine. So do I. If you want to know the truth, I don't think we should put your name on the book. You hardly wrote any of it."

"You're a liar."

"Which part did you write, Melly? Show me."

Amelia's nostrils flare. She storms toward the foldout table, taking hold of the spiral-bound copy of *The Road Trip*. The way she flips through the pages, it's like she's possessed. A few of them tear from the binding. Then, she rips a handful out herself and throws them at Willow. "This entire section was my idea."

Another rip and toss. Chapter Twenty-One's pages fall like snowflakes onto the vinyl floor. "And this one. Your idea for the first plot twist was lame. Even Mr. Spellman thought so. I spoke to him last night, you know. About the query letter. He said I really know how to sell a storyline."

The mention of Sam sticks like a barb in her skin. Willow can't hold back anymore. Suddenly, she's crying and yelling and stomping like a toddler. She wrestles the remnants of the book from Amelia and turns straight to the dedication page. Crumpling it in her hand, she flings it down the aisle.

"Forget. The. Book." Each word, a nail in the coffin of their friendship. They both stare at the balled-up paper, breathing hard. "What about this trip? The crazy way you've been acting. You stole money. Two men are dead because of you. I can hardly stand to say it out loud, but it's true. You killed them!

And you haven't once tried to explain yourself. I don't know you anymore. Maybe I never did."

"Do you think I wanted this? I had no choice."

"That's insane. You sound certifiable."

"Trust me, you can't handle the truth. If I tell you the whole story—" Amelia slips on one of the pages, clinging to the foldout table to stay on her feet. Willow has an overwhelming urge to push her.

"*What?* It couldn't possibly be worse than what's already happened."

"But it is," Amelia hisses. "You didn't get into Northwestern."

"Yes, I did. I can show you the letter on my phone right now."

"That's not what I mean. You didn't get in on your own. I took the SAT for you. Your mom paid me. I've done it for other people, too. A bunch of times. The test proctor and I have an arrangement. For a cut of the money, he lets me in after the test, and I change the answers. *Voilà!* You get a 1450, and I get five grand."

Willow stumbles back and drops onto the sofa. Her face, hot. Her legs, heavy. She tries to pin down a thought. "I don't believe you."

"Think about it for a second, Will. Do you really believe you raised your score by two hundred points with some weekend tutoring? You're horrible at standardized tests. Your mom knows that. So do I. I only offered to help because I care about you, and she told me how important it was to you to get into Northwestern."

Willow concentrates on the rapid flutter of her heartbeat in her neck. She waits for her heart to burst through her skin and fly away.

"You wanted an explanation. That's how it started. That's how everything went sideways for me. Another test proctor named James found out about the scheme. He got angry when I refused to cut him the same deal, and he started to blackmail me. At first, he said that if I didn't pay up, he'd tell my mom. Then, he threatened to go to the dean. Then, the cops. And then I got into some bullshit trouble at school. And my mom got fired for botching a bypass surgery. And—"

"What? Your mom..."

"I wanted to tell you. But everything started to spiral out of control. That's partly why I agreed to your mom's deal. I needed the money, and she was so desperate I convinced her to pay double. It didn't help, though. James kept calling me from an unknown number. When I saw the cash in Jackson's saddle bag, it seemed like an easy answer, so I took it. The restaurant tips, too."

Willow can only stare at her, numb and confused. She wants to shout at her, to tell Amelia she can't have the money. That it's locked away, forever out of her reach. But the words don't come.

"I know you're mad at me. So, I'm just going to get it over with. I'm going to say it fast, like ripping off a Band-Aid. I slept with Sam. It was a one-time thing, like a month ago. I invited him to this poetry reading at Northwestern, and it just happened. But he made me swear not to tell you or anybody else. You know, I was kind of into him for a while, and I thought he actually liked me. That's why I sent those photos. It's stupid. I'm mean, I'm like a walking cliché, right?"

"Who?" Her own voice sounds far away. Like she's floating away from herself.

"Sam. Mr. Spellman. *Hello?*"

An unexpected burst of adrenaline pushes Willow forward. She lunges for Amelia, and they fall onto the floor. Onto the papers strewn everywhere. No thought, only heat in her hands. Heat and motion. She grabs, kicks, punches, snarls. In the melee, her laptop tumbles from the table and lands with a crash.

"Get off me!" Fingers claw at her neck, breaking the leather cord, then at her hair, pulling hard and tearing her scalp. She screams at the awful ripping sound until Amelia lets go.

Willow scrambles up and crawls away like a frightened dog. Finally, she finds the strength to stand, though her legs can barely hold her weight.

"I hate you! I never want to see you again. I'm going to tell everyone what you did. All of it."

Amelia raises her eyes and lets out a ragged breath. They both see it at the same time. The clump of Willow's hair in her hand. "If you breathe a word, I'll kill you."

Still barefoot, Willow runs from the school bus. Past the monkey bars, warm from the sun, and empty picnic tables, sticky with ice cream and ketchup. Toward the tree line, where the shadows gather like a mob and the smell of the campfire fades like a flower pressed between the pages of a book.

She stops at the edge of the woods, where she can hear the roil of the river, and checks her pocket for the burner phone. That's all she needs. She could leave the bus here. Let Amelia deal with it. She can call a taxi and be at Sam's cabin by morning. *Sam.* Then, the truth of it all settles in.

She can't go to the cabin alone. She doesn't have the key anymore. It's somewhere on the floor of the bus, lost in the struggle. Her hand traces the back of her head and finds a small angry spot where her hair used to be. At least it's a tangible kind of pain. The kind time will fix.

But Sam. She can't call him. She can't look at him. Can't speak to him. Even the thought of him hurts. Still, a part of her holds out hope.

Amelia *must* be lying.

About everything. Just a few months ago, Dr. Ford had been honored by Mercy General as Surgeon of the Year. She didn't lose her job. Willow had turned in her exam bubble sheet to the proctor like everyone else. She earned her spot at Northwestern. Her mother would never betray her like that. She's always believed in her.

Amelia *is* a liar. Anything else is unthinkable.

Still, she can't help but think it. The soul-crushing doubt forces an indignant sob from her raw throat. When she rears back and prepares to unleash another furious scream, a twig snaps behind her, clean and sudden, like a small bone breaking.

TWENTY-SIX

NOW

It's been eighteen years since Tracy endured this level of exhaustion. Back then, she'd branded herself the mom-zombie. The mombie, who ran on caffeine and oxytocin, would sleep-walk with eyes wide open from feeding to burping to changing and back again. Even when she could rest, when she should, she'd resist the pull of sleep, anxious that she'd miss something essential. That Willow would stop breathing. That her baby would disappear into the void.

Now, her baby *is* gone, and she's running on pure adrenaline.

At 7 a.m., she brews another pot of coffee and turns on *WGN Morning News*. In a late-night email exchange, Amanda Robles promised her the story would get top billing. It's certainly worthy of the lead. When the intro music plays, Tracy takes a nervous breath.

> *"Good morning, and welcome to* Wake Up Chicago. *My name is Amanda Robles, and I'm reporting to you from the news desk with an important update to a story we've been covering for the*

past week. Last night, in an effort to generate proceeds to fund a private search for her missing daughter, Tracy Barrett self-published Willow's unedited manuscript, The Road Trip. *The book is available now for download on all platforms in e-book and paperback. Tracy hopes that the publication of the novel will bring even more attention to her daughter's story and help to support her efforts to find Willow. As you may recall, Willow Barrett vanished without a trace from the White Water Campground nine days ago. Her best friend, Amelia, returned home shortly after but hasn't been seen since she issued a statement here on WGN four days ago. With Willow still missing, a candlelight vigil has been planned for the Kildeer neighborhood tomorrow night, and WGN will be there, bringing it to you live. In the meantime, I know what I'll be reading on my lunchbreak."*

Tracy's tired eyes burn, but it's there on the screen. It's undeniable, and with the edited cover, just the way she wanted it. The way it always should have been.

The day passes in a blur. Tracy ignores the shrill ring of her cellphone, the ding of her Facebook notifications. She watches in awe as the numbers climb on *The Road Trip*'s sales page, wishing Willow could be here to see it for herself. Her book skyrocketing on its way to bestseller status.

As the sun sinks lower in the sky, she patiently watches the Ford house for signs of life. The blinds stay shut, the front door closed. The only movement comes from the squirrels, mad-dashing across the lawn and scaling the large oak tree that Candice trimmed herself in the spring. Like Grandma Ruth, Dr. Ford insisted that a woman should be self-sufficient, which meant scaling a ladder with a pair of lopping shears.

While keeping tabs on the squirrels, Tracy Googles Moroccan beaches and imagines Amelia there on the white sand, soaking up the sun. She never thought it would come to this. An invisible battleline drawn down the center of Glendale Street. On impulse, she texts Ray.

Would the cops let Amelia leave the country?

WTF?

Just answer the question.

Yes. She hasn't committed a crime.

That we know of.

When Ray calls her, she doesn't answer. She phones Sam instead.

"Hey." Her voice croaks out of her.

"Are you okay?"

"I think it's all finally catching up to me. The lack of sleep. The constant worry. The up and down emotions. I Googled flights to Morocco."

"What? Why?"

"Long story." She hesitates, then, "Did you see it?"

He laughs a little. "Yeah, you stole my idea. I told you that you should've published it days ago. It's at the top of the charts. Willow would be so stoked."

"Yeah, she *will* be."

Sam takes a breath, a purposeful pause. "You made a few changes."

"Necessary ones."

Smartly, he doesn't argue. "Well, at this rate, I wouldn't be surprised if it sells more than ten thousand copies in its first week. There's a good chance it could end up on one of the best-seller lists. I shared it in my English teacher Facebook group."

A photo comes through via text with a screen shot of the book's cover and a post from Shams Spellman. She puzzles for a moment over his unusual username. *My students wrote this! Couldn't be prouder! #whereiswillow*

"Thanks for sharing it, and you were right. It was smart. I can't believe I was ever worried about something as trivial as editing. I don't care about sales either. Or those stupid lists. I just don't want people to forget about her."

"How could anyone forget Willow?" He sounds so wistful, it breaks her heart. "That girl is one in a million."

Tracy spends the evening holed up inside the house, poring over the messages and comments on her Facebook page. The early reviews read more like a police blotter with amateur detectives freely offering their theories as facts. Tracy realizes she stoked the fire by changing the character names—crazed killer Jenna to Amy and innocent Lacey to Wendy. An A and a W, just like Amelia and Willow. But she never expected this level of interest—borderline obsession—and it's both encouraging and terrifying. No fewer than twenty emails arrive in her inbox from the major networks, true-crime podcast producers, book bloggers, all wanting a piece of her story. She responds to a few, but the constant barrage of new messages starts to remind her of a twisted game of whack-a-mole.

Then, she spots the notification at the top of her inbox. A Google alert for the name Jeffrey Wilkes. She'd set it up after her last meeting with Detective Delgado. Her mouth already dry, she clicks into the article. What she reads steals her breath.

> The body discovered days ago by a local fisherman has finally been identified as thirty-nine-year-old Chicago native Jeffrey Wilkes. Wilkes' partially decomposed body was found lodged in a tangle of branches and other debris on the shore

> of the Saginaw River near Bigelow Park. Pending autopsy results, authorities have not yet confirmed the nature of his death, but foul play has not been ruled out. Wilkes was recently released on parole from Metropolitan Correctional Center last year, where he served a ten-year sentence related to the armed robbery of a tourist in 2013.

Tracy closes out of the story, shuts down the browser, and tosses her cellphone away from her like she can unsee it, undo it. Every thought that flits through her brain makes less sense than the last. Two men, dead. But how? Why? Detective Delgado will have a field day with this. It's more ammunition for her victim blame game.

Tracy tries to remember the last time she'd seen Willow angry. Once, when Tracy grounded her for staying out too late, Willow kicked the coffee table, sending Grandma Ruth's thrift store vase to its demise against the hardwood. That thing was worthless, anyway. Amelia, on the other hand, had been a biter. Candice told her so. Three kids in preschool and one in kindergarten. Tracy had seen her pinch a girl in dance class, when she thought no one was looking. Then, there was that fight freshman year that left Darcy McGuffin with a bruise on her arm and a scratch across her face. A quarter sized bald spot on the back of head too. The principal had ruled Darcy at fault for bullying Amelia, though Darcy had taken the brunt of the injuries.

Tracy retreats beneath the comforter. She can't shake the image of Willow's hair and the thought of Amelia pulling it hard enough to rip it from her scalp. Guilt kicks her in the gut, and she doubles over. When she'd changed the character names, she only meant to punish Amelia—and by extension, Candice—for her silence. To stir up a bit of controversy to keep Willow in the spotlight. But now, it seems possible that it's more truth than fiction. What if she really had sent her daughter on a road trip with a killer?

She takes hold of Willow's graduation photo from the nightstand, thankful she'd thought to return it here after the interview that seems a lifetime ago now. She hugs it to her chest under the covers. "Come home to me," she whispers.

TWENTY-SEVEN

The morning of the candlelight vigil commences with a cease-and-desist notice in her inbox from the law firm of Franklin & Pierce, with DocFord@ymail.net cc'ed. She skims it, rolling her eyes at the legalese meant to intimidate her into compliance. *Please accept this correspondence as a formal notice to blah, blah, blah... The nefarious actions you continue to undertake against Amelia Ford constitute tortious interference and blah blah blah... If Ms. Ford is required to initiate a lawsuit to address these actions, we will seek recovery of blah, blah, blah.*

With no regrets, Tracy clicks delete. Between the media and the lookie-loos, she's already become a veritable prisoner in her own home. She won't be held hostage by a frivolous lawsuit. Willow's laptop contains the only evidence she needs, even if it is still in the possession of Chicago PD. A good accountant's daughter, she feels certain Willow had saved every draft, every email between herself and Amelia. Tracy never could understand why she agreed to share the byline when she'd done all the work. But now she wonders if the novel was a last-ditch effort to save a dying friendship. Like the makeshift deckchair rafts the crew tried to assemble while the *Titanic* sank beneath them. Too little, too late.

A quick review of social media reveals that #theroadtrip is trending, alongside #whereiswillow. Tracy scans some of the newer posts, her heart swelling with pride.

> Five stars!

> Read it in one day… couldn't put it down.

> Need a sequel NOW!

But then, BookBetsy5 takes a pin to her balloon.

> Meh. No offense to @writingontheroad but my fifth grader could have done better. I saw every twist coming from a mile away.

The post has over 1,000 likes.

Then, UserAnon88 levels Tracy with a crowbar to the knees. To be fair, Detective Delgado had warned her.

> Remember #crookedray? The cop from Chicago that supposedly took a bribe to frame an innocent man for murder. @writingontheroad's mom dated him. #fishy

Beneath the post, another anonymous user commented with a photograph that Tracy recognizes. Her last public appearance with Ray outside the swanky Four Seasons Hotel at the Policeman's Ball in Chicago.

> Looks like her to me. #veryfishy

Her heart racing, Tracy quickly clicks on the option to

report abuse. Surely, this qualifies as harassment. Thankfully, the photo only has a handful of shares and likes. She doesn't want Willow's name tarnished by Crooked Ray. God, is that really what they call him?

She slumps back on the sofa, disgusted with herself, until the ring of the doorbell snaps her upright like an electric shock to her back. When this is over, she vows to replace it with a new sound. A buzzer, a theme song, a hail of gunfire even. Anything but the peaceful chime that's started to haunt her dreams.

"I know you're in there." Detective Delgado rings again, and Tracy starts to sweat. She's one of Pavlov's dogs now unable to control her visceral reaction.

Seeing no reasonable alternative, she opens the door. "I told you I don't want to—"

"I know, I know. You don't want to see me again until I find Willow. Trust me, between the shouting and the slamming door, it's burned into my brain." Still, she steps across the threshold without an invitation. "But you don't make the rules, Ms. Barrett. If you want Willow found safely, we have to work together. I'm not any happier about it than you are."

Tracy follows her into the living room, where the detective perches on the armchair like she owns the place. In protest, Tracy lingers in the foyer.

"Remember that mugshot I showed you? Jeffrey Wilkes."

Suppressing a groan, Tracy nods. She should've known this would come up, should've shut the door in her face. "Save me the speech. I saw the article online."

"I spoke with Mr. Wilkes' brother. From what he could piece together, there was about seventy thousand dollars in the backpack that drug runner lost, as well as a knife Wilkes had given him for protection. And we've got two fishermen who heard multiple gunshots at the Saginaw River Campground just before dawn on Sunday morning."

"Okay." Again, Tracy laments her draw of the short straw. A

grizzled veteran detective like Ray would've dusted his hands and said good riddance to a lowlife like Wilkes. But this lady won't let it go.

"I took another look at the bus this morning. On the edge of the front passenger rim, there's a small dent. It's not inconsistent with a bullet strike."

"What are you implying?" Tracy asks. "That two nineteen-year-old girls, who've never been in trouble a day in their lives, killed a hardened criminal for his backpack? What reason could they possibly have?"

"Seventy thousand reasons, I'd say. It's only a theory at this point. But we have reason to believe that Amelia was being harassed by someone at Northwestern. According to her phone records, she received at least fifty calls in the last few weeks all traced back to a courtesy phone in Engelhart Hall. It's a dorm for graduate students."

"What does that have to do with Willow? Or the money?"

"I wouldn't be here if I had all the answers. Like I said, it's a theory."

"Well, it's a bullshit one, and you're no closer to finding my daughter. The *true* victim. I hope you'll at least have something positive to say about her at the vigil tonight."

"About that." Detective Delgado takes a weary breath. "The Department wants to call it off. To reschedule. Different day, different location. One we can manage more easily."

Tracy flies into the living room, frothing. "What?"

"This thing is blowing up on social media. You must know that. It's what you wanted, right?"

The detective knows all the soft places to stick it to her. "I never wanted any of this. I just want my daughter back."

"Well, the Fords have received death threats and demands for Amelia to show her face, and we're expecting a large number of outside agitators. It's a serious risk to public safety."

"Death threats? *Please.* No one knows where Amelia or her

mother are." When Detective Delgado doesn't answer, Tracy adds, "They need to answer to someone."

"Amelia's just a kid. Same as Willow."

"She's *nothing* like Willow. She's conniving."

"Is she like you?"

Tracy flinches like she's been slapped. "What's that supposed to mean?"

"It means I read your grandmother's case file. You were only seventeen when she was arrested, but the detective believed you played a significant role in forging the signatures on the artwork. Ruth took the fall for you, didn't she?"

Tracy retreats to the hallway and holds open the door. Her whole body burns. "The vigil is happening tonight. Here. With or without Chicago PD."

The detective brushes past her, leaving Tracy on fire. "I hope you don't regret this."

At 7:30 p.m., Tracy still stands in front of her closet, lost. What does she wear to her missing daughter's candlelight vigil? Not a black dress. She pushes it aside with a shiver. Certainly not the red mini she bought last summer at Ray's encouragement. Or the shimmery gown she'd worn in that cursed photograph at the Policeman's Ball. Even the frumpy floral number she inherited from Grandma Ruth feels wrong. Instead, she selects Willow's favorite. A teal jersey knit that hits her just below the knees. They'd picked it out together for Willow's high school graduation.

At least she's dressed now. But it does little to quell the churn in her stomach, especially after the morning visit from Detective Delgado and the sounds of the crowd growing restless down the street. She hopes Candice hears it, too. Hopes it disturbs her, knocks her off balance inside her feng-shui perfect house. She'll never forgive Candice's deliberate silence. Not after thirteen years of mothering Amelia like her own daughter. Candice always took credit for Amelia's successes. Why should her failures be any different? Whatever went wrong with her, Tracy lays the blame squarely at her mother's feet, and she wants her to know it, to feel it in her bones.

A quick glance out the window only worsens her nerves. Amanda Robles stands near the podium, speaking into the camera. Across the street, the neighbors have laid out a table of refreshments, decorated with pink and white daisies. Tracy recognizes her daughter's bookstore friends posted up in front, each holding a sign with Willow's face and the now-famous hashtag. Behind them, a sea of blank faces. Detective Delgado's voice lingers in her head.

I hope you don't regret this.

At the fringes of the mob, she sees them, dressed in black. Masks on their faces. Their signs read: *Justice for Justin! #crookedray*

I hope you don't regret this.

Another group lingers at the back, holding a banner in support of Amelia. Tracy presses her nose to the glass, convinced it's Candice hidden among them, wearing a baseball cap. As the woman turns to reveal a very pregnant stomach, she releases her breath but feels no better.

I hope you don't regret this.

When Detective Delgado arrives and joins an army of uniformed officers at the edge of the mob, Tracy backs away from the window, overwhelmed. She steels herself like she's preparing for battle. Like she's walking into a warzone.

Armor up, she tells herself, before she slips on a pair of sandals and smooths her wavy blonde hair in the mirror. She studies her face like a stranger. Her crow's feet, deeper than she remembers. The lines in her forehead, more pronounced. She looks exactly like she feels. Old and worn out. As if decades have passed since she stood on the porch and waved goodbye to the skoolie. She wonders if she'll ever resemble herself again.

In the hallway, she pauses to retrieve the remarks she jotted on a notepad. Then, she hurries down the stairs and out the door before her fear slows her down. It's now or never. From her porch, she watches the sun slink toward the horizon. The candles are lit and glowing. They remind her of fireflies, flitting on this warm summer night. They remind her of torches in the hands of the villagers, come to burn her house down. Either way, the scene is beautiful and sad and terrifying all at once. She wishes Willow could see it.

"Tracy!" She turns toward the sound of her name. Sam emerges from the crowd and steps onto her porch right into her personal space. With his navy cardigan, tousled hair and five o'clock shadow, he looks every bit the tortured poet. She freezes for a heartbeat, uncertain what to do.

"Hi."

"Hey, this is amazing, isn't it? All these people here for Willow. She'd be amazed."

"Yeah," she concedes. "She'd love it. Well, most of it."

He follows her eyes across the masses, grimacing when he spots the masked protestors. Suddenly, his hand is on her elbow. It's just a hand, just an elbow, but Tracy pulls back, fearing the camera flashes will capture something else. What would Willow think of her and Sam together?

"You alright?" When Sam abruptly drops his hands to his sides, she regrets caring what anyone thinks. She's a grown woman. "Do you want me to join you on the stage? It might be lonely up there."

Grateful for the offer, she nods. One of the uniformed police escorts them toward the podium, where Detective Delgado waits, glaring at her. Honestly, Tracy expected her to sit this one out. To call in sick.

As Tracy approaches the small stage, the crowd goes quiet.

Then, a heckler calls out, "Where's Willow?" and Tracy stumbles on the step, nearly losing her footing. Another voice from the crowd responds, "Where's *Amelia*? That's the question."

The detective hurries to Tracy's side in a way that softens her vitriol. "Are you sure you're up to this? It's not too late to back out."

"I'm okay. I'm okay. I'm okay." If she says it enough times, it must be true. "I need to do this. I have to do it for Willow."

"Please keep it brief. This thing is one step away from going sideways."

Like a gladiator in the center of the arena, Tracy gazes out into the massive crowd. It's a blur of eyes, all fixed on her. It's up to her to speak for her daughter, and her knees tremble at the gravity of it. One side versus another. Everyone with their own agenda. She clears her throat into the microphone, and an eerie silence descends over the pulsing mob.

"Good evening." Her voice echoes back to her, and the microphone screeches. It momentarily disorients her, and she imagines passing out right here. She grips the sides of the podium to steady herself. "Thank you all for coming to my neighborhood. To the neighborhood where my daughter grew up. I can't believe it's been ten days since Willow went missing from the White Water Campground, and seven since the skoolie I refurbished for the trip returned without her."

Sam appears in her peripheral vision, smiling and nodding encouragingly. She forces her eyes down to her notes. But in her head, she's back in the motel in Buffalo. She hears the gentle clink when he sets his glasses on the nightstand and puts his mouth on hers. She can't believe she did something so reckless. That she wants to do it again.

"Where *is* Amelia?" The same voice shouts again, dragging her into the present fast, too fast. Sensing the crowd's growing restlessness, she presses on.

"This has been the longest and most difficult two weeks of

my life. My daughter is my best friend. She's my confidante. My everything. I appreciate all your support in purchasing her book, *The Road Trip,* and keeping her story at the forefront of social media. In one of the last conversations we had, Willow told me that she wanted to write a book that matters. That means something to people."

"It sucks," one of the #crookedray hecklers says, just loud enough to be heard over the din. A few people laugh. Others boo. Tracy suppresses her rage. She wants this to be perfect for Willow.

"Looking out at all of you, I know she's done just that. I couldn't be prouder of her. I hope and pray that she'll be found safe and—"

"What about your boyfriend Ray?" someone yells. A candle goes flying and lands near the stage. "Investigate *him*!"

Detective Delgado motions for Tracy to hurry it up, as the officers spread like tentacles, pushing their way through the throng. "If you have any information about Willow's disappearance, please contact the Chicago Police Department tip line. Thank you for—"

"Where is Willow?" Another voice joins in, then another. Until the chant becomes an anthem, a demand. A threat. Suddenly the crowd seems to throb with its own heartbeat. A large group begins moving down the street toward the Ford house with alarming speed.

"Wait. Stop." Tracy's cries sound pathetic. No one stops. No one listens to her.

She stands there, frozen, as the chanting grows louder. A scuffle breaks out between the cops and one of the masked protesters. When she feels a hand grab her, she instinctively thrashes her arm back, nailing Sam in the nose. He doubles over. Blood gushes through his fingers.

"Shit. I'm sorry. I panicked." It all happens so fast. A flurry of motion. The sound of glass breaking. Police sirens. Running.

Within seconds, Tracy finds herself in the middle of a candlelit riot.

She and Sam duck for cover and flee toward her porch, staying low like soldiers on the battlefield. At the front door, she fumbles with the keys, nearly drops them. Then, she's inside and breathing heavy and leaning against the wall for support. She hastily turns the deadbolt.

Sam gapes at her. His face, a contradiction of ghost-white and blood-red. He wipes his nose again with his shirt. "What just happened?"

Tracy peeks out the window at the chaos on the street. Several of the masked protesters are handcuffed and seated on the curb, their faces revealed. "I don't know," she admits. "I lost control."

"You?"

She nods. Because that's how it feels. Like she unknowingly unleashed a monster. "I just want her home safe."

"Me, too." Sam comes closer to her. He touches her, leaving a red smear on her arm. "But I keep thinking, what if she's gone? What if Amelia..."

"What if Amelia *what*?"

"Hurt her."

"You think my daughter's dead? Is that what you're saying?"

Tracy listens to the wailing. It's so loud and so close that she can't tell if it's the sirens or Sam or her own voice screaming in her head.

* * *

Hours after the last police car drives away and Sam reluctantly leaves her alone, Tracy still can't stop her heart racing. She takes a warm bath and downs two glasses of wine. She talks to Ray and pacifies his worry by pretending to let him tell her what to do. Then, she cocoons herself on the sofa, puts on the cable news, and watches the horror all over again. Her speech interrupted by hecklers. The amoeba-like crowd advancing on the Ford house, upending their mailbox and leaving it discarded in the street. Her own terrified face captured on camera. The aftermath is worse than she'd realized. A small fire scorched the Fords' front lawn. Their front window was broken.

> *"Police say it was not immediately clear what sparked the chaos but noted that social media discourse in the days leading up to tonight's vigil had been increasingly contentious, with some pitting the girls, Willow and Amelia, against each other, and many speculating that Amelia was involved in Willow's disappearance. The situation became particularly tense after Willow's mother self-published the novel the girls had been working on and reduced Amelia to a footnote on the byline, By Willow Barrett with Amelia Ford."*

When a soft knock comes on the back door, Tracy freezes. She mutes the television and listens hard, finding nothing but the hum of her laptop. Moments later, she hears it again. Her body numb with fear, she forces herself to sit up. Images from the night rush back in. The crazed eyes on her, Sam's blood, the tangle of bodies fighting in the street.

The back doorknob makes a jiggling sound. Tracy leaps up and hurries to the kitchen, where she retrieves a knife from the drawer. Holding it at her side, she slinks past the stairs, down the hall, and toward the window that opens to the fenced backyard. Peering through the blinds, she holds her breath. She expects to see one of the #crookedray mob, clad in black and ready to punish her for loving him, or a sneaky reporter, lens poised to trap her in an unexpected photo op. With a yelp, she jumps back. Her heart pounds. This is much worse. It's like seeing a ghost.

"You're still here." All the online talk had practically convinced her otherwise.

"Where else would I be?"

Morocco. Tracy keeps the thought to herself.

With a delicate turn of the lock, she opens the door and lets Amelia inside. She stares at her for a heartbeat, trying to read her green eyes. Red-rimmed but still shimmering, they make Tracy nervous. So nervous, she holds on to the knife. She doesn't understand this girl at all. The last week proved that. What makes her tick. What's brought her here. What she'll do next.

"Does your mother know you're here?"

"Of course not. I snuck out the window after she dozed off on the sofa. It took her forever to fall asleep. She was pretty worked up tonight. Things got really crazy. They threw a brick through our window. The cops boarded it up, but my mom is scared they'll come back. She's pissed about the byline, too. I tried to tell her it's no big deal. It's all about finding Willow, right? But I can't believe..."

She sweeps her arms wide, as Tracy nods in agreement and waits for Amelia to fill the silence. "A part of me thought she'd come back tonight. That whoever had her would let her go. That maybe she did run away. But now, I have to face facts. She's really gone."

"What the hell happened at that campground?" Tracy asks. "And before that?"

Amelia gives a girlish shrug that pulls at her heartstrings and boils her blood, both. She points her to the kitchen table, where she and the girls had exchanged countless giggles over bowls of ice cream. Amelia slips into her usual seat next to Willow's, like nothing has changed. But Tracy stays on her feet and keeps the knife close, because everything is different.

"Willow did some messed up stuff, Ms. Barrett. I tried to stop her. That night she disappeared, we had an argument, just like I said. A really bad one. I said a lot of things I shouldn't have."

Tracy braces herself for the inevitable. The train that's been zipping down the tracks for months now has finally arrived. Its headlight bears down on her. She's tied to the rail, bound by her stupidity. "You told her, didn't you? About the exam?"

"I didn't want to, but she kept pushing and pushing. Deep down, I think she knew she wasn't up to snuff."

Tracy wrings her hands. It's back again, the urge to slap Amelia's smug face. So much for sympathy. "You promised me you wouldn't. You swore."

"I couldn't hold it in anymore. It just came out. Like a sneeze or something."

"A sneeze?" Tracy rolls her eyes at the ridiculous simile. Amelia will never be a writer. "Does anyone else know?"

"Just this asshole proctor that threatened to rat me out. He started blackmailing me. Apparently, his dad is a senator."

"Is he the one who was calling you from the Engelhart dorm?"

"Yeah. He's a grad student in political science. How did you know?"

Tracy shakes her head. "The detective told me. *Fifty calls?*"

"He wanted me to know that I owed him. That he hadn't forgotten. But every time I paid him something, the debt just kept growing. He swore that if I didn't settle up, he'd tell everyone. I'd be the one to take the fall."

"It won't come out. It can't. Ever." This is it. The moment of impact. Train meet Tracy. Feeling utterly run over, she lays the knife on the table, drops into the chair across from Amelia, and asks the only question that matters to her. "How did Willow react when you told her?"

"Shock. She didn't say much then. I'm not sure she believed me about that, or any of it."

Relief washes over Tracy. She can still salvage this. But

then, she watches Amelia's mouth twist to stop from crying. Her tears leak out anyway. "There's one more thing that I blurted out. After I said it, she went crazy. She lunged at me like she wanted me dead—I've never seen her like that—and we started fighting. I had to pull her hair to get her off me. Then, she ran into the woods toward the river. After I realized what I'd done, I was so sick to my stomach that I couldn't even clean up the mess. The campground staff let me sleep in the main lodge. I just wanted the bus gone out of my sight. I shouldn't have told her. I should've taken it to the grave." She swipes a hand across her cheek. "What if she hurt herself on purpose?"

Tracy can barely stand to look at her, to listen to her snuffling. "What is it? What did you say?"

Amelia levels her with five words she can never unhear. "I slept with Sam Spellman."

"You... what?"

"I slept with—"

"I heard you. Please don't say it again."

Amelia looks at her. Her green eyes, sharp. "It made me wonder..."

"Wonder what?"

"I mean, I know I've never had a real boyfriend. So, what do I know? But it seemed like jealousy to me. Like Willow thought she had a claim to him. If he did it with me, then—"

A loud knock at the front door startles them both. Then, a panicked voice. "Tracy! Is Amelia in there? I can't find her anywhere."

"Shit. It's my mom."

"What are you going to tell her?" Tracy can hardly think straight. She keeps hearing Amelia's confession. *I've never seen her like that.* How upset Willow had been. *What if she hurt herself on purpose?*

"Nothing," she whispers, already on the move. "I'm going out the back. I'll sneak in the same way I came, across the

Millers' yard and over the Forresters' fence. Just stall her for a few minutes."

Her legs move her down the hallway. Her hand turns the knob. She gapes at Candice. No words come.

"Well, is she here?"

Tracy shakes her head.

"Are you drunk?" Candice narrows her doctor's eyes, examining Tracy's blank face. She grabs her arms and gives her a shake. "Are you on something? *Hello.* My daughter is *missing.*"

"She's not here."

Candice lets out a frustrated wail that snaps Tracy back to attention.

"Now you know how it feels."

With Candice gone, Tracy runs up the stairs to Willow's bedroom. She flings open the drawers, pulls back the bedspread, sweeps her hand under the mattress. A single moment plays on repeat in her scattered head. The shuffle of Sam's boots against the carpet. The stack of notes in his hand. *Just a few dust bunnies*, he'd said. *And some handwritten notes for the book.* But where did they go? Ray and the detective had shown up, and she'd forgotten all about them. Did Sam take them?

She drops to the floor and directs her cellphone flashlight into the dark space beneath Willow's bed, where Sam had volunteered to search after conveniently directing her to the closet. Moving aside a few old Nancy Drews she'd gifted Willow from Grandma Ruth's stash, she peers into the void of pen caps and hair ties and unmatched socks. A single lime green Post-it has attached itself to a store receipt. The paper looms at the center like a prize in a game of Capture the Flag.

Tracy pushes herself flush against the bed frame and reaches for it, seizing it between her fingers.

First, the receipt. A $75 purchase at Macy's department

store for Davidoff Cool Water men's cologne. She tosses it on the bed and turns her attention to the grimy Post-it.

> *Rumi wrote, Set your life on fire. Seek those who fan your flames. You set me on fire with your touch, and all I want to do is burn, burn, burn. I can't wait to make love to you in our "Paris." Yours, Shams*

Tracy crumbles. This can't be undone. She can't fix it. It will leave a permanent mark, an ugly scar. Now, there is no doubt that the Willow she knew—her sweet, carefree girl—is lost forever.

INSTAGRAM

writingontheroad If only this post was real and not a figment of my writer's imagination. If only someone could read it. I'm all alone, and I don't know how much longer I can stand it. But I'd rather be alone than... the alternative. #dayten #kidnapped #isanybodyoutthere #losingmymind

1 bajillion likes 6 comments 0 shares

melthebookworm Be smart. Make a weapon. Find a way out. And... I'm sorry for everything. #bffsforever #channelyourinnermelly #whatsonemoredeadbody

> **writingontheroad** @melthebookworm I'm sorry too. I miss you. I wish you'd told me sooner about your mom and the SAT and the asshole proctor.

tracythetaxtamer I love you, Will. I'm looking for you. I won't give up.

> **writingontheroad** @tracythetaxtamer Why didn't you believe in me? #idontcheat

writingontheroad @tracythetaxtamer I love you too. #stillmad

shams Amelia lied to you. You're the only one. Every night you're in my dreams. I want you there when I wake up. Please come back to me, my love.

TWENTY-EIGHT

It's the morning of the tenth day. A simple digital clock in the corner of the dimly lit room keeps the time. Willow makes another mark on the wall with the end of a plastic spoon so she won't forget. It would be easy to lose track in a place like this. A place with no windows and a metal door that never opens. Hasn't opened. Won't. She would know. She's beaten her fists bloody against it. The scabs on her knuckles still ache.

She rehearses what she remembers, hopeful that one day, it will matter to someone. She posts about it in her mind and makes funny little hashtags and silly comments to herself. Sad ones. Things she would say if she had the chance. She repeats the story out loud sometimes too, so she can recall the sound of her own voice.

One hand over her mouth, a strong arm around her neck, squeezing. Her vision went starry and faded to black. Then, she woke up here, groggy and confused. Like the time she and Amelia snuck the good stuff from Dr. Ford's liquor cabinet. Amelia had been too scared to take more than a sip, leaving Willow hunched over the toilet alone.

Since she's been here, she's pressed her ear to the wall and the door, listening for outside noises. A forest or a highway or a distant planet. But there's only the sound of her breath. Her heartbeat. In the stillness, she can hear her body. She notices every rumble of her stomach, every wet whisper of a swallow. On the fourth day, she'd managed to work herself up into a frenzy, convincing herself she'd been buried underground. Days five and six were no better. She felt certain she'd died that day by the river. That this was purgatory. Would a dead girl bleed like this? she'd wondered, picking at a scab on her knuckle. Then, there are the days she thinks only of her mother. How devastated she must be. She wills herself into her mother's dreams. *I'm here. I'm okay.* Then, she gets angry with her all over again. *How could you do that? How could you make me a cheater? Did you?* She doesn't know what to believe.

But there are things to be grateful for too. Like the mini-fridge that's stocked with water and yogurt. The two loaves of bread on the counter. The extra-large jar of peanut butter and a single plastic spoon. The small bathroom, with a working sink and toilet, and the air mattress, where she spends the day. Most of all, the battered nature book she found in the otherwise empty dresser. Her situation could be a lot more dire, and that terrifies her somehow. That she's waiting for the worst of it to unlock the door and stalk toward her and grab her by the neck, claiming her like a calf he's been fattening for slaughter.

TWENTY-NINE

Tracy steps into the steaming hot shower and closes her eyes. She welcomes the punishing sting of the water against her skin. She makes it so hot she can barely stand it. She can't get clean enough. Not after what she's done. What she's failed to do. The signs she missed.

A Google search for Shams had confirmed what she remembered from her freshman poetry class. The mystic Shams had served as Rumi's beloved companion, his rumored lover, and his mentor until he had disappeared under mysterious circumstances. Some believed he'd been murdered by Rumi's jealous disciples. Beneath the deluge of scalding water, Tracy cringes, wondering how many teenage girls knew Sam by his skeevy nickname. She scrubs at her neck, her collarbone, remembering how he'd kissed her there.

When the water finally turns lukewarm, then cold, she forces herself to shut the faucet. To step back into her nightmarish reality. She throws on a fresh set of clothes and returns to Willow's room. To the photo her daughter had printed and tacked to the wall. In it, she and Sam stand side by side, blatantly *not* touching, with matching Cheshire grins, backdropped by the Eiffel Tower. Now that she suspects, it seems obvious. The little tells. The picture, clearly photoshopped. Thinking back, she recalls how strange it seemed that Willow had only taken a few snapshots. *I was in Paris for a writing workshop, Mom. Not to play tourist.*

My God. She trusted him with her daughter.

With herself.

With all of it.

She let him into their home. What did she know about him, really? Turns out, Ray's instincts about Sam had been right along. She needs to talk to him, to figure out what to do next.

She considers the words Bobby had scrawled before he died, certain now that her hunch had been right. He'd directed that message at Sam. *U were there.* But still, she's clueless as to what it means. She thinks of the found burner phone too. Of how long Sam carried it in his pocket. Who knows what he'd done to it? Erased messages, calls. Destroyed evidence of his perversion.

At 2 a.m., Tracy taps out Detective Delgado's number, her finger hovering over the dial icon. She tries to imagine what the detective will say. How she'll blame Tracy for not turning over the burner or Bobby's note. She might even blame Willow for seducing her teacher. That would be unbearable. Tracy decides to play it cool. The detective probably won't answer anyway, not this early.

After four rings, there's a groggy voice on the other end of the line. "Ms. Barrett? Are you alright? We have uniformed patrols making the rounds for the next forty-eight hours."

At least it's not an *I told you so.* "Yes, I'm fine. There's no trouble. The neighborhood has been quiet since..." She can't quite bring herself to put a word to what happened. "I'm not calling about that. I was wondering if your team had a chance to review the contents of Sam Spellman's cellphone yet."

"Oh." A lifetime passes in that pause. "Was there something

in particular you were concerned about? I thought you two were... close."

"It's probably just the situation. My paranoia. But he told me about those sexy photos and messages Amelia sent him. He seemed reluctant to share that with you, which is understandable, I suppose, given the circumstances." Tracy sighs. She knows she's rambling. "But I started to wonder if he and Willow might have had a relationship beyond the classroom and his mentorship this year. He chaperoned a trip for her over spring break, and I... I guess I'm just covering all the bases."

"I see."

Tracy hates these cop games. Ray always played them too, without even realizing it. Never giving it to her straight. "Please, Detective. Do you have children? Never mind. It doesn't matter. Just have some mercy on me."

Detective Delgado's voice softens. "We did a cursory examination of his cellphone. So far, the digital evidence was consistent with his report. At this point, there's no reason to suspect that he was romantically involved with your daughter. Or quite frankly, with Amelia either. He's got a clean criminal record. The principal says he's well-respected, responsible. I hope that brings you some peace of mind."

Tracy can only hear Amelia in her head. *I slept with Mr. Spellman.* She could tell the detective right now, but the words stay locked inside her. She needs to think this through.

"Do you have any other reason to believe that he might have kidnapped Willow?"

"Kidnapped her?"

"I assume that's what you were getting at. That they had a relationship that went awry, and he took matters into his own hands. Most young girls that go missing know their abductors."

"I suppose I didn't let myself go that far. But he did mention something about owning a cabin in Lake Moodie. It's close to Niagara Falls."

"Did Willow know that? Is it possible she could've gone there to hide out?"

Tracy feels utterly defeated by the question. By the detective's assumption that Willow chose this. By her insinuation that Willow had something to hide. By the vast distance between what Tracy knows of her own daughter and the truth. "She's never run away before. She has no reason to hide out."

"Not to belabor the point, but we have two dead bodies on the girls' route. Their families might disagree with that. No matter, we'll check it out."

Tracy remains civil. She doesn't have time to argue.

"You want answers," the detective says. "I do too. We're on the same team here."

It's more of the same standard cop speak. Total bs. Since the day the cops took Grandma Ruth away, Tracy's been on her own, and she knows it.

Ray picks up on the first ring like he always does, unless he's angry with her. At first, she found it reassuring, endearing. A sign of his devotion. But over time, it grated on her, especially after he got ousted from the force. She became the center of his small world. Too small to breathe. Now, she's grateful for his voice on the other end of the line. For his laser focus.

"Something's happened. I need you to come over."

"Now? After what went down at the vigil? I'm not sure that's a good idea."

"I need you, Ray. I wouldn't ask if it wasn't important. Park on Buchanan, and go around the back. I'll be waiting."

INSTAGRAM

writingontheroad I'm dreaming of pizza. Hawaiian, of course. Sourdough crust, fresh pineapple chunks, Canadian bacon, and gooey mozzarella. The perfect combination of salty, sweet, and cheesy. Our favorite. Right, @melthebookworm? #dayeleven #kidnapped #iwouldkillforapizza #seriously
3 gazillion likes 4 comments 0 shares

melthebookworm Like the one we had in Green Bay before everything went to hell. #sals #whereareyou

tracythetaxtamer I remember your first bite of pizza. You were two years old and I made it myself, baked it in the oven of Grandma Ruth's old farmhouse. That was the year I sold it. I didn't have much for toppings in the fridge but we had some canned pineapple, so I figured why not? Your little face lit up like Christmas morning when you tasted it. A love affair was born. #pineapplelover #imissyou

shams I keep replaying our last conversation and blaming myself. I was so stupid. If you come back, when you come back, I promise we'll be together forever. #yours

writingontheroad @shams But I need to know the truth. I can't get Amelia out of my head. She said she missed your lips. Missed. Past tense. That means she kissed you, doesn't it?

THIRTY

I can figure this out, Willow tells herself. She's a thriller writer, after all. She can tell a red herring from a green one. *Why am I here?* While she prepares another peanut butter sandwich, pretending it's pineapple pizza, she makes a mental suspect list, cataloguing the evidence for and against.

1. *Allen from White Water Campground. For: Creepy vibes, definitely into me. Likes knives and ghost stories. Against: Seemed nice, not physically strong. Eagle Scout.*

2. *A random stranger Amelia stole from who I don't know about. For: Money is the root of all evil. Against: Wouldn't he want Amelia instead? Unknown: Is there a ransom demand?*

3. *Mom's ex-boyfriend, Ray. For: It's always someone you know. History of shadiness. Ex-cop. Against: He showed me how to change a tire. Thinks he's a hero.*

4. *Amelia. For: Unpredictable, acting crazy, needs*

money. History of violence. Against: That wasn't her hand. Unknown: Is she working with someone?

5. Milo Bernstein, former manager at Chapter and Verse. For: Asked me out at least three times. Coordinated our schedules. Against: Once screamed like a child when he saw a spider in the travel section. Needed help carrying the boxes of new releases.

With nothing but time, Willow memorizes the list, the same way she'd studied the stupid SAT vocabulary list. Repetition, repetition, repetition. A lot of good that did her. There's a sixth name that she holds secret even from herself. But sometimes, it slips through when she gets really low.

6. Sam. For: Doesn't want to be found out, could be desperate. Good at lying and sneaking around. Against: I love him. Unknown: Slept with Amelia too? Are there more? Does he even love me?

THIRTY-ONE

Tracy wakes in a cold sweat. Her heart throbs, as if she's been running through the woods with a wolf at her back. She sits up and lets her breathing settle, warily assessing every shadowed corner for a threat. But it doesn't take long for the nightmarish reality to rush back in, to overwhelm her. Sam manipulated Willow. Defiled her. Used her. Who knows how long it went on? He's so much worse than the monster in her dreams.

Tracy focuses on the sliver of moonlight through the closed blinds. It spotlights the John Wayne portrait. What would Grandma Ruth do? she wonders. Sweet Grandma Ruth, who had sacrificed everything for her. Tracy reaches for her cell-phone and checks the time. It's 4:30 a.m. It seems impossible that Ray left only an hour ago. That she stood barefoot at the back door and let him kiss her. That she felt reassured, resolved. An hour of sleep, and she's questioning herself again. Retracing every decision she's made. The ones she's yet to make.

With one last look at John Wayne, Tracy scrolls through her contacts and finds Sam's number. It rings forever. She almost gives up. She reconsiders, almost changes her mind.

"Tracy?" He sounds as muddled as she'd expect. "What time is it? Are you okay?"

"I had a dream. An awful dream."

"Okay. What can I do?" Already, she hears him springing into action—the shush of the bedcovers, the click of the light. This is why Willow fell for him, she thinks. No different than Ray, really, he wants to be the prince on the white horse.

"This is going to sound crazy. Just promise me that you'll believe me." When he doesn't answer immediately, she begs him. Her voice, insistent. "Promise me."

"I promise," he says. "I'll believe you no matter what."

"Willow was there in my dream. It was so real. She was at your cabin. She told me."

"*What?*" Sam sounds incredulous. "My cabin?"

"You promised."

"I'm not saying I don't believe you. It's just that... um..."

"She's hurt, Sam. I saw her there." Tracy begins to cry. Nothing feels real anymore. She's outside herself, floating. All she thinks of is Willow, cold and scared and just out of her reach. "Oh, God. What if she's there, suffering, lost in the middle of nowhere? Or worse."

"Did you call the detective?"

"And say what? That I had *a dream*? She already thinks I've lost my mind. Maybe I have."

"What about the sheriff?" he asks. "Detective Delgado told me that she had asked him to send a few deputies out to the cabin, just to check it out. But it belongs to my grandfather. I haven't been there since I was a teenager. He rents it to tourists to pay his fees for assisted living."

Tracy sniffles, sits up. "I thought you said that you camp there all the time."

"Oh, yeah. I do. But not *there*. I camp at my place, right around the corner from here, up by Barber Creek. After my dad died a few years back, I used some of my inheritance money to build a small cabin in the woods. It's my slice of heaven."

"What does it look like?"

"The cabin? It's nothing fancy. Two rooms and a fireplace. The best part is that it's a stone's throw from the creek. I can practically cast a fishing line from my back door."

"Did Willow know about it?"

He sighs. "I guess so."

"Sam, that's it. Willow is at *your* cabin. That's exactly what she said in the dream. I didn't realize what she meant. But there was a little creek out back. I could hear it." Tracy stands up, cradling the cellphone to her ear and tugging on her jeans. "Can we go?"

"*I* can go. Not you. Not with what happened last night at the vigil. It's not safe right now. There are too many crazies dying for a photo-op, trying to make a name for themselves."

"But you won't know exactly where to look. You won't know how to find her like a mother would." There's a sharp edge to her doubt. Like she's on the verge of hysteria. "I need to be there. She's my daughter!"

"I'll call you as soon as I arrive. We can even videochat if you want. If she's there, I'm not leaving without her. I care about her, too. I care about both of you."

Tracy sits back on the bed. She wonders how Sam would explain it to Willow. The kisses he shared with her. Somehow, she fears Willow would turn on her. That it would be her who Willow would hate. "Okay. But call me the minute you get there."

"I will."

"And Sam?" The urgency in her voice sparks like a live wire. "Please find her."

Tracy exhales a ragged breath. Then, she rummages in her nightstand to find the secret cell—her very own burner phone—she'd purchased ten months ago at Ray's insistence, after the

Internal Affairs investigation spooked him. *They might subpoena your phone records*, he'd warned her. *They'll try to spin something against me.* She powers it on, taps out a text, and returns it to the drawer until she needs it again. There's no turning back now. If her suspicions about Sam are correct, he will pay for what he's done to her daughter.

INSTAGRAM

writingontheroad Someone is coming. #dayeleven #kidnapped #imnotaloneanymore #sandalwood

0 likes 0 comments 0 shares

THIRTY-TWO

A soft rumble awakens Willow from a light sleep. That's the first sign. She lies still under the blanket, holding the spoon—handle-up—like a knife in her fist. She waits, listening with every cell of her being. She stares into the pitch black, in the direction of the door, and counts her heartbeats.

When the floor vibrates beneath her hand, signaling the approach of heavy-soled shoes, Willow knows it's time. Time to run. Time to fight. Time to live. But her brain gets stuck on a loop—the hand over her mouth, the snake of an arm that choked her, the world fading to black. She pinches herself hard to focus her mind on the here and now. Holding tight to her weapon, she stands up and scuttles toward the door.

Countless times she's practiced this. Still, the moment the door opens, terror floods into her limbs. She sees only a masked figure, practically invisible in the dark. Like Ray taught her, she flails at him, aiming for the eyes. But he's too fast and too strong. All she stabs is air. He catches her and pins her to him like a bug wriggling on a display board. The spoon clatters against the floor, filling her with a horror that's almost too much to bear.

Willow drives her heel into his shin, satisfied by his yelp.

His grip loosens, and she springs forward, lunging toward the open doorway. Beyond it, she glimpses only more darkness. For a single glorious breath, she knows freedom.

Then, a hand seizes her ankle, and her whole body goes airborne. She lands with a thud that leaves her stunned.

He hovers over her. Paperweighted beneath him, her body goes still. His hot breath warms her cheek. He smells familiar.

Something stings her neck. Burns, burns, burns. She tries to swat at it—at him—but her arms go weak. Legs, too. Her mind holds on to the bitter end, fighting to stay alert and alive. She recognizes that scent. She bought it for him at Macy's with her bookstore money.

"Sam?"

THIRTY-THREE

Tracy watches the dawn from the picture window downstairs. After yesterday's chaos, the police cordoned off the neighborhood and sent the reporters packing. Still, it looks like a warzone out there. Broken bottles and discarded signs litter the trampled grass. The broken top of the Fords' mailbox—a quaint miniature house with their surname painted on the side—lies on the sidewalk like an upended statue. In her own front lawn, the mementos left behind for Willow have been scattered far and wide.

It's been two hours since she heard from Sam, when he texted her the location of the cabin at her request. Her last three calls have gone unanswered. Unable to endure the wait, she tries again.

"Tracy? I... trying... reach... My reception—"

"Hello? Sam?"

The phone cuts out. She dials again. Straight to voicemail.

Where is he? What's happening? Has Willow been found?

The questions multiply like a virus, and full-blown panic sets in. She can't sit here any longer. She's mucked it up enough already. She grabs her car keys and screeches down Glendale, heading for Barber Creek.

THIRTY-FOUR

A sudden terror grips Willow, and her eyes dart open. She squints against the sun and gulps the fresh air, remembering the scent of Sam's cologne and the sting of a needle in her neck. Like the sharpest knife, fear slices through her brain fog. *What happened? How long have I been out?*

Though it's daylight, time means nothing anymore. Still, there are other clues. The grogginess. The pounding in her head. The disorientation. She's been drugged, the same way she was days ago at the campground.

Where am I?

Outside. In a place that's vaguely familiar. With trees above her and dirt beneath. A small log cabin in her peripheral vision. When she hears the scuffle, the shouting voices, she has no more time to assess her situation. It demands action.

She tries to stand but finds her feet bound together with duct tape. Hands, too. She rolls toward the sound of the commotion, trying to make sense of it. Her mind feels so muddled, so slow. She must be seeing things. Hallucinations, that would explain it. The two men fighting.

Sam rears back and punches Ray in the jaw. This is not the

Sam she knows, the Sam she loves. The Sam she slept beside, curled in the cocoon of his arm. This Sam looks angry, vicious, unhinged. And Ray? He's out of place here. Like the wrong piece in a puzzle, she can't make sense of it. It's all static up there. Static and horror.

When she attempts to cry for help, her throat closes. Her desperate croaking gets lost in the melee. She works on freeing her hands instead, pulling as hard as she can muster. The tape loosens a bit, but doesn't budge.

"You pervert!" Ray shouts, before he comes back swinging and lands a solid hook. With both men staggering in her direction, she realizes what's at stake. "You seduced her. She's practically a kid!"

A gun lies in the dirt a few feet away from her. Moving her body like a worm, she wriggles toward it. So close. Closer, closer.

"Get back!" Ray shouts at her. "He's dangerous. He hurt you. I saw him moving you out of his house. You were just a lump in a blanket. Who knows what sick shit he had planned?"

"What the hell are you talking about?" Sam yells, as he lunges for Ray's leg and drags him back to the dirt.

"I'm talking about you, asshole. What you did."

"Are you okay?' Sam calls to her, with Ray pinned beneath him. It hits her then, where she is. Why it looks familiar. This cabin belongs to Sam.

"You kidnapped me."

Sam stops, looks at her. Willow flashes back to the lonely stretch of Route 23, to the dark shield of Jackson's helmet. Sam's eyes are like that now, unknowable. Time plays tricks with her, slowing to a crawl.

Ray rises up and delivers a savage blow that leaves Sam stunned. Blood erupts from his busted lip, and he spits out a spray of it. She stares at the red drop on her wrist.

Her fingers brush the gun. It's nearly in her grasp.

Ray, too, hurries toward it. But Sam recovers fast, and now he's armed himself with a rock. An alarming sense of déjà vu washes over her. She's watched this scene play out before at the Saginaw River Campground, in real life and a thousand times again in her mind. She watched and did nothing. A man died because of her hesitation, her inaction.

Sam hoists the rock over Ray's head. She understands what happens next. The rock will crack his skull like an egg. After, he won't look human anymore.

She opens her mouth, but nothing comes out. It's a silent scream.

Her hand closes around the grip of the gun. She aims it at the man she once loved. Still loves, in a twisted way. Even if he broke her heart. Even if he snatched her from the edge of the forest and locked her away.

She does what she must.

The shot rings out.

Blackbirds take to the sky like ink exploding across a blue canvas.

She squeezes her eyes shut, praying that when she opens them this will all have been a dream.

THIRTY-FIVE

Five miles from Barber Creek, Tracy can hardly stand it. Inside the tight wall of her chest, her heart pumps like a fist, and she lays her foot on the gas, blazing down the two-lane road like a woman possessed.

Her poor GPS can't keep up, and when the pavement turns to dirt, she takes the turn too fast. Her tires skid in the gravel, and she white-knuckles the wheel, willing her vehicle to stay on the road. With a quick breath to steady herself, she's off again.

The path winds through thick tree cover and across a bridge over a trickling creek. One more turn, and she spots the cabin nestled between the pines. She finds a spot in the makeshift parking lot of the forest bed. The two other vehicles she recognizes as belonging to Sam and Ray.

Her car chirps at her. "You have arrived at your destination." As if she'd planned this. As if she'd known all along that it would end here, this way. With Willow sobbing in the dirt. Blood stains the front of her shirt, but she appears unharmed. Two arms, two legs. The blue eyes she would know anywhere.

Before the shock of it hits her bloodstream, Tracy flings off her seatbelt and throws open the car door. She needs to feel her arms around Willow, to convince herself that it's real. That it's finally over. She flashes back nineteen years to a lonely delivery room. To the moment the nurse laid her baby on her chest, skin to skin. It felt like this. Like coming home.

"Mom?" Willow tries to stand, stumbles forward, collapses against her.

Tracy grimaces at the discarded duct tape near her daughter's feet.

"Sam..." Willow breathes his name into her shoulder.

Tracy finally raises her head and looks up. Sam's body quivers in the dirt, slumped in a pool of blood near a pair of broken glasses.

"I had to," Willow tells her, between blubs and breathy gasps. Tracy can't bear to see her this way. "But he's... is he... *dying*?"

"It'll be okay. Just breathe."

"It was him. It was him. It was him."

"I know," Tracy coos, trying to reassure her.

"No, you don't. I lied to you. I was so stupid. I thought he loved me."

Tracy cradles her daughter. Since Willow disappeared, she'd pictured this moment countless times. But she imagined it differently. Reuniting with her daughter in a triumphant haze, not feeling Sam's cold, sticky blood against her own chest. She squeezes Willow harder, waiting for the nausea to pass.

"Mom, I thought..."

"I heard you, honey. It's okay. I'm not mad. I'm just so glad you're okay." She pulls back and meets her daughter's eyes. "*Are you?* Okay, I mean."

Willow doesn't answer, and her tears don't stop.

"Where's Ray?" Tracy asks. But already she hears him, sees him, running toward them. His clothing, dirty and rumpled. His lip, busted. A purpling bruise colors his jaw. She lets him hold them both, lets him play the hero. The wounded warrior.

"You found me." The words rush from Willow in a weepy gasp. She looks at Ray. "How?"

Tracy leaves Ray to explain himself and approaches Sam with urgency. The police will be here soon. The ambulance too. Some things are not better left unsaid. She nudges Sam's boot, and his glazed eyes creep open.

"Tracy. I..." His voice falters.

It's hard to look at him like this, with blood bubbling from his mouth. Life leaving him one breath at a time.

"I... didn't... kidnap... her." It might be all he can muster, this declaration of innocence, but it's enough to refuel her rage.

"You had sex with my daughter," she hisses. "You stole her innocence. She's only nineteen years old. She was your student, and so was Amelia. You manipulated *me* too. I trusted you and you lied to me. You made a move on me. Did you honestly think I wouldn't figure out what kind of monster you are?"

Tracy wants him to fight back. To defend himself. To answer for what he's done. She wants to tell him how he ended up here and why. She wants him to leave this earth with that realization. But he only gasps and gurgles. Then, his body stills. His head slumps to one side. She kneels beside him and holds two fingers to his wrist for confirmation. All his reasons, his distortions, his excuses die with him. For that, she has no regrets.

Twenty minutes later, Tracy holds Willow close with a protective arm draped around her shoulder. From the back of the ambulance, she can hear Ray—his policing tone, sharp and authoritative—as he recites his story again to the detective. He, too, wears Sam's blood, mixed with his own.

Detective Delgado scribbles on a notepad, then looks up at

him. Her disdain leaks through. "I know you've already been through this with the responding officers, but I need you to walk me through it again, Mr. O'Grady. From the beginning."

Tracy homes in on Ray's voice, while Willow sits numbly beside her.

"I met the guy a few times last year."

"The guy?"

Ray points his thumb in the direction of the body. At least it's covered now. "The dead guy. Sam Spellman."

Willow whimpers. Tracy wants to whisk her away far from here, but she needs to hear Ray's explanation.

"I tried to tell Tracy that he made my Spidey sense tingle, but he had her snowed with his Harry Potter glasses and his fancy PhD. Trust me, after twenty years as a cop, I know a pervert when I see one."

"Are you saying that you knew he had kidnapped Willow?"

"Of course not. I'm a lawman, not a psychic. But then, I saw him with my own eyes. Right here!" Ray gestures wildly, overselling it. He doesn't do subtle.

The detective gives a stoic nod. Tracy can't tell whether she believes him until she says, "So, you stumbled upon a kidnapping? Exactly how did that happen?"

"Like I told the other cop, Tracy calls me last night and says she thinks Spellman might've had a thing with Willow, which honestly didn't surprise me. He spent way too much time with that girl, trying to pass it off like he cared about her writing. But Tracy is a trusting person. She was pretty broken up. Apparently, she called you and tried to tell you about it, but you blew her off."

Ray pauses for effect, but Detective Delgado makes no attempt to defend herself. She simply waits for him to continue, which only revs Ray's engine.

"Well, somebody around here had to act like a cop and investigate, so I figured I'd drive by his place in Kildeer and have a little chat. See if I could get him to talk man to man. Next thing I know, he's coming out of his house and hightailing it to his ride like his pants are on fire. I had to act fast. On instinct, I followed him out here. Sure enough, by the time I pull up in front, he comes around the back carrying a lump in a blanket. I saw a goddamn foot hanging out of it."

"He was coming from inside the cabin?"

Ray shrugs. "I assume so. With Tracy asking questions, he was probably starting to feel the heat and thought he'd better cover his tracks and get her out of here."

"Why didn't you call us right away?" Detective Delgado asks.

"Are you sure as shit asking me that? That's rich coming from you. Didn't you call me Crooked Ray?"

"Just answer the question, Mr. O'Grady."

"First off, the reception is shit out here. Half a bar, if you're lucky. Second, nobody was gonna believe me. Certainly not you. I had to handle this myself, and it's a damn good thing I did. No telling where he was taking her or what he was planning to do. We may never have seen her again. For all I know, he was about to get rid of her permanently."

"Then what happened?"

Tracy doesn't want to hear any more. But there's nowhere to run, and she can't bring herself to leave Willow alone.

"I followed my training. Pulled out my concealed carry weapon and told him to set whatever he was packing on the ground. Out of nowhere, he drops her and charges at me. The gun goes flying, and we get to fighting. Exchange a few blows. He got me good on the jaw. At some point, I guess Willow came to. She saved my life."

"She *what*?" Tracy blurts it out without meaning to. Willow clutches at her, gulps back another sob.

"Yeah, you should've seen her, Trace. She's fierce, just like her mama."

If not for the detective, Tracy would backhand him. The smug way he looks at her, like he can lay claim to her. Like he had any part in how Willow turned out. Like they're a team.

"How did she save you?" Detective Delgado asks.

"She managed to get to the gun first. She shot him."

THIRTY-SIX

A thunderstorm rolls in that night. Tracy insists that Willow sleep in her bed. She needs to keep watch, the way she did when Willow was just a baby. She smooths her hair back, taking comfort in her peaceful expression. From here, Tracy can't see the small bald spot on the back of her head, where the hair has begun to grow back. She can't see the scabs on her swollen knuckles, the red marks around her wrists, or the pronounced jut of her clavicle. She lost five pounds.

Tracy blames Ray for that. For all of it, really. He couldn't follow a simple plan.

It should've been Amelia in that room, locked away for a week and surviving on bread and peanut butter. That was what Tracy had intended all along.

It should've been Willow here with her, leading the search efforts for her best friend. But Ray had mucked it up. He told her it didn't matter. That he'd grabbed Willow out of convenience that night, since she'd wandered off on her own. That he was the one taking the risk, the man in the arena. Tracy was only a spectator, criticizing him from afar. But it *did* matter. It mattered more than anything. She wanted Willow safe, soaring above it all like a shooting star.

It should've ended with a walk away. With Amelia's release in the woods near Niagara, where she could find her way back to the campground and the girls would be publicly reunited, as their book sales soared. Not with a dead man.

It should've been the perfect road trip, not a crime spree with bodies mysteriously piling up on the route and cash stashed in the secret compartment.

Tracy still couldn't explain it all, but she had done her best to salvage an absolute disaster. In fact, she couldn't have written a better ending with Sam as the perfect fall guy. Her silly, made-up dream story had sent him to his doom. That and the specific brand of cologne she'd told Ray to pick up at the all-night drug store and douse himself with, knowing that Willow would recognize Sam's signature scent. Her only regret was that Willow had pulled the trigger.

Detective Delgado could be a problem, the single snag in her perfect silk sash. She didn't seem to buy Tracy's explanation for how she'd arrived on the scene so quickly, though Tracy mostly told the truth. *A dream? Really?* The detective couldn't refute it.

But lying next to her daughter, listening to the rain pound the window, Tracy's stomach turns with guilt. She only wanted to give Willow the world. Her first-choice college. The spotlight she deserved. Tracy knew how impossible it would be for her to come by it honestly. Life didn't work that way. It certainly hadn't for Grandma Ruth, who had spent her last dime trying to save the farmhouse and to keep Tracy fed and clothed and capable of dreaming big. Maybe too big.

Tracy rests her head on the pillow. She closes her eyes. Tomorrow, Amelia will come over. WGN will be here when she tells Willow about the launch of *The Road Trip*. They'll celebrate together.

A crack of thunder wakes Willow with a start. She sits straight up, her eyes wide.

Tracy tries to soothe her. She would hold back the storm if she could. "It's okay."

Willow turns to her mother, and Tracy prepares herself for the same question she'll be answering for the rest of her life. *Why didn't you believe in me?* Willow had already asked her three times since Tracy had driven her home from the hospital. Damn Amelia, for opening her big mouth. Tracy couldn't make her daughter understand that she'd done it not because she *didn't* believe in her but because she *did.* No standardized test could measure Willow's worth, and she certainly wouldn't let a meaningless number hold her back.

"How did you know about Ray?"

"What do you mean?"

"Today, at the cabin, you asked where Ray was. But you couldn't have known he was there."

"I saw his car when I pulled up." She wraps her arms around her daughter, who can never know the truth. She would never forgive her. Tracy will be hard pressed to forgive herself. "Try to sleep. We can talk about it in the morning."

Willow nuzzles against her, hiding her face in Tracy's shoulder. "Did the police find the place where Sam was keeping me? They kept asking me what it looked like, but it wasn't any place I'd been before. It wasn't inside his cabin."

"I don't think they know yet. They may never know." Ray had promised her they would never find the tornado shelter at his uncle's house in Fox Lake. No one had lived on the property for ten years, since Ray's aunt had broken her hip and wound up in a nursing home. Ray had stashed the bribe money there too, in a hole beneath a massive elm out back. Tracy knows the whole truth about Crooked Ray. But the saddest part of it all, Ray isn't that crooked. Not as crooked as her. He loves her, still.

He would've done anything to get back in her good graces, even a staged kidnapping.

"Where was he taking me? What was he going to do? He never even came in that room to see me. It was so quiet and so lonely."

Tracy sighs under the weight of it all. She wants to fast forward through this part. To excise Sam from Willow's memory. Hers, too. To cut him out like a cancer.

"It's hard to understand a person like that, honey. He was sick."

Her daughter says nothing for a while. The rain keeps falling against the window. "Is it wrong that I still love him?"

"Of course not." Together, they shiver at a furious flash of lightning. "Grandma Ruth once told me that love is just like a Midwestern storm. It might blow your roof off. But as long as it doesn't kill you, it'll pass."

Long after Willow falls to sleep, Tracy drifts downstairs. When Ray knocks softly on the back door, she lets him in. Rainwater drips from his jacket onto the kitchen floor. His dark, wet hair looks almost black.

He makes it as far as the kitchen table before Tracy whispers, "How could you let her shoot him? That wasn't what we discussed. How hard is it to follow a simple plan? I said, set him up, make him pay. Not end his life. And most especially, don't have her end it. I don't want that on her conscience."

Ray shakes his head, hissing back at her. "Oh, but you're fine with it on mine."

Tracy hushes him. Willow can't hear this. "Well, honestly, yeah. Because your screw-up set this whole thing in motion. My daughter was supposed to be here, safe with me. You didn't even bother to tell me that you took her. You could've used the burner phone. But no, you just waited for task rabbit Allen to show up on my front doorstep and scare the hell out of me."

"We've talked about this, Trace. I did it for your own good. You needed to be believable in the part of the frantic mother. The less you knew, the better. Besides, isn't my screw-up the only reason you found out about Spellman and Willow in the first place? If you ask me, I did both of you a huge favor." He sighs. "But I didn't come here to argue."

"Then, why did you come?"

Ray holds out his arms. It's part invitation, part surrender, part plea. "To check on you. To hold you. Haven't I finally proven that you can trust me? That I'm worthy of a second chance? I swear I'll be a better man. I'll give you all the space you need."

Though he waits expectantly for her to step into his embrace, Tracy doesn't go to him. "I need time, Ray."

"You're wearing my T-shirt. That must mean something."

She gives him a sad smile.

"Promise me you'll think about it. You'll think about us. We *do* make a great team."

His words hit her in the gut. How many times had she said that to Grandma Ruth, as she painstakingly copied the signatures on the worthless portraits her grandmother salvaged from the junk pile? "I promise."

THIRTY-SEVEN

For the third time in one week, Tracy sits in the same awful interview room across from Detective Delgado like she has nothing to hide. She could've lawyered up like Ray, but that would only give Willow a reason to doubt her. Tracy can live with a lot. She can live with Willow knowing that she paid Amelia to change the answers on her exam. She can live with Willow questioning her decision to release the book, to reduce Amelia's name to the smallest legible font on the cover. But she can't live with her daughter realizing that she concocted the entire kidnapping to boost book sales. To launch her career. To make her into the star Tracy should have been.

"It just doesn't make sense, Ms. Barrett." It's the detective's favorite line. The old Columbo strategy. "We've scoured every inch of Spellman's cabin in Barber Creek, his home in Kildeer, and his grandfather's property at Lake Moodie. There isn't a single room like the one Willow described."

"But you said that the cabin door was a match for that key you found on the bus. That's where he took her over spring break when she told me she was in Europe. The room must be there somewhere. Hidden in the basement. Or in a shed out back. Maybe there's a separate lodging on the property you haven't located yet."

Detective Delgado sighs. It's not the first time she's heard this. These are Tracy's favorite lines. Along with this one: "Sam Spellman was a predator. He started an inappropriate relationship with my daughter and her friend, both his former students. He was grooming them the whole time."

"No one is disputing that his behavior was inappropriate. As you know, we obtained statements from Willow and Amelia. IT recovered deleted messages on the burner phone that corroborated her report, and we found those Post-its you mentioned, mostly love notes. Cellphone data also confirmed that Sam met up with Willow in Milwaukee at the start of their trip. He used his credit card for the hotel. Even his ex-girlfriend, a teacher at Dearborn High, reached out to us to share her concerns that he'd been too interested in some of the female students. But none of that proves that he kidnapped Willow."

"Then, who did?"

"That's what I need you to tell me. I get the feeling you know more than you're saying. To me, the whole thing screams set-up. A staged kidnapping. You were the one steering this ship, posting on social media, giving interviews. But I know you didn't do it alone."

Tracy barks out her usual laugh.

"Are you protecting Ray? I still don't buy that he just showed up at Sam's house for no reason."

"Of course not. I'm grateful to Ray for listening to me. For believing me. For trusting my instincts." The implied subtext, *unlike you*, hangs in her long pause. "And most of all, for saving Willow. But, if he did something wrong, I'd be the first one to turn him in. I put up with his bs for too long. I'm not going backwards." Ray would be heartbroken to hear her say that. She made promises to him, knowing she couldn't keep them. She didn't want to depend on him or anyone, no matter how strongly he felt about her. Her true love is her daughter. Always has been, always will be.

"Were you and Amelia in on this together? Was it her scheme for attention? For fame? Book publicity?"

The poor detective keeps launching her doomed questions. Each one drops straight to the ground in a fiery explosion. "You think Amelia and I plotted a crime together? I can barely stand to look at that girl. She did nothing to help find Willow. In fact, why don't you ask her what happened to Bobby Jackson? To Jeffrey Wilkes?"

"We have. We've asked your daughter as well. They both claim to know nothing." Her cynical smirk makes Tracy nervous. "I wish seventy-five thousand dollars would turn up in my vehicle out of the blue for absolutely no reason."

Tracy plants herself solidly in the chair and shrugs. Then, she asks her favorite question. "Am I under arrest?"

"You're free to go."

For the third time in one week, Tracy prepares to leave the same awful interview room. But she can't resist one parting shot. "Do you really believe I would plot my own daughter's kidnapping? That I'd put her through something like this? And for what? Fame, fortune? *Book sales?*"

"In the end, you got all three." Detective Delgado twists her mouth, pondering. "Ever heard of Jamestown Publishing Company in New York?"

Tracy remembers the shiny floors, the fancy elevator. The feeling she could belong there. "It doesn't ring a bell."

"Interesting. They're defunct now, but one of their editors remembers you quite well. Well enough to reach out to our tip line. You wrote under a pseudonym, Ruth Barrett."

"Oh, gosh. That was a lifetime ago. I submitted a novel to them. I couldn't have been more than eighteen. They expressed some interest, but it didn't work out. If you ask me, they were trying to take advantage of a young person, thinking I wouldn't recognize my worth."

The detective studies her. Tracy doesn't flinch. She can't afford to drop the mask of confidence. More than once, it's saved her.

"They saw it a bit differently."

"I'm sure they did, especially now that my daughter is famous." Tracy reaches for the doorknob, securing her escape route. "What did they tell you that's got you so worked up?

"That large portions of your manuscript were plagiarized. That Grandma Ruth kept a stash of unpublished manuscripts she purchased dirt-cheap from the estate of James Wiley. He acquired fiction for HarperCollins for twenty-five years before he retired. You stole your words from the slush pile. They went easy on you because of your age."

The door is open now. All she has to do is walk through it. "That's quite a story, Detective. After you hang up the badge, maybe you should write a book."

THIRTY-EIGHT

TWO WEEKS LATER

Tracy can hardly stay focused on the thoughts that pinball through her brain. She presses her sweaty palms against her jeans. When the cops arrested Grandma Ruth and drove her away from Tracy in the back of a patrol car, she felt just like this. Like everything that mattered was moving further and further away from her. She couldn't control the outcome anymore. Could only watch the dominoes she set in motion. How could she know her grandmother would take the rap for her and claim she was the one who forged all those signatures? It's no different now.

Even from here, Tracy can feel Willow's fear. How she's not sure what to say. How she doesn't want to mess it up. How reality is so much scarier than fiction. Next to her, Candice looks on stoically. Silence seems the best way to maintain their uneasy truce. The less they speak about the road trip, the better. At least they could agree on that.

"Good morning, Chicago. I'm Amanda Robles. Today, we're joined live in studio by best friends Willow Barrett and Amelia Ford, whose story has captivated the nation. One month ago, Willow was kidnapped from the White Water Campground by her former English teacher, Sam Spellman. After being held against her will for nearly two weeks, Willow was rescued at Spellman's cabin in rural Illinois, where her captor was shot dead. Following her release from the hospital, WGN was there for the emotional moment when she was reunited with Amelia."

Amanda cues up the footage, which runs for two minutes. The hugs, the tears, the apologies, the laughter. By the end, Amanda's eyes glisten.

"Willow, I think I speak for all our viewers when I say, we are so glad to have you with us today. How are you feeling?"

A softball question. An easy start. "Today, I can say that I'm doing great. I feel so lucky. But I'm learning to be okay with not being okay. After the trauma I experienced, I know I can only move forward. I can't go back to who I used to be. Fortunately, I'm blessed to have my mom and my best friend"—she squeezes Amelia's hand—"and our fantastic readers to support me. Everyone has been so kind and gracious. It's truly restored my faith in humanity."

"Amelia, you went through a lot as well. There was speculation that you played a role in Willow's kidnapping. That you fled the country. Rumors circulated about your status at Northwestern. There were allegations of cheating. Your home was attacked in what some have dubbed The Candlelight Riot, and you and your mother received death threats. That can't have been easy."

Tracy glances sidelong at Candice, searching for a hint of emotion. She knows Candice blames her for all of it, but that doesn't seem fair. After all, she'd lied too about her termination to save face and instructed Amelia to do the same. And the publicity has been good for her. Just last week, she landed a new job as the host of a medical miracle show on TLC.

"Honestly, as hard as it was, it was nothing compared to what Willow went through. I'm just so relieved to have her back in my life. I decided to take some time off from school for a while, and I'm feeling excited about the future."

"What about the two of you? Are you in a good place?"

Willow smiles. Only Tracy recognizes the uncertainty in her eyes. "We're in a good place now. A lot of the negativity was manufactured by social media. All best friends go through rough patches, but at the end of the day, we are each other's biggest cheerleaders."

"What about the online conjecture, the rumors of a crime spree? An ill-fated road trip?" Amanda tosses the phrases out casually. Like it means nothing. Like she's talking about the latest trends in footwear.

The girls turn to each other and laugh the way they used to, when Tracy would catch them in Willow's bedroom, giggling over shared secrets. To Tracy, it sounds rehearsed. There's none of the old, unbridled joy beneath it. "Some people really need to put down their devices and step away from the conspiracy theories. Both Amelia and I have talked extensively with detectives from the Chicago Police Department. There is no evidence linking us to any crimes. Of course, we feel terribly for the families of Bobby Jackson and Jeffrey Wilkes, and we've committed a portion of *The Road Trip* proceeds to GoFundMe campaigns established on their behalf."

"What about the byline? Willow, shortly after your rescue, you announced on social media that Amelia would be given equal billing on the cover. Why was that important to you?"

"We're partners. We worked on this book together, fifty-fifty." It's total bs, but Tracy catches the hint of a smile tugging at the corner of Candice's mouth. Tracy hopes her show tanks.

"Do you blame your mother for shortchanging your friend?"

Willow's eyes flit in her direction, just off set. Tracy nods at her. "I mean, who doesn't blame their mother at one point? She made a mistake, and I wanted to rectify it right away. But I want to add that my mother's quick thinking is the reason I'm sitting here. My mother and her friend, Ray O'Grady. Without them, I would have disappeared forever."

Amanda nods gravely. She graciously sidesteps the Sam discussion, per their agreement in the contract. "Let's talk about next steps. The book has already sold over one million copies to date and counting, and it's snagged the top spot on the *New York Times* Bestseller List. Our viewers will skewer me if I don't ask. Will there be a sequel?"

"Right now, we're taking it day by day and enjoying our success," Amelia begins. "But we are excited to share that we will be taking the skoolie on the road again this fall with stops at bookstores all along the famous Route 66 from Chicago to Santa Monica. You can find all the details @writingontheroad."

"Wow. That is amazing. Our viewers will be thrilled, pun intended."

Tracy hangs on every word now. It's nearly over. "Girls, we have a special surprise to share with you today. We've just learned that Netflix has announced production of a movie based on *The Road Trip*."

"It's a dream come true." Her hands clenched in a death grip in her lap, Willow speaks right to the camera. Tracy can sense her struggle. But she feels her triumph too. She clings to that until it disappears. "I'm grateful I could do it with my..."

"*Your...?*"

Willow turns to her mother again. In her, Tracy sees a bold and courageous young woman so different from herself. So much better in every way. Yet, she raised her. She did that right, at least. She takes comfort in that last look.

"I can't do this anymore." It tumbles out of Willow's mouth. "This isn't a dream. It's a complete nightmare. I can't lie any more. Two men are dead because of us, and I strongly suspect my mother was—"

Tracy desperately wants to hear the rest. She wants to see Candice's face. Amelia's too. But she knows what will happen next. The whole house of cards will fall, and she'll be crushed beneath it. She's no Grandma Ruth. She knows when to jump ship. She can't bear Willow visiting her in a jail cell, or worse, blaming herself for putting her there. Without a word, she slips out the back to the taxi that awaits her. After a quick stop at the elm tree on Ray's family land, she'll be on the next plane out of here.

EPILOGUE

FIVE YEARS LATER

writingontheroad First selfie on #dayone of an epic road trip through Morocco to launch my latest novel, *Nightfall in Marrakech*, an international spy thriller. Reading and signing tonight at Marrakech's Rooftop Café. #theroadtrip #morocco #seeyouthere #bookten

15,734 likes 3,444 comments 989 shares

ilovepuppies Ten books… I'm so proud of you!

bookbetsy5 OMG. My favorite author. I can't wait!

radreviewer I hope it's better than your last nine. #disappointed #onestar #whydoikeepreadingthem #sobaditsgood

therealmelthebookworm Déjà vu?!? J/K. Good luck on #bookten! #theroadtripthesequel #bringpepperspray #whereistracy

> **truecrimelover44** @therealmelthebookworm Are you seriously impersonating a criminal? The real @melthebookworm is in jail, loser. You should be too. #leavewillowalone

chicagowriter @truecrimelover44 what if it IS the real @melthebookworm from @illinoisdeptofcorrections? #sheneedsattention #orangeisnotthenewblack

therealcrookedray @truecrimelover44 @chicagowriter has a point. There's nothing you can't get in prison, including a cellphone and an Instagram account.

amandarobleswgn Love this author's story and her stories! Can you believe it's been five years since #whereiswillow? Remember when @writingontheroad dropped some major bombshells live in studio? Check out our latest interview, where I ask her all your burning questions, including #whereistracy

chaosismyfriend Anybody else find it interesting that Morocco has a no extradition policy? #whereistracy

Willow positions herself on the stool at the front of the café and raises her eyes to the crowded room. In her hands, she holds her tenth novel, opened to Chapter One, but her mind is four thousand miles from here. In the house on Glendale Street she can't bring herself to sell, even though she hasn't spent a night there in years. Still, when she thinks of home, it's that house she pictures. Not her fancy Chicago brownstone.

She steadies her breathing and smiles at the audience. At the handsome artist in the front row who slipped a rose-cut sapphire on her ring finger at dinner last night. Who cried when she said yes. In a certain light, from a certain angle, on certain days, he reminds her a little of...

No, she won't let herself go there. He's nothing like Sam. Sam took advantage of her when she was only a girl with dreams. Sam slept with her best friend. Sam lied to her mother.

That five-year anniversary interview with Amanda Robles really did a number on her. All the barbed questions she fired had hit their mark.

Are you in contact with Amelia? No. After I testified against her in court, which resulted in convictions for second degree murder and grand theft, I was advised by my attorney to cease contact. I have abided by that recommendation. As far as I know, Amelia will be eligible for parole in forty-five years.

Some of your fans theorize that Amelia lost her mind writing about the Great Lakes Slasher. That she blurred the line between reality and fiction. What do you think? Amelia is not an evil person, far from it. But when she started cheating on the SAT for money, she got in over her head. She didn't reach out for help. Instead, she stubbornly tried to fix the problem by creating so many more. I still feel a lot of guilt that I didn't see the signs sooner. That I couldn't help her. Honestly, I miss her.

Did you know your mother staged your kidnapping? I knew something wasn't right, but it took me a while to put the pieces together afterward. I told the police everything I could remember, and it wasn't adding up. That's why I spoke up at the interview, in front of the whole world. I didn't want to lie any more about any of it. The police eventually located the bunker I described on a parcel of land that belonged to the O'Grady family, and Ray confessed. It's a painful time in my life that I try not to revisit. Sometimes, I fail. But writing helps. Writing gives me closure.

Where is your mother? I wish I knew.

What would you say to her? For a long time, I was furious at her for being so selfish, but with a lot of therapy, I've made peace with the past. I forgive her. In her own troubled way, she was doing what she thought was best for me, and I hope to see her again someday. Even if just for a moment. Just to know she's okay.

Willow lets her gaze wander to the fringes of the room, where a woman in a fuchsia headscarf catches her attention.

"Good evening," she begins. "Thank you so much for being here tonight. I'll be reading the first chapter from my soon-to-be-released tenth novel, *Nightfall in Marrakech.*"

As she begins to read aloud, she can't look away from the woman. The audience disappears, even her striking fiancé. She directs every word, every pause, every emotion on the page to her. When she nears the end of Chapter One, she decides to continue. It's more a feeling that she can't stop. She'll read all night if she must.

A small part of her mind drifts to a time and place she rarely revisits. The back cab of Ray's pick-up truck, where he'd stashed her on the drive to Sam's cabin, rolled in a blanket. When she'd come to briefly, fleetingly, she saw him there behind the wheel. Like a strange mirage, it didn't make sense at first. Not until later. When she woke up again, bound in the dirt, and heard the two of them arguing. Only Willow knows the dark truth she harbors. The ways that she's more like Amelia than anyone else could fathom. That she shot Sam, not because she thought he kidnapped her and not to rescue Ray, but because Sam deserved it. He hurt her. He lied to her. broke her heart. It turns out she doesn't mind a shocking twist.

The woman in the headscarf nods at her, as if she can see right through her. All her secrets laid bare. Then, the café door opens. A young couple make their way inside with apologies and tuck into a space on the periphery. Willow drops her eyes for a moment to find her place on the page. When she looks up again, her mother is gone.

A LETTER FROM ELLERY KANE

Thank you for reading *My Missing Daughter*. With so many amazing books out there, I am honored you chose to add mine to your library.

Want to keep up to date with my latest releases? Sign up below! We promise never to share your email with anyone else, we'll only contact you when there's a new book available, and you can unsubscribe at any time.

www.bookouture.com/ellery-kane

One of my favorite parts about being an author is connecting with readers like you. You can get in touch with me through any of the social media outlets below, including my website and Goodreads page. Also, if you wouldn't mind leaving a review or recommending *My Missing Daughter* to your favorite readers, I would really appreciate it! Reviews and word-of-mouth recommendations are essential, because they help readers like you discover my books.

Thank you again for selecting *My Missing Daughter*! I look forward to bringing you many more thrills, chills, and sleepless nights.

ACKNOWLEDGMENTS

In the summer of 2021, the tragic case of Gabby Petito captured the nation, after she went missing during a cross-country road trip in her conversion van. Investigation revealed that she was murdered by her fiancé, Brian Laundrie, who returned from the trip alone claiming he had no idea as to her whereabouts. His parents, too, came under intense scrutiny, as many questioned what role, if any, they had played in covering up his crime. Like so many others, I was gripped by the story and found myself riveted by the haunting idea of two travelers departing on a road trip together. Only one returns. But why? That question led me down a twisty path—of best friends turned enemies, of mothers and daughters, of a book within a book—until I arrived at *My Missing Daughter*.

Writing is a bit like a road trip with its inevitable potholes and rainstorms and flat tires. Breathtaking sunsets, too. I started writing *My Missing Daughter* well over a year ago, and the journey to completion did not go as planned. Somewhere in the middle, I took a detour back to Texas to relocate my elderly father to a nursing home here in California. Then, I picked up an unruly hitchhiker in the form of my rapidly expanding private practice as a forensic psychologist. After a few unexpected pitstops, I hit my stride and reached my destination, but this book, more than any other, truly felt like a journey from start to finish.

I owe a tremendous debt of gratitude to you, my avid readers, for joining me on my writing adventure. Hearing that my words have impacted you is a little bit of magic, and knowing that my stories have a special place in your heart makes it all worthwhile. A special thanks to Ellery's Entourage, whose members go above and beyond in supporting my work!

I am fortunate to have a fabulous team of family, friends, and work colleagues who have always been there to support and encourage me on this journey. Though my mom is no longer with me, she gifted me her love for writing, and I know she's cheering me on even though I can't see her. Thanks, too, to my dad, who's never been a reader but thinks I'm brilliant anyway.

To Gar, my special someone and partner in crime, thank you for patching all my plot holes without complaint; for cheering me on when I need it most; and for championing my dreams as much (and sometimes more) than I do. I know you don't believe me, but I couldn't do any of this without you.

I have been unbelievably fortunate to be matched with a fantastic editor, Lucy Frederick, and a fantastic publisher, Bookouture, who truly value their authors and work tirelessly for our success. It's been a pleasure to team up with Lucy and the entire Bookouture family, who have worked so hard to spread the word about my books.

Lastly, I have always drawn inspiration for my writing from my day job as a forensic psychologist. We all have a space inside us that we keep hidden from the world, a space we protect at all costs. So many people have allowed me a glimpse inside theirs—dark deeds, memories best unrecalled, pain that cracks from the inside out—without expectation of anything in return. I couldn't have written a single word without them.

PUBLISHING TEAM

Turning a manuscript into a book requires the efforts of many people. The publishing team at Bookouture would like to acknowledge everyone who contributed to this publication.

Audio
Alba Proko
Melissa Tran
Sinead O'Connor

Commercial
Lauren Morrissette
Hannah Richmond
Imogen Allport

Cover design
The Brewster Project

Data and analysis
Mark Alder
Mohamed Bussuri

Editorial
Lucy Frederick
Melissa Tran

Copyeditor
Liz Hatherell

Proofreader
Becca Allen

Marketing
Alex Crow
Melanie Price
Occy Carr
Cíara Rosney
Martyna Młynarska

Operations and distribution
Marina Valles
Stephanie Straub

Production
Hannah Snetsinger
Mandy Kullar
Jen Shannon
Ria Clare

Publicity
Kim Nash
Noelle Holten
Jess Readett
Sarah Hardy

Rights and contracts
Peta Nightingale
Richard King
Saidah Graham

Printed in Great Britain
by Amazon

57492142R00179